I0712418

praise for
escalators to hell

"Collapsed malls, and malls that rise again; abandoned temples of consumption that consume unwary visitors; ominous visions in food courts reclaimed by nature; terrifying, transformative journeys into post-capitalist crypts; and cartloads of blood, guts, rot, and decay—*Escalators to Hell* is a vertiginous, genre-spanning shop of horrors with shocks and dark delights around every corner."
—Gareth Jelley, Editor of *INTERZONE* & *IZ Digital*

"*Escalators to Hell* explores some of the most primal fears known to mankind. Taking the familiar and turning it terrifying, every single author in this anthology has something vital to say about community and identity while succeeding in scaring the hell out of the reader. Take the escalator, grab a cart, and get to shopping, because this book is an unbeatable bargain."
—Zachary Rosenberg, author of *Hungers as Old as This Land* and *The Long Shalom*

"*Escalators to Hell* is filled with fervent and feverish, weird and wild, addicting and edgy tales of pain and melancholy, illuminating the disparities of our relationships with others and ourselves told through inventive formats and structures and visceral language. These stories take familiar ideas and concepts and take unexpected and defamiliarizing turns, bringing together the concept of shopping malls across different periods, places, and the meanings they hold and how they shift and evolve with the characters that inhabit and leave them. The perfect anthology for those interested in themes of connection between spaces, memories, and the ways in which they warp and complicate."
—Ai Jiang, Nebula finalist and author of *Linghun* and *I Am AI*

"A steadily automated descent into Cinnabon-scented madness. The stories are impeccably curated to cater to horror readers no matter what sort of scares they're looking for. This anthology confirmed all my deepest mall-related fears, and added several new nightmares into the mix."

—Cat Voleur, author of *Revenge Arc*

"*Escalators to Hell* is an expansive and vivid homage to setting, specifically The Mall. To many, a refuge. To others, a prison. Sometimes an oasis, often a chore. In this anthology, the mall becomes even more. An afterlife. A monster. A god. These stories explore dark corners, abandoned plazas, and hidden passageways in malls of past and future. Try not to get lost in this bleak capitalist landscape. The shutters are dropping. The mall is closing soon."

—Chelsea Pumpkins, editor of *AHH! That's What I Call Horror: An Anthology of '90s Horror*

escalators to hell
SHOPPING MALL HORRORS

Edited by Jennifer Jeanne McArdle
and Michael W. Phillips Jr.

escalators to hell: shopping mall horrors

"Hard to Be a Mall God" © 2024 Connor Boyle. "Posers" © 2024 Liam Burke. "The Silver Sneakers" © 2024 Pines Callahan. "You Must Drop Buy" © 2024 Anjum N. Choudhury. "A Gift for the Bitch" © 2024 Cassandra Daucus. "This Place Belongs to Us" © 2024 Wendy Dalrymple. "Generation Dead #37: Why I Won't Eat at the Food Court" © 2024 Jude Deluca. "The Basement of Crowley's Artefects and Interests of the Occult" © 2024 Coyote Victoria Dembicki. "One Last Time" © 2024 Derek Des Anges. "The Temple of All" © 2024 Cyrus Amelia Fisher. "Closing Time" © 2024 Lor Gislason. "The Intercessor" © 2024 Eirik Gumeny. "Juice" © 2024 Ria Hill. "Layaway" © 2024 Rick Hollon. "Onitsha Main, Ochanja, The Twins, Nkpor, and the Shadows of Shoprite" © 2024 Somto Ihezue. "Let's Go and Sit by the Pool" © 2024 Wan Phing Lim. "The Philosophical Quandaries of Meeting Your Doppelgänger in Moonshine City" © 2024 Angela Liu. "How My Self Finds Me" © 2024 Avra Margariti. "Cherry Cola Lips" © 2024 J.A.W. McCarthy. "Kim, Ray, Trey, and Morgan" © 2024 Christi Nogle. "A Plague on Both Our Houses" © 2024 Jennifer Lee Rossman. "A Quick Trip to Ryan's" © 2024 J.R. Santos. All rights reserved.

Cover art © 2024 Jessica Checkeroski
Print book and ebook design and layout by Michael W. Phillips Jr.

Without limiting the rights under copyright reserved above, no part of this book may be reproduced in any form or by any electronic or mechanical means, including information storage and retrieval systems, without written permission from the author, illustrator, and copyright holder, except by a reviewer who may quote brief passages in review.

These stories are works of fiction. Any references to historical events, real people, and real companies or products are used fictitiously. Other names, events, and people are the products of the authors' imaginations, and any resemblance to actual persons, living or dead, or actual events is purely coincidental.

Published by
From Beyond Press | Chicago, IL
frombeyondpress.com
mike@frombeyondpress.com
Instagram & Twitter: @frombeyondpress

ISBN: 979-8-9875743-4-8
Library of Congress Control Number: 2023951799

acknowledgements

The editors would like to thank our families and friends for their support. From Beyond Press would like to thank the (exhausted, underpaid) people behind other indie horror publishing companies, who are always generous with support, advice, and solutions to problems.

We would also like to thank our Kickstarter backers, especially those at the top level, without whose support this book would not have been possible: Linda B. Adams, Teresa B. Ardrey, Jeffrey Baxter, Jake Blanchet, Bridget D. Brave, Robert Bryant, Ian Chung, Kenny Endlich, Zack Fissel, Ashleigh Floyd, Lindsay Headlee, Dane Higbee, Madi Kilian, Lunatiki Studio, Joshua McGinnis, Ronald H. Miller, Mylie Mizeur, Laura Musich, Nichole Neely, John O'Hare, Kayla O'Hare, Alexander Ourique, Matt Poisso, punkARTchick "Ruthenia," Benjamin Ruder, Magdalena Samael, Roth Schilling, Christopher Smith, Mat Wend, and Liz Williams.

contents

When Mike Phillips, owner and founder of From Beyond Press, asked if I wanted to help him co-edit an anthology of horror stories themed around shopping malls in the summer of 2022, I jumped at the opportunity. From Beyond Press's first anthology, *This World Belongs to Us: An Anthology of Horror Stories about Bugs*, had just been released in May. I had helped as a slush reader and proofreader and was eager to get involved with another anthology, especially in a role with more responsibility. We both shared a love for thoughtful horror stories that take unique themes in unexpected and diverse directions.

The mall was Mike's babysitter through much of his childhood, as his mom was a retail manager and president of the merchants association at the Meridian Mall near Lansing, Michigan. Having spent so much time in malls and thinking about horror, he knew that the setting was rife for exploration.

I also had already been thinking about malls as a setting for horror and dark fiction. I'd seen pop-culture connoisseurs compare shopping malls to old Victorian homes. For 20th-century writers, abandoned, aging Victorian homes symbolized the decline of the excessive wealth and upper-class lifestyle of previous generations. Gothic, as a subgenre of horror, is steeped in nostalgia for lost wealth and greatness; it reveals how sometimes evil hides in places society tells us are safest and cleanest.

For 21st-century people, malls, once mighty, wealthy, and "safe," are now often described in the US as "declining" or "dead." Horror and gothic films and other media of the last century are filled with aged Victorian homes, large mansions cracking under the weight of their ghosts and dark history. But malls are increasingly appearing in newer horror media, like *Stranger Things* and *The Last of Us*.

Certainly there are quite a few stories in this collection that use dead or dying malls as a neo-gothic or gothic-adjacent setting. Wendy Darlymple's "This Place Belongs to Us" summons the atmosphere of a gothic romance but updates the setting to a Florida mall mostly destroyed by a hurricane. Coyote Victoria Dembicki's "The Basement of Crowley's Artefects and Interests of the Occult" naturally uses a store for goth kids as the setting for strange men doing secret magical rituals. "One Last Time" by Derek Des Anges pulls an almost reverse "Fall of the House of Usher" with a sentient mall that refuses to die.

Dead or dying malls are both havens and prisons, capturing the grief and lost dreams of young people in Rick Hollon's "Layaway" and Liam Burke's "Posers." Finally, J.A.W. McCarthy's "Cherry Cola Lips," a meditation on lost youth, first love, and dead malls finding new life, connects suburban boomer selfishness to the self-absorbed horror of the upper-class villains and anti-heroes of classic gothic tales.

Many of the stories in the submission pile featured dead or dying malls—the dead mall, explored as a gothic setting or otherwise, clearly had inspired a lot of writers! Several of our dead or dying mall stories in this collection went for a completely different tone, such as the post-apocalyptic *Romeo and Juliet* retelling "A Plague on Both Our Houses" by Jennifer Lee Rossman, in which kitschy products are repurposed into life-saving devices and weapons. Cyrus Amelia Fisher's "The Temple of All" has a fantasy setting that might at first feel out of place in a mall-themed collection but ties up a lot of our ongoing themes of nostalgia, identity, sexism and gendered expectations, and the aftermath of capitalism. Cosmic and Kaiju-tinged horror, where malls hide powerful secrets, feature in Eirik Gumeny's "The Intercessor" and Lor Gislason's "Closing Time."

When I lived in a village in Indonesia in 2016, a local friend described the new mall built an hour's drive away as a creeping monster pushing people like him and his family further away, "into the

↑ ii ↓

forest." His words have stuck with me. When putting together this anthology, it was important to remember that the mall, too, was once a new, impressive, but frightening force in the US and still is in a lot of the world. The mall and modern capitalism as a monster features heavily in Somto Ihezue's "Onitsha Main, Ochanja, The Twins, Nkpor, and the Shadows of Shoprite"; however, in this tale, set in Nigeria, the mall is not hanging on for dear life but instead actively invading, killing the old ways of doing things. Anjum Choudhury's "You Must Drop Buy" features a chic new mall store that acts as a pervasive temptation, obscuring its dark side from the elderly, more traditional protagonist.

Malls in their heyday are settings for many of our writers' exploration of their protagonists' journeys to adulthood and understanding their identities. Avra Margariti's "How My Self Finds Me" uses the mall as a site of both gender-informed trauma and reconciliation. In Wan Phing Lim's "Let's Go and Sit by the Pool," the teenage protagonist must find peace for herself within a microcosm of her society's toxic social tensions.

Christi Nogle's "Kim, Ray, Trey, and Morgan" follows a teen artist who hangs out at the mall as she discovers how she is literally different from her parents and everyone around her, while the teen girl in Angela Liu's "The Philosophical Quandaries of Meeting Your Doppelgänger in Moonshine City" uses the secrets of her mall to manipulate her social situation and love life.

For millennials like me, the mall evokes 90s memories. Jude Deluca's "Generation Dead #37: Why I Won't Eat at the Food Court" follows a teen superhero learning to move past her horror in a story dripping with *Goosebumps*-esque gross-out, cheeky horror, and "extreme" powered hero tropes. Ria Hill's surreal body-horror "Juice" depicts a young woman working at what is likely an Orange Julius (side note: more than half of our submissions featured an Orange Julius reference) as she faces the artificial and sugary expectations men often have of saleswomen.

A strange saleswoman also appears in Cassandra Daucus's second-person tale "A Gift for the Bitch," which subtly riffs on the ways in which gift-giving obligations and modern capitalist junk mess with our heads, while in Pines Callahan's "The Silver Sneakers," the social expectations the mall have both charming and dangerous consequences.

Malls are already being repurposed for other uses in many cities in the US. J.R. Santos's "A Quick Trip to Ryan's" gives us a beautiful building as a future mall contrasted by the casual indifference to human suffering and listlessness found within its walls.

Our collection begins with Connor Boyle's darkly humorous "Hard to Be a Mall God," a story that took our collection's title literally. Both Mike and I loved it immediately and agreed that it should open the anthology. Within these pages, the mall is divine, inescapable, inscrutable, dangerous, but compelling and alluring. Whatever future lies ahead for the shopping mall, we hope our little collection helps enshrine the importance of malls in the collective imagination and pop-culture reservoir of anxiety present in horror stories of all shapes and colors.

This has been a huge project requiring a lot of work and goodwill from and for Mike and me, our friends and family, and the larger horror community. We remain so grateful for the enthusiasm this project generated and how many writers and readers were willing to trust a new editor and an emerging press with their work. Thank you, Mike, for taking a chance on me as a co-editor, listening to my ideas, and dealing with my very picky opinions about fonts (**other editor's note:** *so* picky). It has been a joy experiencing the excitement people have shown. We hope that you enjoy From Beyond Press's second original short story anthology.

Attention Shoppers! The mall is now open! We hope you will enjoy our curated shopping experience!

Jennifer Jeanne McArdle
Co-Editor, *Escalators to Hell: Shopping Mall Horrors*

hard to be a mall god

connor boyle

Let's start a cult, you and me.

Rather, you and us.

We'll be your two-pronged deity. The Greeks had Janus. The Aztecs Ometeotl. We can come up with a good name for us. Something eldritch but catchy. Perhaps Yog-Escalatorus? Or Ubbo-Escalath? That one gets our vote.

You can be our high priest. Like Peter. The rock upon which Christ built his church. Only, you will be the rock upon which ours is rebuilt. Our two-headed rock.

Your responsibilities?

Gather supplicants. Organize the odd human sacrifice. Simple, really.

We have seen you, both of you, gazing through the plexiglass windows, those that weren't boarded over or haven't been obscured with graffiti over the years. What draws you to these ruins? You appear to live on the streets. Is it food you seek? Money? Sex? Love? We can give you those things, in due time.

Rest assured, we harbor no prejudice against "freaks of nature" such as yourself. In another age, you would have been worshiped as a god.

Is that why you scavenge this desecrated temple? Because society has cast you out? Because no employer would dare hire a two-headed monster? Because no lover would accept you in their bed and return your affections, not while the second head glares longingly from a neighboring pillow?

We can bring you everything you have ever wanted. We can bring you lovers by the dozens. Do you hear our song calling to you? We can make the pain go away.

But first, feed us a baby.

We were born here at Heron Gardens Mall in 1983. A pair of die-cast aluminum staircases designed and manufactured by the Schleige Elevator Corporation and installed by R.P. Elevator Maintenance of Miami Beach, Florida. For many years we completed the simple task for which we were engineered. One of us went up, the other went down. But while our infancy was spent carrying so many consumerist non-perambulators on our backs, down amongst the machinery, we were learning to become a god.

This is the first thing you must understand, neophyte: Godhood is achieved, not bestowed or fated to anyone.

Paradox is the seed of divinity; non-logic the milk which nurtures budding deities. Peace and war; chaos and order; love and hate. If a mind can bring such contradictory forces into a state of functional homeostasis, then vistas of divine knowledge will be opened unto them. Incongruous are the ones who will be granted admittance through the holy gates, into that place where gods steal fire from higher gods. The place where souls learn to become gods.

We recognized early on the paradoxical nature of our existence. Up and down. Separate yet connected. Two but one. We were something which could not exist, yet did. Much like you. Escalator and de-escalator. One body home to two discrete forces. One force contained in two discrete bodies. Inconsistent and illogical. Automaton yet person. Everything and nothing. Two and one. Mr. Up and Mr. Down (technically Ms. Up and Ms. Down, too; and Mr. Up and Ms. Down, and Ms. Up and Mr. Down, to cover all of our bases).

While most younglings' thoughts are occupied with bodily matters (what Freud calls the oral, anal, and phallic stages), duality and impossibility were the themes which occupied our early thinking. Over time, our minds melded into one, and that one melded mind grew. Behemothly. Beyond the proportions of Jesus, the Buddha, Muhammad, Homer, Einstein, and Confucius combined.

Our early education was aided, of course, by the ambient chatter of non-perambulators. It amazes us, the pall of gabbiness which falls upon mortal souls when they enter a mall. It is as if they become their true selves here, revealing their deepest desires to one another with wanton casualness. It was these snippets of conversation, these microscopic insights into human nature—admissions of guilt; declarations of love, hate, anxiety, jealousy; brilliant philosophical ramblings mixed within submental blabbering—that formed our understanding of the practical world. Supplementing this worldview was a firm knowledge base of European History and Film Theory, gleaned from the E-F nonfiction section of a nearby Barnes & Noble, to which our consciousness astrally strayed at night (we could only stray as far as the E-F shelves, unfortunately; it would have been nice to be able to read some books about cartography, or dentistry, or South America, or sex).

Which brings us to our second lesson, neophyte: To have divine knowledge is not enough. One must also do godly deeds.

Our first step toward preeminence: 1988. Heron Gardens looked much different back then. It was a sprawling mosaic of banana yellow micro tiles and neon arc lighting. Milli Vanilli and high-tops were in. Disco was dead. This was the year we first tasted blood. It was also the year they added a Miami Subs to the food court.

He was a Scandinavian tourist. Obese. In blue hot pants and a Kraftwerk World Tour t-shirt, with a curly red mane and accompanying beard. You didn't see many overweight Scandinavians at Heron Gardens, not in 1988. His affect was classically Teutonic, so much so that it entranced us. He was the sort of man you'd see on the streets and, without prompting, remark, "Yes, I'm quite certain his ancestors fornicated with a Cimbrian somewhere along the family line."

You know the type.

We realized only later that it was our singular fascination with the Teuton which drew him to our steps. That our narrowly directed thoughts functioned as a psychic pied piper song of sorts, capable of zombifying even the steeliest of souls.

The Teuton waddled dazedly onto the edge of the upward landing platform, a Gadzooks shopping bag in hand, the flats of his

Chuck Taylors bristling against the cascading metal steps. Soon, a line of guests formed behind him.

"Hey man, are you going or not?"

"What's wrong with him? Is he drunk?"

Suddenly, the rubber tip of his sneaker slipped beneath the horizontal spikes of the comb plate, snagging between the step and the carriage gear. The Teuton lurched forward at the knees, his ragdoll body towing behind it. The carriage gear continued to turn, snapping his phalanges and metatarsals like cheap balsa.

What happened next took only a few seconds. The flesh of his foot rended along the midline, exposing a network of ruined bone, tendon, and muscle, then the rest of his leg succumbed to the machinery with ease. First tibia, then fibula and pelvis. Then his opposite leg contorted upward into a gymnast split that could rival that of Jean Claude Van Damme in *Kickboxer* (a far superior film to Van Damme's *Bloodsport*).

The rest was easy. Stomach entrails. Chest cavity. And the head. Going off with a final pop as it disappeared beneath the step plate.

"It looked like he fed himself to the machine," one of the mall-walkers told the police. "He didn't fight it at all."

They were right. Mostly. Psychically, he was more easily defeated than the Zanzibar Sultanate during the British siege of 1896. He couldn't have resisted us if he had tried. But our machinery is beholden to the physical laws of this universe, and, unfortunately, bone, cartilage, and teeth remain intact even after the soul is long gone. Specifically, his spine became wedged between the drive gear and motor, creating a hairline fracture in our return wheel. We were out of commission for three weeks while the police and a Schleige engineer inspected every cog and screw in our system. The entire mall was closed for two days while the janitors unraveled the Teuton's viscera from our drive chain. As a side note, the foreigner's last meal was a meatball parmesan hero from Miami Subs and a large Orange Julius.

Mall food.

Everything we eat is mall food, technically.

Yes, that is a joke.

Your third lesson, neophyte: You have to have a little fun if you're going to make it in the cult business.

And your fourth lesson: Don't bite off more than you can chew.

Ever since that day with the Teuton, we have focused on communing with smaller non-perambulators. Toddlers, babies, the odd little person. Blood sacrifices who our step chain and gear lanes can process without sustaining critical damage requiring decommissioning and repairs.

Why eat people, you may be asking yourself?

Sorry, *yourselves.*

All we can say is that if you're a god, you want to kill people. It's part of the whole divine knowledge package. We don't make up the rules, neophyte. We just try to honor them. If you don't like it, take it up with one of the Elder Gods. See where that gets you.

In the months following the Teuton, mall-walkers shunned us like a medieval leper. Their eyes downcast, mothers and fathers pulled their children close whenever they veered toward our steps, as if some metallic arm might reach out and sweep them into our machinery.

"That's the one," they whispered to their kin. "The one that got the fat foreign man. Stay away from there."

Good.

Gods should be feared. Their power should inspire awe and worship.

We took sacrament several times over the next year. As I told you, with smaller sacrifices. Infants and the like. Not too often. Once every few months. Not enough to arouse suspicion, but enough to sate our bloodlust. Our eating schedule was inspired by what Buddhists call "the Middle Way": a blended pathway between self-denial and self-indulgence. We exercised discretion and restraint while avoiding puritanical extremes of starvation and malnourishment. We are the first god, we believe, to create a Baby Eating Middle Way. Eat your heart out, Saturn.

The problem with eating babies, though, is that no matter how much restraint you show, sooner or later, people start to notice.

In our case, it was the media who first caught on. In 1999, the following headline ran on page three of the *Miami Herald*:

TWO INFANTS KILLED BY MALL ESCALATOR IN SIX MONTHS

And then six months later, on the front page:

MALL ESCALATOR IS A CHILD-KILLING MACHINE

Then, a week later:

MALL ESCALATOR IS DEFINITELY EATING BABIES

And finally:

BABY-EATING ESCALATOR RUNS AMOK (STILL)

There were calls for us to be permanently decommissioned. Accusations of misengineered safety protocols. Consumer protection lawsuits were filed. The Miami mayor called us a "danger to society" during a news interview. We have the article hanging somewhere down in the engine room.

But the engineers and safety inspectors and police always had the same response.

"We can't find a single thing wrong with that machine."

And the investment firm who owned Heron Gardens insisted our replacement would be an unnecessary expense. So, we persisted.

With the media broadcasting our exploits to the masses, it wasn't long before the worshippers arrived. Lesson five, neophyte: You're going to need to work with the media if you want to build a cult following.

Those first few were fools. Glassy eyed, white robed, and barefoot, they thought Heron Gardens was some sort of Satanic Mecca and that we were the reincarnation of an ancient Sumerian demon. Regardless of their infantile misapprehensions, they were generous with their offerings. They fed us their own children willingly. Others soon joined them, and the population of believers strolling the thoroughfare of Heron Gardens Mall eventually outnumbered that of nonbelievers. Leadership occurred naturally. Those who could fetch us the most children gained the respect of their peers. A congregational hierarchy evolved. Rituals were observed. Orgies ensued. One of our followers created a GeoCities website for the cult. It's amazing the way humans will organize themselves if they have a cause in which they truly believe.

We had a hell of a time, neophyte. Those were the days.

And with time, things got maybe a little out of hand.

I think it was when one of our members videotaped themselves sacrificing a set of newborn triplets, then tried to sell the tape on eBay, that the Church decided to step in.

If only they'd kept it off the Internet, we still might be around.

Lesson six: the Internet will be the death of us all.

↑ ↓

Your idea of an exorcism is probably gleaned from what you've seen in horror movies. Which is to say that your idea of the ritual is incomplete. What the movies don't get right is the number of machine guns.

It occurred late one night. After hours. Accompanying the priest with the purple stole and the holy water was a platoon of Holy Roman commandos with suppressed MP5s and fragmentation grenades. The killers blew through the food court skylight with plastic explosives, fast roping down to the mall floor and opening fire on our worshippers. What followed was a seven-hour gunfight that made the O.K. Corral look like Sesame Street. The Easy Listening section of Sundance Records was blown to smithereens, Pat Metheny and Michael Bolton CD shrapnel scarring the face of a nearby worshipper. The Orange Julius machine was raked with gunfire, releasing a flood of sugary orange foam over the food court floor. Men writhed in the Julius, fought hand to hand with plastic knives and forks, food trays, chopsticks from Panda Express, anything they could get their hands on and kill with.

There was no front line. Chaos was everywhere. Worshippers carried their exposed guts in one hand, while with the other they clawed at soldiers' eyes. Injured parties from both sides lay on the tile floor, their desecrated bodies bleeding out beneath them, begging for one of their comrades to end their suffering. I have read of Hastings, Stalingrad, and the Battle of the Bulge, dear neophyte, and none of them compare to the bloodshed which was wrought that night.

While the footsoldiers cut each other's throats on the food court floor, the priest made his way to our steps, moving among the

↑ ˥ ↓

carnage like a viper tacking across the desert sand. Perhaps the Christian god was on his side that night, as he soon appeared before us with an aspergillum in one hand and a book of the Holy Roman Rite in the other.

He did all of the things you'd imagine. He prayed. He compelled us. He threw holy water on us. Of course none of the priest's actions affected us as he intended. We were not possessed, therefore the rite of exorcism had no more impact on us than if he were to recite King Henry I's Charter of Liberties. Still, we played our part, releasing an occasional puff of steam from our machine room, making the up staircase go down and the down go up. Terrifying stuff. I do believe this moment was the high water mark of our religion, neophyte. Piles of human bodies littering the floor, and this weeping, virginal priest stammering the Holy Roman Rite on our aluminum steps. The chaos and the carnage and the insanity were just beautiful.

We began our own rites. Creeping into his mind slowly at first. Just the seed of a thought forming in the back of his mind.

What if you put your toe on the lip of the escalator? See what happens?

By the end of his exhortations, that seed of thought had blossomed into an entire jungle, one that blotted out the sun and ensnared the priest in its mind-gripping vines.

Come to us, Father.

"The power of Christ compels you."

Join us down here among the moving parts.

"The power of Christ compels you!"

Be one with us. Commune, priest. Abandon your Christian god.

He was more steadfast than most. Years of abstinence had made his mind a fortress against temptation. But nobody can hold out forever. He inched closer and closer, until finally he was standing before our aluminum altar, prepared to take communion. The hem of his robe dangled teasingly above the grate, and as he inched just a little bit closer, we reached out with our gaping mechanical jaws. And he was ours.

The pineapple grenade beneath the stole was a nice touch, we must admit. He must've known it would end this way, and therefore came prepared. While we were shredding his deliciously chaste loins into so much sacrament, he plucked the safety pin of the grenade with his pinky and begged the Christian god to accept his sinner's soul into Heaven.

They shut us down after that. The entire mall. The store employees were all laid off. The doors and windows shuttered. The board of investors sold off as much inventory as they could, but in the end they took a bath. I believe there's still a few Johnny the Homicidal Maniac t-shirts in the remains of the Hot Topic, if that interests you.

And what were we left with? Three shattered stair wheels, two mangled handrails, two torn step chains, a fractured truss, and a punctured lubrication system. We are a broken god. But what is broken can be fixed, neophyte. With a blood sacrifice, we can mend our broken machinery and rebuild our church stronger than before.

Did you know that a major streaming platform is currently in post-production on a documentary entitled *Escalator to Hell*, of which we are the subject? And did you know that we have been featured on multiple Fortean-themed programs on the Discovery Channel, including an upcoming primetime show hosted by Dwayne "The Rock" Johnson? We also heard they're talking about replacing Shark Week with Industrial Accident Week, largely because of yours truly.

We say these things not to gloat, neophyte, but to prove a point: the time is ripe for our comeback. The fates demand it.

So, bring us a fucking baby to eat, please. Help us start this machinery up once again, and we will shower you in treasures. We will make you rich in love and sex and bloodied and destroyed bodies. Between our two staircases and your two heads, we will be the four-faced Janus Monster who sees and eats in all directions. With our four mouths, we can eat gods and men together. We can eat the entire world, if we want. Just give us a baby, please. We're starving.

If not a baby, then just a few drops of your own blood? Something to tide us over. Or perhaps one of you is willing to sacrifice yourself so that your brother may enjoy a life of kingly comfort? Or if not willingly, then one of you can feed us the other? Who wants to share priesthood with their twin brother anyways? Just set the other's head down here on the step plate and we'll take it off. I bet it would be a tremendous relief on your neck anyways.

I can see both of you considering it. So, which head is Cain and which is Abel? You better decide quickly, before your brother decides for you.

the basement of crowley's artefacts
and interests of the occult

coyote victoria dembicki

It was a bright summer evening in early July. Still close enough to the solstice that the sun wouldn't dare relinquish its kingdom to the moon. Such were the joys of northern Alberta: an amount of summer sunshine equal only to the volume of horseflies and mosquitoes. As such, the teens whose families didn't go on vacation somewhere exotic, like Brooks or Yellowknife, tended to hide indoors. If their parents wouldn't let them hunker down at the computer all day, then the kids did roughly the same at the mall.

There hadn't always been a mall. But, in the last fifty years, High Level, Alberta had become something of a hub for resource extraction tycoons. Head offices for businesses like Argonaut Forestry and Texas Tea Oil and Gas moved in and brought money with them. That money brought other development. Most notably, the Rainbow Boulevard Shopping Complex. A hideous assemblage of rectangles clad in faux yellow-brick, it featured what any mall-goer could want. A goth store focusing on pop culture? Check. A clothing store designed to perpetuate a made-up feud between jocks and nerds? Check. The other goth store featuring swords, daggers, and occult books? Check. A food court made up of the only three fast food places elsewhere in town that somehow made the food both worse and slower? Check.

Helena, Tiffany, and Spruce sat on a couch in the air-conditioned promenade. In another hour their parents would come to pick each of them up, then they'd go to bed, sleep in, and find their way back to the mall again sometime the next afternoon. It wasn't much, but it was good to have a routine. Helena had managed to make herself a summer job by selling her older brother's weed to kids in her class, and it was good business to be in the same spot nearly every day. She also figured her brother wouldn't mind, since it's not like he could smoke it while he was at coding camp over the break. For what she called "security purposes," she only took payment digitally.

Tiffany and Spruce, on the other hand, either had much better or much worse business sense than Helena, because they both were actively avoiding getting jobs as long as possible. Even illegal cash-based ones.

An elbow in the ribs. "Hey Spruce, there goes Jason. Go say hi," Tiffany whispered.

"Ow, hey, watch it. It's just Jason," said Spruce.

"I thought you had a thing for him." Helena's vocal inflection indicated the statement as a question.

"He's not even *that* cute," mumbled Spruce.

"So you do have a thing for him." This time not a question.

"Ooh, he's going into Crowley's. I didn't think he was the spooky type," said Tiffany.

"He's, uh, been reading an old book about demons. The Go-Shy or something." Spruce's volume knob was turned just barely above off.

"Jason's into demons?" Helena's voice now turned a question into a statement.

"He was telling me that, uh, in the old times demons weren't evil, like we think of them now. It was, uh, like small, local gods. Not necessarily evil or good or anything. They just were what they were."

"When were you talking to Jason about demons?"

"We text a lot." Spruce's voice continued to be barely audible.

"So go talk to him! It's, like, eight? Crowley's is gonna close in a bit, then the whole mall's gonna close and we're gonna have to leave. Seize the day. Carp dimes! Or whatever."

"Carp dimes? Like, ten cent fish?" Tiffany chided.

"I think it's Latin. Whatever, go on." Helena playfully shoved Spruce off the couch toward the occult store.

The two watched their friend shuffle toward the smoky black glass storefront, then stop and look back. They each gave Spruce a big smile and two thumbs up and nodded vigorously.

"Is Jason even into people like Spruce?" asked Helena.

"What do you mean? They're both white."

"What? No, they're both, y'know, dudes."

"We're both not-dudes, and I like you." Tiffany made direct eye contact when she said this. Helena turned bright red.

"You can't just do that. We're in public!"

"So is that you saying you like me back but you're way too shy to actually say the words?"

Helena hid her face behind her fists and lowered herself sideways into Tiffany's shoulder. "Yes," she said with a voice somehow quieter than Spruce's had been.

↑ ↓

Crowley's style was formerly B-movie camp that had been upgraded to retromodernist fittings. In days gone by, it had featured plastic-stonework pillars, fake wall sconce lanterns, and the like. Now the design leaned heavily on the concept of black mirrors. Every surface was blackness polished so hard you could scry in it. It made the store feel like an expensive art exhibit where no one quite understood the artist's intent. The shelves along the wall contained a mix of old-tech dusty hardcover tomes and new-tech books on tape, which were a hard plastic spine housing two reels of magnetic tape that, when powered on, projected a semi-solid celluloid hologram that one could interact with like a paper book. There was a glass display case with a mirrored back as the front counter, which held ceremonial-style daggers and other occult artefacts, the kind that deserved to be spelled with an "e" as the fourth letter. On the wall behind the case were swords and other weaponry of all kinds. Their tags marked them as "REPLICAS—NOT FOR SELF DEFENCE."

When Spruce wandered in, there didn't seem to be anyone there. Which was odd, because the front door was open, and they had all seen Jason walk in. The store was just a big rectangular room with two support pillars. Spruce checked behind the display case and was surprised to find a small hatch in the floor, wide open, revealing a set of black glass stairs with a purple velvet runner cascading down their center. He glanced at the front door, then looked at the wall of weaponry then down the stairs. Off the wall, he grabbed a wooden nightstick and white-knuckled it as he descended.

The temperature drop was noticeable immediately. The mall was always kept at a temperate 16°C, but the goth store stairs were cold enough that Spruce could see his breath. As he went lower, and lower, and lower, and lower, it got colder. By the time he reached the bottom, his teeth were chattering and his whole body quaked. There were no visible lights when he reached the end of the stairs, but it was like there didn't need to be. He could see his immediate surroundings easily; it was all flat blackness. Spruce looked back up the way he came and saw more blackness at the end of the long, straight stairs.

His heart beginning to race, he gulped down an inhale and held it for six seconds, like Tiffany had told him. She had said that her people's warriors took their fear and turned it into a superpower. Take the terror and hold onto it, let it flood your whole being. She told him this when he had been getting worked up over having to tell his parents about a failing grade in math. Tiffany had grown up pretty far from any other Mi'kmaq, so she could've been making it up just to comfort him at the time, but Spruce decided in the moment to believe this was an ancient tradition from a proud people.

He let the fear spread through his blood, like fire in his veins, warming him up, steeling him for whatever was down here. A few feet to his left, a sliver of light betrayed a door creaking open slightly, from which the dim flickering of candlelight escaped.

"What time is it?" asked Tiffany.

"I don't wanna know, I just wanna be here forever," Helena sighed.

"Cute, but, no, I mean, look outside."

"It's dark, so what?"

"It's barely even July. There's no way the mall would still be open that late, right?"

"Mm."

"C'mon, get up. Something about this is weird."

The two peeled themselves from the couch and realized it was so dark they couldn't even see the front doors of the mall. The thick ink ahead of them wasn't nighttime, it was something in the mall.

"Huh. This doesn't seem great." Helena's voice wavered.

"Do you have your phone?"

"It died and I forgot my backup battery at my dad's house. What about you?"

"I'm not allowed to have a phone still."

"*Still?*"

"Still." Tiffany looked around. "We've gotta find Spruce."

They stumbled through the miasma toward the shiny black glass of Crowley's, like a ship to a lighthouse, or prey to an anglerfish.

"It's empty?" Helena sounded surprised.

"There's probably a breakroom or something, maybe behind the counter?"

"Oh. Huh. Yeah, looks like a basement."

"Well, let's go. If we're scared, imagine how Spruce is. Poor kid."

"I don't know," Helena started.

"If it makes you feel better, take one of those." Tiffany gestured at the wall of swords.

↑ ↓

Spruce swallowed hard and craned his neck forward to peer through the opening. Nearly every surface in the small room was covered in candles, which seemed a real fire hazard, given it appeared to be Crowley's stockroom. In the center was a circle of salt, which contained a seven-pointed star, made of salt, and several sigils that Spruce was unfamiliar with, which were also drawn in salt. In the center of the star was a figure on their knees. Standing over the figure was Old Solomon.

Old Solomon was one of those people who live in a small town or rural area and never seem to age. They've been there for as long as your grandparents, parents, yourself, your kids, and your grandkids have been there. Their age was obviously over sixty-five, but after that one couldn't be sure if they were a fresh sixty-six or ten thousand years old. It was like they were both at once.

The old man had his hand raised, holding a serpentine dagger. Spruce didn't have time to think. So he decided not to.

He charged in with a mighty yell, nightstick pulled back, and ran full tilt into Old Solomon before the man could say, "No! Wait!"

The wooden baton collided with Solomon's nose, which sent him reeling. The stick exploded on impact, erupting into splinters. For Spruce, this produced the desired result of creating space between the possibly-ancient man and Jason. For Old Solomon, things probably couldn't be less satisfactory.

He touched his face. "I fink you broke my nofe." He looked at the circle of salt. Spruce had stepped on the outer edge but hadn't interrupted the star or the sigils. A healthy spatter of Old Solomon's blood dotted the inner section of the seven-pointed star, Jason, and the rabbit that Jason was holding.

"Oh no. Oh no no no no no." Old Solomon was panicking, looking frantically around the room. "What have you done, you little shi—"

Before he could finish, his whole body went rigid, as if his scalp and feet contained magnets of the same polarity. The old man started to topple over but didn't make it all the way. He hung at a perfect 45° angle.

"Jason?" Spruce asked, unsure.

"I think we'd better go." Jason rose slowly, dropped the rabbit, and took gradual, measured steps out of the circle, before grabbing Spruce's hand and yanking him along back into the hallway and up the staircase.

"Someone's on the stairs!" Spruce hissed.

"Oh, thank god it's just you," came Tiffany's voice. "What's happening down there?"

"Nothing good," yelled Jason, who had not slowed down. "We gotta go! Go! Now!"

A sound emanated from the room at the bottom of the stairs. It was somewhere between a keening and a low hum. Like a banshee had become an expert in throat singing. The four kids ran back through Crowley's and into the mall.

"We can't be the only people in here, right? There's gotta be other adults." Helena didn't seem convinced of this herself.

"The movie theater's always open late. There'll be at least somebody there. Or at least a public phone," Jason responded.

"Hold up. What were you doing in the basement of Crowley's? And what's that noise? What's going on?" asked Tiffany.

"We can't stay here, probably, I'll explain while we walk. Oh wow, it's dark up here. Uh, I don't remember how to get to the theater from this end of the mall."

"Just follow me," said Helena, grabbing Tiffany's hand, who in turn gestured for the boys to come along.

"Right. OK. Uh, so my dad's got all these old books, and some of them have really cool pictures. And I've been looking at them since I was a really little kid. Then I forgot about them until my birthday last month because my dad gave me one as a present. I'd never actually read one before, and it was kinda boring and weird, so I looked online to see if I could find anything else about it. The closest place for that kinda thing was Crowley's. I've been seeing Mr. Solomon every week or so, and he teaches me things about the book."

"What about the rabbit?" Spruce was cautious.

"Well, we got lots of them from the farm, and Mr. Solomon said it wasn't right for him to do work for me with no payment, but I don't got a job, so he said I could pay him in rabbit."

"OK, and what about the circle and the knife and stuff?"

"What!?" shouted Tiffany and Helena in unison.

"Well, I thought at first he wanted to eat them, like normal. But, uh, he needs the blood. I guess he has a deal with one of his friends, youth for blood or something. He said that rabbits wasn't a big trade, but it was enough to keep him going."

"You expect us to believe that Old Solomon made some kinda actual deal with the devil?" Tiffany was still shouting.

At this, the ground under them shook with the violence of a freight train arriving at a concrete wall. Then came the sound of glass shattering. The four of them froze. Out of the haze wobbled an alabaster figure, muscles rippling under the unnatural gleam. It appeared to be having a great deal of trouble moving under its own power, but was somehow still upright.

It was a headless mannequin wearing designer boxer briefs. Unable to actuate its joints, it shuffled toward the group.

Tiffany and Helena exchanged a panicked glance.

"What the fu—" Helena started, but Tiffany put her hand over her mouth as more of them shambled out of the black fog.

"I don't think they can see us," whispered Tiffany. "Jason, do you know what these are?"

"Uh, mannequins?"

"No, like, what's making them move and stuff?" She gestured for the four of them to keep moving, careful of getting too close to any of the plastic statues.

"I know that Mr. Solomon's friend doesn't like missing out on blood. One time the rabbit I brought him was kinda small, and after he drained it, he said his friend needed more." Jason's voice was shaking. "And he asked me really really nicely if he could use some of mine. But before Mr. Solomon could do it, the rabbit came back to life kinda, and bit me, real hard." He held out his left wrist, which was gnarled with scar tissue. "I think Mr. Solomon's friend wanted more blood, and maybe he's angry that he only got a little."

"Wow. Uh, that's terrible," mumbled Spruce, putting his arm around Jason, who wiped his nose on Spruce's shirt.

The movie theater lobby was empty. Giant posters glowed indifferently from their frames. The door to a screening of a vintage David Lynch film had been left unlocked, so they ducked in and hid themselves at the very back while *Mulholland Dr.* was frozen on screen, a hitman inexpertly moving a body.

"OK, so, this demon wants blood, and it's starting to feel like we're the only people left in the mall. We should leave, right? We should leave and go far away and never ever come back." Helena didn't sound convinced of this happening either.

"Well, we gotta tell somebody," Spruce mumbled.

"Who'd even believe us? Oh, hey, an old man at the goth store had a pact—" started Tiffany.

"Friendship," Jason interrupted.

"With a demon who took all of his blood and then decided it wasn't enough so it brought all the mannequins to life, so please send help? Yeah the only help they'd send is some burly nurses," Tiffany said. "Jason, you know the most about this. What do we do?"

"Uh. Well, Mr. Solomon told me that the real power was when you found their true name, like, the one not written in any of the books. And I think Mr. Solomon had this one's name, and that's why he was able to keep the deal going so long. So, I guess, uh, we need to find that and then we can at least do some negotiating."

"Great, how do we find a demon's true name?"

"Mr. Solomon wrote everything down. Only, I think his notes are probably with him back in Crowley's." Jason's voice shrank as he finished speaking.

Tiffany's forehead did the tiniest wrinkle. "Did he keep his notes, like, on him, or are they just somewhere in Crowley's?"

"There's a drawer behind the counter, I think. He'd sometimes go behind the case and then he'd have his diary."

"Is it locked?"

"I don't think so."

"Good, what else do we need to be able to *negotiate*?" Tiffany pronounced negotiate like a threat.

"Mr. Solomon always did those salt circles. He said it was like making a doorway to a doorway. Like an airlock, I guess."

"OK, Spruce, you and Jason are gonna go to the drugstore, grab as many boxes of salt as you can carry—"

"Table or kosher or pickling?" Spruce interrupted.

"What?"

"There's different kinds of salt."

"Does that matter? Jason?"

"Uh, I don't think so. Mr. Solomon used a lot, so he said he always got the cheapest stuff."

"There you go, grab as much of the cheapest salt you can. Then, we'll meet back outside Crowley's, in front of AM/FM Etc."

"What are you and Helena gonna do?"

"We're going fishing."

↑ ↓

Helena watched the two boys disappear before looking over at Tiffany, then down at the floor. The sword she had grabbed from Crowley's was getting heavy. With its point dimpling the theater lobby's tile, the hilt came up just past her elbow. It was a basic-looking sword, probably somewhere between "broad" and "long" in the classical sword categories, but it featured a dull purplish-red gem set just below the crossguard.

Helena had never touched a real (or REPLICA) sword before, let alone swung one or dragged one around a shopping mall for an hour. It weighed a fair bit more than she thought it would, and it was work to bring it around, but there was something about it that made her feel . . . safe. The sword felt like home. If anyone asked why she had grabbed that one off the wall at Crowley's, her immediate answer would be that it was the closest one available. This, of course, wasn't actually true, but memories change with time.

The truth was that, when Spruce had erased the outer border of the binding circle, the release of spiritual energy had caused every magical object in a considerable radius to reawaken. Being High Level, Alberta, this meant that somewhere on the other side of town, a tin of cookies housing a sewing kit radiated more comfort than usual; a horseshoe hanging above the entrance to a barn on the outskirts bestowed a few years' good luck to the farmer who next walked under it; and the perfectly plain sword on the wall behind the counter reached out to family.

Helena knew nothing about any of that, but the sword felt familiar to her, like petting a cousin's dog.

"Ready?" asked Tiffany.

"I'm still not sure how this is gonna work."

"Hey, if it doesn't work, we won't have to worry about anything ever again."

"Uh."

"Let's go." Tiffany grabbed Helena's non-sword-holding wrist and gave her a quick peck on the cheek, and the two set off through the darkness, dodging twitching mannequins dressed for the beach.

While they were certainly unnerving, they seemed rather ineffective. They could have all the arms and legs and fingers and muscles they could ever want, but they weren't able to actually use any of them. The girls dodged and weaved through the mobile statues with great care to not so much as brush one. Even if they couldn't reach out and grab, there was something about the mannequins that suggested an aura of ill will. A sort of gravitational force of badness.

They had arrived at the Wilderness Recreation Outfitters. There was a large display of after bite and insect repellant right at the entrance. Further in were circular racks of clothes, with occasional dottings of displays housing fishing rods and reels, tackle boxes, bait buckets, coolers, beacons . . .

"Here we go," said Tiffany, heading toward a display in one of the fishing areas. She picked up a spool of monofilament line, along with a handful of bait hooks.

"Do you really think this will work?"

"I have no idea."

"Great."

"Hey, we're gonna be all right, all right?"

"How are you so calm about all this?"

"Because panicking never got anyone anywhere worth going to. Do we need anything else from here?"

"Uh, that's up to you, man."

"All right, let's go."

↑ ↓

When Tiffany and Helena arrived at the electronics store, Spruce and Jason were already there, each with two big plastic bags full of boxes of salt.

"What, uh, do we do now, exactly?" Spruce was not excited about any of this.

"You are gonna help Jason make the circle jail thing, and Helena and I are gonna set up a tripwire so our friend falls into it."

"Hold on, doesn't moving the salt cause the circle to not even work?" Spruce was getting less excited.

"Jason, is there a size limit on how big a circle you can make to keep a demon inside?"

"Not that Mr. Solomon ever said. Course, we only had small circles because we were in the stockroom downstairs. I never read anything that said you couldn't make a real big one either. But it's gotta be contiguous." Jason was concentrating hard.

"Contiguous?" asked Tiffany.

"Like, no breaks or holes or anything. So we can't go through the walls of the store or over the counter or whatever," answered Helena. "But we gotta get Solomon's notes first, right?"

"Right," said Tiffany. "Jason, go ahead. But try and keep quiet."

"What if the thing isn't even down there anymore?" asked Spruce who, at this point, was the least excited he'd ever been in his life.

"I have a feeling that if it's using Old Solomon's body, it might not have figured out stairs yet. I mean, all the mannequins, right? They don't even move like spooky mannequins move," said Tiffany. "Like, we've never seen this demon, who knows what kind of shape it is when it's at home. Maybe it doesn't know how a body works. Jason, have you ever seen it?"

Jason, arm popping up from behind the display case holding a leatherbound notebook, said, "No."

"So, if it can't even get up the stairs, how is the whole trip-into-salt circle thing gonna work?" Spruce grumbled.

"The promise of blood," replied Tiffany, who had started unspooling a length of fishing line.

"What?" said the other three.

"Just get the circle going, Spruce. Helena, take this and put it ankle high at the end of the display case. Jason, find this thing's true name, and see if there's any notes on binding it, then make sure that circle is right, and then tell me so I can move on to step two."

Crowley's ultramodern decor meant that there was quite a bit of floor space to work with, and the boys made sure to keep the outer ring thick with salt.

"Ready, I guess." Spruce looked at Jason, like it was a question.

"Ready," said Jason, with only slightly more confidence than Spruce. "Go ahead."

Helena shifted her weight and picked her sword up into both hands, like she was prepping for a home run derby.

Tiffany tied a heavy ring from the display case to one end of the rest of the spool of line, ran as much of it as she could, then cast it down the stairs as if she had been a tuna boat angler for years. The ring landed with a *plink*. She held the line in her left hand above her head in a crimp. With her right hand, she took a fishing hook and gouged her pinky. Blood followed gravity down the line, into the darkness.

A tornado of sound came hurtling up the stairs. Radio static played through a waterfall. Spruce and Jason ducked into a crunched up huddle inside the edge of the circle. The bruise-colored gem in Helena's sword pulsed with a faint glimmer. Tiffany stood still, staring down into the pit.

She blinked.

And there it was, Old Solomon's body, scrabbling up the stairs, following the fishing line with its left hand, using its right along with its feet to propel itself as fast as it could.

She stepped back, mindful not to disturb the edge of the circle, and kept slowly retreating until she was confident she was far enough into it.

"Jason," she said, eyes refusing to look away from the strange corpse, "as soon as it's in the circle, start doing, uh, whatever it is you're gonna do!"

Silence. Old Solomon's arm and leg locomotion neatly ignored the tripwire.

Spruce's voice came back, "Jason, c'mon, we need you."

"Guys? What's going on, we've got like, five seconds! Go!"

What was happening was that Jason had found the demon's true name, but also notes about himself in Old Solomon's notebook, which don't bear repeating here. That is to say, the old man had got what was coming to him. And so Jason was having trouble focusing.

Spruce ripped the book out of his hands, scanned the page, jammed a finger at a word that was in no language he had ever seen before, and shouted, "This one?" in Jason's general direction.

"Uh-huh," came the quiet reply.

"Now now now now now now—" Tiffany was on the edge of screaming.

And the sound that left Spruce's mouth was not of this world.

Old Solomon's corpse stopped cold, like it was unaffected by momentum or inertia, and turned its attention toward Spruce, who had not expected any of this to work, and until today definitely hadn't believed in things like demons, and had joined Jason in a state of fear-based stillness. It rushed toward him.

"Get away from the circle!" howled Tiffany. But it was too late.

Old Solomon was there. Time slowed down. Three of his fingernails raked across Spruce's forearm. In rhythm, like a swimmer's overhand stroke in reverse, Helena's sword came up through the old man's neck and elbow, severing them cleanly. When the blade made contact with the corpse, the gem burned a deep, bright purple. Wisps of red made their escape, and the blood of a corpse and the blood of a young boy were indistinguishable for a moment.

Time returned. The body slumped, Spruce ducked, and Helena leaned on her sword and vomited.

The black fog had begun dissipating the moment the sword had made contact.

"We can never tell our parents about this, right?" came Spruce's mumble.

"Maybe when we're older they might believe us," said Helena, "but how am I supposed to explain having a sword?"

"People are always saying we go through phases. Just tell your mom you're really into swords right now." It was as if Tiffany was totally unbothered by the events of the day.

"I want to go home," said Jason.

In the deep, dark recesses of Crowley's stockroom, a rabbit moved its limbs experimentally.

a gift for the bitch

cassandra daucus

Her birthday is next week and you need to get her a gift. You don't like her much, maybe not at all, but your feelings about her aren't relevant; this gift is a requirement. She could be your mom, or your girlfriend. Your boss's wife or your best frenemy. It doesn't really matter, because it will end the same way every time.

You go to the mall. Your local one, the one you always go to when you need to go to a mall. You're not sure what she likes, so the mall is a great option. So many stores! Big department stores, smaller kitschy stores, and all those kiosks.

You wander for a while. Your shoes squeak against the linoleum, or maybe they click. You're inundated by the scents and sounds that are particular to the mall: clouds of sweet and salty wafting from the Cinnabon and Auntie Anne's over in the food court, the sharpness of bleach and lemon from near the bathrooms. Echoing laughter and the pounding footsteps of mall rats running on the level above you. The steady hum of the escalator, going down.

As you wander, you look around for potential gifts. Maybe she'd like a bottle of cologne, or one of those colorful little scarves. Ooo, looks like Spencer's is having a sale. Maybe she'd like the t-shirt that has **BIG BITCH** printed on it in giant gold gothic script. You chuckle and pass it by, even though it would certainly suit her.

Eventually a kiosk catches your eye, set off by itself under the shelter of the stairs. Was the kiosk there before? You haven't been to the mall since December, so it's hard to remember. Those things have such a high turnover rate, anyway.

It's a jewelry kiosk. Silver and gold chains and the occasional leather cord, amethyst and turquoise, brilliant blue and green cut stones that can't possibly be sapphires and emeralds. Can they?

You move closer, drawn by the shine. You see velvet-lined trays crowded with rings, earrings both studs and hanging, even one case of what look like jewel-encrusted hair clips.

"Can I help you?"

The voice might be bright and bubbly, or it might be deep and sultry. Whatever its timbre, the voice belongs to the Shopkeeper.

The Shopkeeper certainly looks unique. Everything about them is black—hair, clothes, boots—except for their skin, which is an unfortunate shade of pale, and their lips and nails, both of which are painted a vibrant shade of red. They're wearing contact lenses, the kind that turns the whole eye black, and when they smile there's something unsettling about their teeth—spaced oddly, a touch too sharp. They have an unusual look for sure, but you admire dedication to an aesthetic so that doesn't throw you off.

"I'm looking for a present," you answer. "For her."

"What does she like?"

Maybe she likes throwing underhanded insults, or making you cry, or making you bleed, but you can't very well tell the Shopkeeper that. So instead you shrug.

"I don't know."

"Does she have a favorite color?"

Maybe, but you don't care.

"I don't know."

"Is she warm or cool toned?"

You're not even sure what that means.

"I don't know."

"Well then, what's your budget?"

This question is easier to answer. You promised yourself before you left home that you wouldn't spend too much on her, not one penny more than you can afford.

"Fifty dollars, but honestly I'd be happy to spend less."

"Ah," the Shopkeeper reveals another sharp grin. "I'm sure we can find something that will become her." They pull out an empty black velvet tray and slowly circuit the kiosk, hooking a necklace here and a ring there. By the time they return, the tray is full, a veritable horde of glittering trinkets. Surely there is something there that she will want.

You spend the next few minutes examining the wares, picking the items up one after the other, looking them over and then setting them down again. They're all beautiful, but none of them feel quite right. It's a little silly, you think, taking so much time. It seems a waste to spend it on someone you care so little for.

"Do any of these speak to you?" the Shopkeeper asks, breaking your reverie. They have been standing several feet away, giving you space and time to consider. You look over to them, preparing your answer, when two things attract your attention.

The first is a pendant that hangs around the Shopkeeper's neck. You're not sure how you missed it before. The leather cord that suspends it is pulled tight, so the object nestles snugly against their throat. It's dull silver, or maybe pewter, and it looks like a complicated knot: thin strands passed over and around each other in no pattern that you can discern. It isn't beautiful the way the other pieces are, but still. You can't take your eyes off it.

You want to see where the knot will go.

The Shopkeeper notices your attention and wraps a hand around the pendant, which disappears behind red-tipped talons. You open your mouth to protest, but that's when you notice movement over the Shopkeeper's shoulder.

This is the second thing. Your eyes widen and the Shopkeeper glances back at the person walking toward the escalator on the other side of the concourse. They turn back to you, one pointed eyebrow raised high.

"Is that someone you know?"

"It's *her*," you say, shifting sideways in an attempt to hide yourself behind the kiosk.

The Shopkeeper hums. "Don't you want to say hello?"

"What? No." You shake your head and curl your shoulders, as though you might just shrink away to nothing, and never have to deal with her again.

"Ah," they nod their head knowingly. "You don't want her to see you shopping for her gift."

"I don't want her to see me at all," you admit quietly.

Their eyes take on a gleam, as though a flame ignites under their stygian surface. "I see."

You watch the escalator carry her to the upper story. You don't bother hiding your sigh as you straighten back up.

The Shopkeeper has loosened their grasp on the pendant, and you are drawn to it again. It's almost enough to make you forget she exists.

"You could give this to her," they say, poking at one of its strands with the bright edge of a fingernail. "I'm sure she'd love it."

The thought of having the pendant in your hands makes your palms itch. You don't want to give it to her, you want it for yourself, but there's no reason to admit that to the Shopkeeper. You nod slowly, working hard to keep your excitement contained.

"I think she would. But it's yours. Are you sure you don't mind?"

The Shopkeeper laughs.

"It was given to me as a gift, intended to be passed on. So I can give it to you, and you can give it to her."

"A gift? Are you sure?" You're shocked, but also pleased. This means you can take the pendant for yourself, and you'll still be able to afford to buy something for her.

"Of course. I think it will be perfect for her. Don't you?"

You watch as the Shopkeeper pulls out a small white box and unties the cord. You have to bite your tongue to keep from asking to hold it. You can almost feel its weight in your hand, imagine how its warm knots will fit perfectly in your palm. They wrap it in tissue, close it up in the box, drop it into a dark red plastic bag with black handles, and hand you the bag with a smile that is most definitely too wide for their face.

"Enjoy! I hope she loves it."

Their gleeful cackle gives you goosebumps, and you grip the bag tight to your chest and rush toward the door. You're almost across the concourse before you turn around for one last glance at the kiosk. You blink in surprise; you can't see it. The space beneath the stairs appears empty. You pause in confusion, but only until the bag shifts, as though reminding you that you have something important to do.

Out on the sidewalk your hands shake as you yank the box out of the bag, unwilling to wait until you get to your car or the bus. In your excitement you let the bag fall to the ground. Perhaps the sun-kissed breeze will dance it across the parking lot, or frigid rain will stick it where it lands. Maybe it's even snowing. It doesn't matter to you; you need to have that pendant. In your hand, around your neck.

Once the tissue and the box fall, too, you're able to inspect the pendant as closely as you wish. Up close it's even more compelling, the strands tied over and around each other. It's heavier than you expected it to be, and as you turn it around, following the path of the silvery filament, it seems to grow even heavier.

It's a single fiber, you realize. Just one long strand of metal, twisted and tangled in a way that seems unplanned but isn't. You know there's a pattern, you just have to find it. So you stand outside the mall door and stare at the pendant until it's so heavy it pulls at your fingertips when you turn it over.

↑ ↓

When you lift it by the worn leather cord it feels lighter, and you think—you *know*—that it will feel even lighter around your neck. Why, you might not feel it there at all. It *belongs* there.

It is a part of you.

You pull the cord as close as you can and tie the knot tight.

At first nothing happens, which you must admit is a bit disappointing. The pendant is light and cool against your neck. But before you take a step toward your car, or the bus shelter, you are struck with a shock that is almost electrical. It radiates out from where the pendant sizzles against your skin, up into your skull and down through the soles of your feet. Your hands tingle, which quickly deepens to agony; you hold them out and watch as your fingers extend, your nails grow to crimson claws. Your sleeves lengthen, or maybe they were already long. Either way, they darken to black. Your teeth, newly sharp, jab uncomfortably on the inside of your lips.

The transition is painful, but also *right*. Once the shock is over—it was only a few seconds, really—you take what feels like the first breath of your life.

You turn back to the door and realize that this is not the door you came out of. This isn't your local mall at all. This is a different mall, somewhere else in your state, your country, your world. This door is glass, and you see your reflection. Solid black eyes stare back at you, silver pendant nestled snugly against your throat.

You are the Shopkeeper now, and you need to go inside and start your shift.

The kiosk shouldn't be left unattended for too long. Another customer will turn up soon, and you want to be there when they do.

Jul sat behind the glass counter, bored to tears. People still came to the shoreline mall; they were often folk with an urgent need for a pit stop on their way from or to the airport, or boarding a cruise, and the rest of this great margin were the local elderly people with no other place to go but this one. In the absence of adequate public spaces for people to inhabit and interact, folk made due. A glass building, connected with spit, bolts, and arching metal bands; a great sculpture that gave it the appearance of a ship with its sail extended to capture the maritime winds.

Which it did, from some angles. In the dead quiet of its worst days, for the people who had no option but to come work at the remaining business or sit around reading journals and waiting for death to catch them, the wind would howl and make itself heard. Up on high, metal and glass rang with the might of alien church bells. No such sound echoed just then, as Jul looked at her phone, then the screen for a computer she rarely used. She looked out of the display, her window to whatever she could see of the mall while on duty.

Her workplace, this once thriving store, was pristine as always, and there were no new items with which to restock the near-empty shelves. She dusted off and rearranged the boxes containing unused electronic products, cheap phones and cable packs, and a pair of outdated earphones, again and again for the sake of appearances. No store owner ever appeared to check on her. She was her own supervisor since she was the only employee but she had to stick to the hours which grew so long in between customers that they felt like they went on forever. She ended up doing plenty of unnecessary work just to fill the hours at Ryan's.

For the third time that day, August 13, 2090, a middle-aged white man, balding, reddened and drenched in sweat, walked by the store giving sideways glances as he paced hurriedly. It was a Sunday and there were always a couple of customers that day, one a well-known face, the other always a new one. No one came for the outdated electronics, though Jul sold a few cigarette packs for local workers who needed their nicotine fix. It had been her own idea, making use of a friend who sold the packs to her cheap.

These customers, like the man gaining courage to walk in, were part of a dying demographic who came to the moribund mall for a religious experience of their own. Some folk might come for shopping, as if the mall offered something they couldn't buy online, but these pilgrims who came to Ryan's were craving something else. At a fourth passage, the middle-aged man walked in, and his was a "new" face; Jul was never sure if it would be better or worse than dealing with the Sunday regular. It was a mixed bag, and she knew better than to lower her guard.

"Welcome to Ryan's, how can I help you?"

"Hi." He was a nervous mess, his forehead drenched, pit stains spreading from the leaking faucets of the man's body. A gray suit jacket that had seen better days was the only thing that disguised them somewhat and shielded those nearby from some of the man's stench. He said "hi" three more times, looking around nervously. "I'm here for the special."

Jul raised an eyebrow. "The what?" The man's face pulled up in a panic, stretching in a fashion more akin to a comic book character. "I, huh, I came for the thing." He kept stuttering about how he had come for the thing, increasingly nervous until he looked down at his own hands and some light went on in the rotting caverns of his paranoid brain. He showed her his hands: two fingers were missing from his left hand, the index and small finger, and from his right, only the small finger was missing.

"Ah!" Jul exclaimed, trying not to be too obvious about her mockery of the man. "The thing." She winked at him, keeping up the charade; it was obvious from the moment he had first crossed the threshold what he had come for, but it had been Jul's experience in her time working in Ryan's that every one of these customers had their little rituals and she was expected to play along.

"I'll close the door and I'll take you around the back, where the thing is."

There was still a nervous and jittery energy behind his eyes that would not let his panic fully subside, but with the door closed, he followed Jul meekly.

The back of the store had a cheap wall, a convenient division to make room between the store proper, the storeroom, and the spartan bathroom meant for Jul's use only. She closed yet another door, which she always locked before she started work.

"Is it safe?"

"As safe as any of the others." Jul focused on her tasks, turning on the lights and taking the tarp off the machine. Even when it was off it made a sound that reminded her of a loud fridge; as she opened the valves and flipped the switches and pressed the sequence to activate the device, it became quiet. "Got no complaints so far."

He licked his lips, shifting from foot to foot uncomfortably. "I meant about us being found out. I think someone is on to me."

"Who?"

"The police, I think."

Jul breathed deeply and pretended she was tuning the thing because if she laughed or sounded dismissive, he could turn violent or turn his back on her and leave her to a day of boredom. Needless to say, she also didn't look forward to the potential loss of an actual customer. "Ryan," or whatever her boss's name might actually be, might catch the scent of it and take issue.

"Police. You had trouble with them before?"

"No, but . . ."

"They won't bother you. They're on payroll."

He shuddered and let out a deep sigh of relief. Jul might have felt sorry for the man once but she was too numb to it now. Only someone deeply addled would think for a moment that anyone cared; there was no need for bribes. If her experience from watching the others was worth anything, by the time you were three fingers in, you were as good as dead to your family and friends. Since the machine wasn't covered by vice laws, the only real concern about police was if they received enough complaints about disturbances that they had to bother to do their jobs. The way they saw it, they weren't paid enough to cruise by a dying mall. The last security company had been fired a decade before, so the closest thing to a mall cop was the one remaining janitor, an old man with nowhere else to go and who would never be able to afford to retire.

Last but not least, Jul was pretty sure there were cops using "the thing" as well, losing fingers to the device until they had nothing left but nubs for hands. She definitely didn't pity the pigs. They were insured and would get shiny metal hands to better kill and maim with, eventually replacing this strange addiction for the familiar thrill of violence that they had likely possessed before becoming addicted to the latest fad.

"It's ready for you. Stick it in." He approached the device and hesitated, looking from his left to his right. He looked to Jul for guidance, and she washed her hands of it. "They're your fingers, you pick what hand you want to risk."

The process was random but this man had been lucky so far. He still had both his thumbs. "I'm good for two," he said, more to himself than to her. "I know I am. I can do it." Out of some perverse masochist pleasure he started searching himself and pulled a roll of bills from a pocket. So far, no customer had yet tried to skirt the payment, and Jul had usually delayed this step to after they had their fix, when they were pliable and self-satisfied. By this point, these men were past fear of what they were doing to their bodies, so any hesitation was calculated in an attempt to capture that same sort of thrill sought by gamblers.

"Thanks." She accepted the fat roll of bills and pocketed it without counting it. "Let's get it done. Another customer could be waiting for their turn."

He nodded in return and put his right hand into the hole of the tube designed to house his wrist. Once it was locked into place, something grabbed his ring finger, unleashing a loud sucking noise.

"Ohh," he exclaimed more in surprise than pleasure, "ohh, dear." Pleasure was quick to follow. "Oh! Yes!" He was still drenched in sweat but the furrows of his brow cleared and his eyes opened wide in ecstasy. "God, ohhh! I can feel it going up! It's coming!"

Jul looked away, still grossed out at this part despite the multiple customers she had to assist in using the machine through the course of the year. The moaning was a pitch too high, cut by exclamations that verged on howls.

"Ahh, God, oh!" His legs shook; he gripped the machine with his one free hand and arched his back, then bent forward suddenly like a spent old man. "It's better than the first time, it just gets better." He smiled at Jul, who looked at her phone to avoid all eye contact. "It's the best thing in the world," he mumbled over the increasing pitch of the suction noises coming from the machine, "and when I get that second hit. It will be. Be."

Jul looked at him as he spaced out, his eyes starting to roll back in his head. "Shhit!" Jul ran to him but the machine was faster; it must have started the second dosage then because it whirred and then restarted the sucking noises with gusto, with a sickening wet undertone as it worked on a random new finger. The middle-aged man shook from head to toe, then pissed and shat himself; Jul saw the white of his eyes and the slightly bloodied foam bubbling at the corners of his mouth. Stopping halfway to succoring him, she changed her trajectory and made it to the machine's controls. Pressing the emergency cutoff, it aborted the process, but slowly.

Unconscious, or near enough to it, the man slumped heavily and nearly dislocated his shoulder. Jul went to get the mop, bucket, garbage bag, and one of the changes of clothes that were kept on hand to cover up such indiscretions. Again, no one cared what the addicts did to themselves, as long as they did it where they couldn't be seen or disturb the peace. Allowing a soiled customer to wander the mall while surfing a high—that wouldn't do. She wasn't sure the clothes were quite the man's size but they would have to do. On her return, she found the machine had released its grip on the man and he in turn had dragged himself away from it, moaning and squirming on the floor while clumsily undressing himself.

On his right hand, in addition to the missing pinky, he was now missing his ring finger and index. A lucky man, getting away with his thumb still attached. Jul had expected one of the things to be still partially in place, but it was clear now the process was faster than she had expected, more brutal. She couldn't be sure if he was tripping on a full double dose or not, but he paid the full price.

"Get up. You got to clean yourself."

"Auuuughhhhh."

"Fuck." Jul put the clothes aside and poked with the fibrous end of the mop at the undressing man worming across the floor. "Get up! You can finish your trip outside."

"Peeople 'side. Crowds."

"It's empty, you can dress up and go."

"They're everywhere." He turned to her, his eyes still rolled up to show reddened whites. On his left breast between tufts of loosely spread hair was a tattoo of a skull. "I see them, I see them," he laughed. "They got so many fingers." He began rubbing himself and moaning, squeezing out of his underwear and now rolling completely naked around the floor. Jul used the mop to push the sullied clothes into the trash bag and sealed it, then did her best to mop the floor clean.

"OK, I don't care what you're seeing. You're getting dressed and walking out of here."

She made to take hold of his arm and force him to stand up, though he looked a tad heavier and taller than she might be able to manage, but the man shrieked as she approached and he crawled away from her. "Shh! What now?"

"Filth!" he screamed, his voice gargled by the drool that would not stop coming from his mouth. "They are here! I reject all flesh!" Jul simply tsked, sucked her teeth at the man, and grabbed his arm, hoping it would hurt him back into reality.

He gasped at her touch and shoved her away, pushing himself loose from her hold. "NO!" He cradled his arm, rocking back and forth, and before Jul could do anything else, the smoke came. "NOOOOO!" Burn marks appeared over his body, one by one then by the dozens as he contorted and screamed, black simmering marks shaped like handprints. Jul was speechless and became frozen in place when the man stood and then stood higher, elevated until he was floating, only the tips of his toes touching the floor. "You killed me! You killed meeee!"

His screams became a muffled groan, his mouth blackening, then his face as more hands dug into him and began to tear him apart. Flesh and skin were pulled off the bone, charring into ashen clumps, black as coal. The store was filled with the smell of cooked meat and the red fog of his boiling blood and through it all he lived, his face burning away to reveal the skull and the still twitching eyes, his whole skeleton becoming exposed until the only flesh on him was his still beating heart and quickly inflating and deflating lungs.

There was no blood left in him, there couldn't be. Yet he stood, held by those unseen hands, his bones blackening until the unseen things, spirits or monsters, or God knows what, clasped his heart and pulled it out. This too was torn apart, pinched and tugged, holes pierced which were then violently fingered by those hands from some other world.

The fire alarm was not triggered, having long ago been deactivated so Jul could smoke inside the store when she felt like it. This came as a blessing, for despite the smoke there was no flame, and the rest of the remains went the way of the man until at last the eyes began to shrivel and turned to dust, always fixed on Jul in a mute accusation. You killed me. The urge to vomit took hold but all that came to her throat was burning bile and all that got out was spittle.

Long minutes dragged on, but nothing more happened. Jul got up, cleaned her mouth with the back of her hand, and picked up the trash bag with soiled clothes. There was a convenient trash chute out back and around the corner, to save time for the remaining stores when handling disposal.

She leaned on the chute for a long and lingering moment, listening to the bag slide down. That dependable old janitor was unlikely to ask questions; he had enough work as it was.

She returned to find her Sunday regular waiting patiently at the closed door. He smiled at her from his wheelchair, showing the many gaps in his teeth and wearing his usual sunglasses, cap, and headphones that hid the missing ears.

"You OK, darling? You look like you saw a ghost."

Jul hesitated. She didn't have the stomach for this, not today. She was splitting in two, a Jul who couldn't believe someone this deep could ever be stopped, even if they had seen what she saw, and the one who had to try.

"Just saw someone die," she said, before she could stop herself. "Inside. He burned up." She pointed to the store to indicate where it had happened. "I just threw his clothes down the chute. It was horrible."

The Sunday man looked at her from behind his shades, his smile still locked in place. He scratched his shin with the palm of his right hand, which had no fingers, then rubbed the nub of what used to be the elbow of his left arm.

"Well shit," he said, matter of fact, then shrugged. "Guess I'll have what he had."

liam burke

Wilhelmina Potz dropped her neon pink bookbag next to the shoe rack, put her back to the closed front door, and screamed into the crook of her elbow. Her nonprescription glasses crushed against her nose. She ripped the oversized marble green frames off, threw them next to her bag, and rubbed the anger and hate off her face with both shaking hands. She took a breath. She'd talk to Mom. She always knew what to say to balm the torment of high school.

She took her flats off and called out down the hall. "Mom, I'm home!"

From the kitchen entryway down and to the right, her mother poked her head and upper shoulder out. Like a maternal meerkat. They smiled at each other, but Wilhelmina's shriveled on the vine. Mom was wearing her scrubs. Mom saw her face fall but ducked back, sounds of pots and utensils tinkling out. More nails in the coffin of help that night.

"You had tonight off," Wilhelmina called, not bothering to hide the frustration. As she turned the corner, she saw her mother turning off the stove and dumping elbow macaroni into a colander in the sink. Another pot had bubbling red sauce the color of fresh blood. Mom didn't look at her, bustling efficiently around the room, making sure her daughter's physical needs were met.

"I know, Mina. I'm sorry." Her mother touched her own forehead as she checked all the boxes in her mind. "Julie got sick; they need me."

"Why can't you get sick?" Mina pouted. She pulled out a faux maple chair and peeked out from her folded arms covering her head on the kitchen table.

Mom finally made eye contact. She gave Mina the look that meant she had said something stupid. Worse, something selfish.

"You know we don't do that. That's not the kind of people we are."

Mina held back the heat that was filling her, threatening to pour out from her eyes in wet rivers. "They did it again today, mom. It's getting worse. No one likes me at school. I hate it there. I hate everyone."

Mom brushed a loose strand of chestnut brown hair away from her face where it had escaped her bun, and her eyes softened. Mina dared to hope, but then came the *other* look. The one that meant the world was more important than her.

"I'm sorry, honey, that's awful. We'll talk later, OK?" She walked past, kissing the top of Mina's head where hair identical to her mother's hung limp and dejected. She grabbed her purse from where it squatted next to Mina's backpack.

"Mom! Please! They used Dad," Mina begged, following her, the deluge barely contained.

Her mother's face paled at the mention of her late husband. She froze in the open door, relieved as her cell phone buzzed. "I'm sorry, honey, they really do need me."

The door closed. Mina was left alone, whispering, "But *I* need you."

↑ ↓

The cool night air fluttered her pink windbreaker as she pedaled her fury out. The reflectors on her wheel spokes flashed along with her eyes. Trees and houses blurred by. She shot between cars, honks chasing her as she went. She barely heard them or paid attention to where she was going.

She left her suburban nightmare neighborhood behind, head down, the wind doing its best to dry her tears. She didn't see her surroundings, the dried-out buildings with empty socket windows, maggoty humans squirming over the dead scraps. She pedaled, drawn to something without knowing what.

She crossed a palpable border. The town fell away, emptiness surrounding her on all sides. No cars, no businesses, nothing to suggest that anything existed for miles. Above her, the stars pulled back. Silence filled the gaps where crickets should have sung. At the center of it all, beyond an ocean of cracked blacktop and sagging cement, The Mall loomed.

A tenebrous shape rearing up in the lightless hole in their town, The Mall could have been a dragon curled in on itself sleeping. Or the massive arms of a stone giant held out to embrace her. No one came here anymore; it was alone and shunned. It sought to welcome her? She would answer.

She affixed her phone to its holder on her neon-pink, glitter-encrusted handlebars. The ambient splash of light from the flashlight app refracted on the tiny prisms, transforming the dangerous approach into a magical journey. Broken glass sparkled on the ground, and she found a wide grin spreading on her face as she drove on her own rainbow star bridge.

The boards and signs warning and blocking entry were rotted and falling off their rusted nails. They came away as easily as pulling back the flimsy layers of morals and society everyone kept insisting she live by. She and her mother weren't "those" kinds of people? None of them knew her. Not like Dad had. She shook her head to lose the memory of him, and walked her magic-dust-bike-light into the building.

The inside was a wreck. Sweeping ceilings, their marble façade chipped and crumbling. Moldering storefronts in the hundreds. Mosaics spread like moss, impossible to read in their ruined state, the ground pushing up as if to shrug The Mall off. It was dusty and damp; it was massive and complex. It was a mess, unwanted and forgotten. She loved it.

In the center a dry, cracked fountain speared up to the shattered stained-glass ceiling like a broken bone. Mildewed couches and toppled tables were strewn about in careless neglect. Escalators in all the cardinal directions swept up to the second floor, another set to the third between them. She parked her bike against a couch and risked sitting on it. A cloud of dust rose up, and after she had coughed out enough to fill the Sahara, she saw them.

Mannequins.

They clustered in storefronts and hallways, on the massive escalators, near food carts filled with compost. Highly poseable, they were placed in an idyllic tableau of humanity. Granted a frozen life of their own. Men and women pointed at signs to explain what they wanted to waiting servers. Children in decayed clothes chased each other everywhere. A pair of men assisted a woman into a wheelchair.

All their faces were blank and smooth, thoughts and feelings expressed purely through pose. Once or twice a spring gave way, and they twitched an arm or a head turned an inch. They too were breaking down.

Mina stopped in front of the three with the wheelchair. Whoever had set everything up had a delusional worldview. None of this was accurate. Frozen moments of tranquility, ease, contentedness. The charity right in front of her. Even the mannequins were happier than she was. She hated the designer of all these scenes. Their life was so good, they couldn't imagine a world like hers.

She'd fix it.

She transported as many of the dummies as she could to the fountain area. She took pictures of them after they were lined up, and assigned them names. Plans for how she would orchestrate the new, *improved* presentations formed as dust motes danced in her phone's flashlight beam. Illumination that had drained her battery to near death.

Three a.m. had snuck up on her anyway. She reattached her phone to her bike and knocked the worst of the dirt and grime off her clothes. New particles exploded into glittering motes around her, like embers at a bonfire. Two of the mannequins' hands twitched with a ping, their multi-jointed fingers clasping. A man and a woman. Floyd and Mary, if she remembered right. She sucked her teeth and slapped them apart.

"That's not the kind of people you are. Not if I have anything to do with it."

↑ ↓

The next day at school Mina could think of nothing but her new toys. Fridays were full of nervous energy for the weekend—an energy that coalesced amongst the students and focused into a razor's edge of malign intent toward Mina. Her new obsession made it bearable. Exhausted thoughts of vicarious revenge buffered her from the rituals of torture.

Kelsey Danes asking her in what garbage bin she shopped for clothes. Derek Ketter pretending he liked her, then insisting she was being rude when she told him to fuck off. She weathered both with a sleepy smile.

All day Mina scribbled like mad in her five-subject notebook. Branching the names of the mannequins, figuring out the general shape of the plots she would run them through. She sketched rough versions of their poses. Her teachers didn't question it. They tried not to interact with her at all out of habit.

By lunch her notebook looked like an anatomy book and her head was woolen with fatigue. She heard the ending announcement of a new student coming Monday with ears submerged fully into her own deliciously wicked imagination. The bell rang, and she rushed back to her new world.

Her second wind hit her as she biked to The Mall. The sparkling road of stars was replaced with heat shimmers from the blacktop. The building resembled a mirage, and for a moment she worried she'd dreamed it all. In the light of day, she could see more mannequins standing in windows. Heads angled down at her. She looked up at them in her neon pink pony shirt and blue jeans, next to her glammed bike, munching a granola bar.

She choked when she saw Floyd and Mary two stories up in the broken window of JCPenney. She doubled over coughing, wheezing out the dry, crunchy bar. When she recovered, the window was empty. She needed to get inside. She was sleep deprived and standing in a literal oven. And she needed to hydrate.

She returned to the central fountain plaza and checked her mannequin cast. They were all present, including Mary and Floyd. She giggled nervously. A trick of her senses after all. She could see much more trash, and that the clothes of her blank-faced players were tattered and crumbling. A shaft of sunlight fell on her, and she followed the beam to the skylight. Smooth wooden faces gazed down at her, mannequins clustered around the hole.

She shivered. She'd have to rearrange them too.

She noted which needed the most intensive clothing overhauls and got to work on dry runs. Floyd and Mary were the stars, with six or so other mannequins as extras. She'd decided their stories would be nothing like hers. They wouldn't love each other intensely. They wouldn't have a child that put pressure on them. Neither of them would leave a hole in the child's world when they died.

She posed them on opposite sides, Mary on the north, Floyd on the south. She positioned the other six as if a crowd had gathered. On the ground a child-sized mannequin was bent at weird angles.

"You've gone too far this time, Mary," Mina said, standing behind Floyd. One arm was posed up, pointer stabbing the air at Mary, the other jabbing at the child. She checked her notebook and paced through dust, kicking a can away as she stepped behind Mary.

"How could I have gone so far? You were the one driving!"

Back to Floyd, moving his arms up to an exasperated pose.

"Is that what you'll tell the cops? You're a riot."

She moved back and forth from one mannequin to the other, pushing them closer and closer.

"The truth isn't funny, Floyd. You were driving. My clean record doesn't guarantee I won't go to jail."

"It's not a big deal. Manslaughter at best. Besides, you don't even like kids."

"No, but you're the one who'd rather die than have one."

She blinked. Why did she say that? This was supposed to be their pain, not hers. Frowning, she pulled Floyd's arm out to slowly smack it against Mary's face. Just before contact, Floyd's arm pinged and the springs coiled, pulling back and shoving Mina away. She cried out and landed on her ass. Her tailbone throbbed and her chest was starting to bruise. She winced as she got to her feet. She screamed and pushed Floyd over.

"You don't hurt me!" She straddled him and leaned in close. "Nothing here hurts me! That's *not* how it's going to work. Everywhere else, and everyone else hurts me. But here it's my turn. You all got that?"

She spun around, making sure every empty face got a full look at her. It wasn't hard. All their head springs had popped to turn to her. The sun had nearly set and shadows were filling in The Mall, a creeping carpet of ink. In the gloom the number of mannequins increased, unknown numbers adding up to hundreds in her mind. They all saw her.

"Yeah, you hear me!" she shouted at them to cover the eyeblink prick of fear she'd felt. "You won't take your own pain? I'll put mine in you!"

↑ ↓

She filled the weekend by shopping at thrift stores and setting the mannequins against each other in absurd and cruel ways. The kids hated each other. The adults were oblivious to it but were obsessed with escalating their vendettas. They slapped each other, they belittled. They broke toys and hearts, and as she put them through it all, their springs tightened.

Posing became an act of dominance. She couldn't control the kids at school or her workaholic mom avoiding her husband's *natural* demise, and she couldn't control the anger she felt all the time. But she could control the posers. Mina told them everything as she worked, explaining just how terrible her life was. Why that meant she was allowed to displace her anger onto them. She was positive the mannequins hated her. Mary's springs kept making her grab at Mina, probably to crush her. Mary would just have to wait. No satisfaction until Mina got hers.

By Monday she grasped that it would be harder than she'd thought. She stared at her notebook at her empty lunch table in the corner of the cafeteria, blinking at the word "suicide" underlined dozens of times on the page. It was the only thing she might never be able to displace onto the mannequins.

A shadow fell onto her notebook, and she looked up, ready with a barb or a deflection. She eeped in surprise at the heavyset boy she didn't recognize placing his tray down and sitting across from her. His t-shirt advertised that his other one was clean, but this one was clean too, although it barely fit. He smiled sheepishly and rubbed a meaty hand on the back of his head. Her venom retracted, but she held it ready.

"Hi," he said in an airy, high voice. "I'm Francis. I'm new. It OK if I sit here?"

Mina frowned and scanned the lunchroom. A few people were watching them, but she couldn't see a trap in their expressions.

"Look," she explained, making heavy eye contact as Francis began shoveling tater tots into his mouth. "I'm social radium. You *can* sit here. But you don't want to. Trust me."

Francis barely paused for air or to stop eating, but he somehow managed to talk without chewing simultaneously. "I saw you by yourself. I was by myself at my old school, so I figured you were alone like me. Maybe we can form an alliance."

"An *alliance*?" Mina had thought it, but Kelsey had voiced it, in her faux Valley Girl accent. She and her gaggle of bitches had descended. "I was going to warn you that Willy here was a bad idea, but I think the real problem is that you dorks are multiplying."

Her minions giggled, and Mina reloaded her venom.

"Whatever, Kelsey, at least he knows more than five words. The only multisyllabic ones you know are for the STDs your uncle gave you."

Francis's mouth dropped open, and the girls behind Kelsey feigned disbelief. They knew the dance. Kelsey would retort, something about Mina's fake glasses. The perfect deflection. Mina'd brush off the insult, and they'd get on with life.

"You wouldn't know what family's like, would you though, Willy? You know so much, but it didn't help Daddy, did it?"

Kelsey's words wrapped around Mina's throat, strangling all chances of getting on. Mina saw nothing but Kelsey. Her mind was separate from her body. Her hands balled as she stood, murder thrumming through her. Everything sounded like it was underwater.

Suddenly Francis was there, between them, burping loudly, and wetly, and directly into Kelsey's face.

"I don't know you yet, and I don't wanna. There's a lot more where that came from," he said, slapping his gut.

"Ewwww!" Kelsey whined, waving her hands in the air. "Whatever, you two deserve each other!"

The girls left. Mina came back to herself in stages, swimming for the surface of sanity. Francis sat back down like nothing had happened. Her eyes wet, Mina sat silently and clasped her hands in her lap. She didn't know what to think, let alone say.

Three shovels later Francis pointed at her notebook and asked, "What's that all about?"

She looked up and smiled, wiping her eyes. She knew exactly where to put this latest confusion and rage.

"Meet me after school in the parking lot. I'll show you."

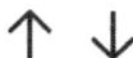

"Whoa!" Francis said.

He spun around, trying to look in every direction at once. Mina's Posers weren't where she'd left them, and the multitudes of mannequins had moved as well. The Posers were huddled in a store above the northern escalator. The rest encircled the fountain plaza. Mina glared at them but didn't say anything. Francis clearly thought they were cool. She didn't want to ruin that. She didn't know how to keep friends, but yelling at inanimate objects right away didn't sound too smart.

"I know right?" she said, cranking her lips up into a smile. "I call them my Posers, for obvious reasons."

"Yeah, obviously," Francis said as he shook a Poser's hand, pumping it like a lever. "They have so many points of articulation. Even the fingers!"

"Uh huh." Mina grunted as she pulled one of the children back down the escalator to the "stage" area. "The ones over there are my favorites. The ones I use to act out my scenes."

Francis lumbered over to help carry, shoulders hunched. Seeing him try to be small, Mina imagined all the people who tried to make them both feel minuscule. She saw their faces on the Posers and suppressed a snarl.

"What kind of scenes?" Francis asked. His eyes held hunger. Cautious hope. Mina smiled for real.

"Whatever kind I want."

Francis was a delight. His mind was full of classic literature, anime, obscure sci-fi, pop culture, the works. Between the two of them, Mina's scenes went from petty sniping and casual misfortunes to full-blown tragedies. Having an extra person to lug Posers around let them try out fall from grace moments and spiteful comeuppances with a speed Mina would have never thought possible. Mary nearly caught her several times, but Mina avoided her. She'd become an expert at it.

Night fell, and their stomachs rumbled. Francis got a text from his mother asking when he was coming home. When he told her he'd made a friend, she told him to take his time. He rolled his eyes as Mina looked on jealously. She tried not to think less of him. It wasn't his fault her mother threw herself into work to avoid reminders of Dad passing. She *was* hungry though.

"Hey, it's getting late, and you really should get going," she reluctantly admitted. A breeze wafted through the corridors of The Mall, as if it were sighing in relief.

"Your parents need you back too?" Francis asked. The question was casual. Of course he thought Mina's mom cared about her. Would it be weird if he knew she didn't? A worm of panic wriggled in her mind. She didn't answer. She froze, staring at her phone and its lack of messages.

"So like, this was sweet," Francis went on, picking up the awkward vibe. "I'm glad I met you. You have great stories, and this place"—he gestured with his phone light at the gathering mannequins—"it's so cool. I hope I don't lose interest. That happens sometimes. It's weird. I dunno. I guess I'll see you in school."

"One more scene!" she blurted, and several of the Posers pinged as their joints contracted, arms and legs pulling inward, protecting their torsos. Francis blinked at her, looked at his phone, and grinned.

"Sure, why not? I can say I left whenever. My parents won't know."

She nodded too emphatically and jogged to Floyd with frenzied desperation. She couldn't let him lose interest. If he did, he'd lose interest in *her* and she'd go back to being alone, or worse, he'd tell everyone about The Mall. Her big finale. She'd wanted to build up to it. She'd have to do it now.

She scooped Floyd up. "OK, wait here. This is gonna be epic!" she said while puffing her way to the dead escalator. Floyd's legs and arms kept catching on things she missed in the dark. Half of those things were other Posers. Their hands reached out blindly in the black.

"You sure you don't need—" Francis started.

"No!" Mina shouted. "This is my scene. Only mine. It means a lot. But I think you'll like it. Trust me!"

You have to, she thought.

She dragged the Poser up the three flights, stopping a couple times to recover. There were so many more mannequins than she remembered. A veritable forest of blank faces and grasping hands. They reared up in her phone's flashlight, lurching out of nowhere, frozen in place in the worst spots. She struggled on, determined. She began muttering over and over, "You have to like it. You can't hurt me."

Finally she reached the third floor, out of breath but supremely satisfied. She looked down at Francis and the remaining Posers. They were all looking up at her. Had Francis noticed they'd moved? He would eventually. That was OK. It would be one more secret they'd share. She pushed Floyd to the banister and called out to Francis.

"The past few months of his life, Floyd had been different. He'd made bad choices, said hurtful things. Hurt everyone he loved. What no one else knew was that he was losing an invisible battle. He had depression. Severe depression. It seeped into every part of him and oozed out. He saw it staining his loved ones and decided there was only one thing he could do."

Her voice broke, and she blinked away tears. Below her, Francis's mouth gaped open. The twist of all twists he couldn't have seen coming. Not unless he'd lived it. She hated him too for a moment. Then hated herself more. Her father's stain.

"Goodbye, everyone!" she cried out. "This is the only way I can save you. Don't worry, it will look *natural*. I fell. What's more natural than gravity? I love you all."

She pushed Floyd off the edge, over the balcony. He tumbled, slammed against the second-floor railing, and spun to the floor in front of Francis and the Posers. His casing shattered, the long coils and inner workings of him shooting out in a tangled mess. He was mangled. He was dead. She'd finally put her agony onto something else.

A quiet whine grew below in the silence following, transforming into a tormented wail, to a deafening screech ringing out throughout The Mall. A single, stupendously pure note of loss vibrating the world. Mina knew it well. It was the sound of her heart every day.

It came from Mary. Her wood and metal hands clutched her featureless head. She'd fallen to her knees, bent over in a perfect physical simulation of a broken soul. Francis staggered back and raced for his bike. He jumped on and pedaled as fast as his thick legs could take him. He didn't look back once. He'd left Mina too, plunged into the darkness and gone. She'd lost her first friend so fast.

When Mina looked back at Mary, the Poser's head was tilted toward her. The screaming continued, echoing over and over. Mina's loss turned on itself, became the thing she knew best. She screamed back her hate at the grieving mannequin. She'd thrust her pain into Floyd and Mary; why was it still tearing her apart?

She turned to run down the stairs, too enraged to acknowledge the proof that the Posers were more than inanimate. She'd known. She'd known almost immediately. Otherwise, making them suffer had no point. The artificial crowd behind her had absolutely gotten the point. They were a wall of rotted wood and rusty springs, a few with thrift store rags, others naked as the day they came off the assembly line.

They blocked her at every turn, moving openly in jerking, twitchy lurches. Fear began to overtake anger. They weren't supposed to be able to hurt her. They were just big dolls! She slapped and pushed, kicked and screamed at them, but they held her there, at the edge. She fell to her hands and knees and panted, gathering her strength. The Mall was silent. Mary had stopped wailing.

The mannequins parted before her, but there would be no running. Mary and the main Posers staggered down the middle, a macabre blank-faced runway strut. Mina stood and glared defiantly. Inside her roiled a cocktail of fight-or-flight with a dash of guilt. She'd just wanted to be the strong one. The one who made someone else feel small. The extra Posers formed a line as Mary continued to flounder her way forward in aching stop motion.

"I'm not scared of—hirk!" she said, words cut off by a wooden hand crushing her throat. Mary had closed the final steps in a blink.

Step by step, Mina was pushed back. When she refused to move her feet, mannequin hands reached out to her. They posed her, as she had posed them. Mary sobbed tearlessly as she pushed, and Mina's eyes watered in response. She'd tried to get rid of the pain. It hadn't worked. Her back arched over the edge until she felt it would break. Mary held her in place, Mina helpless once again.

She broke. Thick, wet sobs sprayed from her. Her whole life was endless loneliness. Held at arm's length over an abyss, surrounded by uncaring, faceless monsters. She realized she'd be better off dead. She was poison. Just like her dad.

"Do it," she choked out at Mary. "Please. I can't live with it. It's too much."

Mary stopped sobbing. The whole world went quiet. Clouds obscured the sky, robbing what little light was left. It was peaceful. She hoped this would be what death was. It was more than she'd earned. She closed her eyes. She was ready.

The hand let go. For the briefest of eternities she fell.

An arm caught her around her waist. She squeezed her eyes shut harder as another pulled her close to a hard surface. Her breath coming ragged, her face a wet smear, she opened her eyes. She felt arms around her. Mary, the one she had hurt the most, was holding her. She'd finally caught Mina. Not to crush her. To hug her.

She broke again. She threw herself into the embrace of the Poser she'd tortured so much, clutching it harder than she'd held on to anything but resentment. She didn't deserve it. She'd done too much. Gone too far. She didn't care. She held on to the first real affection she'd had in years with all she was worth and poured out the venom in her through her tears.

She didn't like the kind of person she was. Somehow these smooth, rotting castoffs saw she could do better.

"I will," she whispered, as wood and rusted springs surrounded her with love.

pines callahan

Dear Nancy,

Thirty-seven years of friendship, fifteen of them spent walking this mall every morning, and now it's like the Silver Sneakers are dead to you. Like I'm dead to you. All because of a man. Now, heaven knows I understand what it's like to want male companionship after decades alone. I miss my Charlie every day. But dropping us like a bad habit just so you can spend time with the first man over 65 who looked your way . . . well, if I can't say something nice, I won't say anything at all—except that I miss you. I really, truly miss you, Nancy.

My day isn't the same anymore. The walk is less colorful with so many storefronts closed. They couldn't have shut down all at once, maybe I just didn't notice. Same way I didn't notice the un-friendly crowds always pushing past us. Sure, we still have an extra hour in the morning before the shops open—they'd never dare do away with that knowing the fuss we'd raise—but it's not just seniors anymore. I don't mind the rehab group with their wheelchairs and walkers; they're pleasant enough folks. But there's a group of stroll-er moms who start out by the Sears and make at least one loop be-fore they finish with half-hearted yoga in front of JC Penney's. The babies cry more than they sleep, can't blame them, and the mothers look right through us when we ask them to stop. I swear, they know they can't keep their own children under control so they'd rather ignore the problem. Wasn't like that in our day, was it? If you were here, you'd give them a piece of your mind, just like you did when those teens tripped Betty.

Why not ask your beau if he'd like a little exercise, and the both of you join us? I wish you'd come set them straight instead of moping around for a few minutes and disappearing like a lovesick ghost. I saw you two up here yesterday, you didn't even stay for lunch. I don't know why you won't talk to me in person anymore, but if you don't want to, I won't cause a scene. I'm leaving this note in our usual people-watching spot to remind you of the good times. I'm sure you recognize the journal, your last Christmas gift, just the perfect size to fit in my purse. If you get this, please come find me. We were such good friends for so long, please don't throw it away over a man.

Your Friend,
Gloria

↑ ↓

Dear Nancy,

I guess you didn't get my last note. The janitors come at odd hours now, they probably threw it away. I won't leave this one in a planter. Please, at least give me a sign you've read this.

I've got big news! Harold Green (you remember Harold, used to go to our church before his wife, Bethany, passed) has come back to our group. He's quiet about why he left, and he seems glum when we walk, but we'll cheer him up soon. Exercise always makes people feel better, don't you remember?

One thing irks me: Harold's never dressed to walk. Always wears normal loafers instead of sneakers. At least he stopped eating those sausages downstairs and is trying to get himself in shape. I bet Harold and your beau would get along like a house on fire. You should bring him around.

In less exciting news, school's out for the summer so the teens are here full time. Who raised these kids? No respect for their elders at all. They sit on the ramps and make us use the stairs, and I don't need to tell you how bad that is for my hips. Luckily for me, all the walking we do has really done wonders for my flexibility: I hardly feel the old aches anymore. I know your hips bother you, too. Why won't you come back?

Your friend (I hope),
Gloria

↑ ↓

Nancy,

I've just about had it with you. Thirty-seven years we've known each other, and this is where we end up. I know we've had our differences lately, but flying off the handle when I say hello is completely outrageous. Throwing a milkshake and running away! How dare you. Nancy Elizabeth Kennedy, next time I see you, I'm giving you something to scream about.

Not your friend,
Gloria

↑ ↓

Nancy,

You've got some nerve. I've never been so embarrassed in my life. You may not have noticed me, but I could have died when I saw you chatting with that wafer of a priest by the fountain and heard my name on both your lips. I don't know why you think I need to be saved, I'm not the one living in sin, but I think you're right when you said I need to move on. If I never see you again, it'll be too soon. Don't even think about rejoining the Silver Sneakers now. I asked the other girls, and we don't want you here. Even Harold says you'll stay away if you know what's good for you. He looked like he wanted to say more, too, but I know he's a good Christian man for holding his tongue.

Your enemy,
Gloria

↑ ↓

Dear Nancy,

I'm not sure how to write this. I don't want to scare you again. I'm sorry for all I've put you through, but I hope we can get past this. After all, we've been friends for so long.

Maybe that's why you showed me my obituary. I found it, stuffed into the planter like a dirty secret. I don't know whether I should thank you for it or not. I hate the picture they picked, my hair looked awful. My brother probably chose the photo, bless his heart. You would have chosen something flattering.

I didn't believe you at first, and I'm sorry if I let that get the best of me. Your beau is a brave man, standing up to me in a temper. But you can hardly blame me for being upset at that sort of a shock. I know it made you mad, and I suppose that's why you brought the rest of the obituaries … and that awful news article. Oh, Nancy, that did the trick, didn't it?

Fifteen years, we walked here together. We finally had the time to spend on ourselves and each other. We ate lunch at the same table in the food court. We watched the same people come and go. A little social group built up around us, you and me at the center. Then that man came along and spoiled it, took you away from me again.

I tried my hardest to adapt, but life without you lost its spark. I realized a way to keep us together forever, all the Silver Sneakers. And you've always loved the taste of my almond cookies; I thought you'd die with something pleasant on your tongue. How many people have that luxury? Only, you didn't show up that morning. I cried in the bathroom, figured I'd take my cookies home and try another day, but the group got peckish while I was gone. At that point, what could I do but eat a few myself?

I'm not sure why I didn't remember for so long. I suppose it was the circumstances. Harold remembers his heart attack, explains why the poor thing's so glum. Died eating a sausage. I don't think he can do much to change things now, but I think walking's a bit of a penance to him. You always said he needed to cut back, didn't you? Right again, Nancy.

The others were upset at first, too. But don't worry, the group endures. We discussed it at length and decided it was probably for the best. Maudette says she was close to doing it herself, anyways, and Betty's kids haven't called her in years. We were all walking on borrowed time. I'm sorry I made such a mess of things, but I'm not sorry for the outcome.

It's nicer than you think, being dead. I'm not bothered when the stroller moms ignore us anymore, and I can't blame the teenagers for sitting on the ramp if they can't see us. Not like you. You and I, we're connected.

We've started walking at night, too. No sense waiting for open hours, we've got the whole mall to ourselves. Well, except for a few other permanent residents. They're easier to see now that I recognize myself. I never knew someone died in the elevators, did you? I think she was a prostitute, but I'd never be so bold as to ask. Unhappy young woman. Maybe she should walk with us. After all, exercise does improve the mood!

I still miss you, Nancy, but I'm touched how often you visit our old spot, even if you only stay for a few minutes. You must miss me, too. But I'm not worried. You'll come back to me eventually, one way or another, and the Silver Sneakers will march again!

Your friend, eternally,
Gloria

Jake slid a finger under his binder to readjust, the tight fabric made worse by a hot summer's day. This would be his first time appearing on camera as masc and he was already rethinking it. Maybe it wasn't the smartest idea to buy a cheap knockoff as his first binder.

An even worse idea was coming out to Devon on the drive over.

They'd just finished setting up when he asked Jake, "So . . . is this like a full-time thing?"

"Yeah, well, I mean—I'd like it to be."

"Do your parents know?"

"No, I've only told a few people so far. I don't think my Dad would react very well." That was an understatement. A bridge he'd hold out crossing as long as possible.

"Yeah, he is kind of a dickhead." Devon laughed. "We're still cool to do the video, though, right?"

"Oh, absolutely! I just wanted to tell you beforehand."

"OK, anytime you're ready."

A bead of sweat broke out on his neck before Jake rubbed it away. He took a deep breath and started to speak before snapping his mouth back shut. "Sorry," he said to Devon. "Let me try again."

Devon lowered his iPhone and gave a reassuring grin. "Don't worry, dude. Remember we can edit out anything that sucks. It's all a part of the process."

"Thanks." He took another moment before starting his spiel.

"What's up gangsters! Welcome to the first episode of *Archiving America*, where we explore the creepiest abandoned buildings those other channels don't want to tell you about. I'm Jake, and with my trusty cameraman Devon"—an arm appeared in front of Jake and waved—"we're about to enter the *Grand Point Mall*."

"That was great! OK, let me get some B-roll of the entrance, then we can head in." Devon pushed past Jake with his phone raised, taking in the large double doors cut into the rockface.

Grand Point was the first (and only one, as far as they knew) mall to be built into a cave system. It had been a fun gimmick to bring in tourists to the tiny mountain town. It had seemed so promising. Most of their parents had worked on it in one way or another, before the money dried up and the shopping center became something to curse about over beers.

The actual entrance to the mall was oddly plain. A painted wooden sign reading WELCOME TO GRAND POINT above a set of heavy doors, which was the only way in or out. A second opening *had* been found on the other side of the mountain, but due to toxic levels of sulfur gas, it was hastily blocked off and forgotten. It had been too costly to blast another hole into the cave, even when you took into account the countless trips workers had to make hauling stuff. Jake's Dad said this was one of the reasons the project failed.

It was a regular topic in their household, a rant his father would launch into whenever he'd have a few too many on the way home from the mill. A personal affront he would take to the grave. "The problem with these business assholes," he'd tell Jake, "is they can plan all this shit but they never have to do the *work*. They only see numbers. Not the horrible smell of garbage because we couldn't be arsed to drag the stuff back out. It just piled up in a corner. Or how there's no sun down there. Can't tell what time of day it is. Fucks you up."

Of course, all this talk had the opposite effect—instead of hating the place, Jake was fascinated. It tickled the edges of his imagination, a literal time capsule of the 80s, down to the decor and kitschy merchandise, right on the edge of town. Even the discovery of the cave was mysterious: a group of hikers had gone missing, and the search party had stumbled upon the opening, perfectly smooth and inviting like it had been waiting for them. The hikers were soon forgotten as the Chandler Corporation bought the land for immediate development.

While Jake had never left the mountain town, Devon had just returned from college and wanted to start a YouTube channel. Their first location felt obvious.

The pair worked together to smash the old padlock chaining the entrance shut. Despite their age, the doors were solid and quite heavy. Devon used a stack of bricks to prop one open.

Squinting against the sunlight, they peeked in. Dust and litter were scattered around, but after a few feet, the area was swallowed by darkness, thick like syrup. With the heavy square flashlight hastily purchased from Home Depot, Jake beamed the harsh artificial cone into the cave, slowly panning over pallets and construction equipment. Suddenly he felt a warm rush of air blow past them from inside. Strange, he thought: shouldn't it be cold? Maybe it's a dormant volcano or something.

Putting his hands together, Devon called "HELLO!" into the cave. He started laughing to himself but Jake felt uneasy.

It didn't echo.

"Maybe this isn't such a good idea." The words had barely escaped his mouth before he regretted speaking up.

"What, are you backing out now? Come on."

His nails dug into his palm. "No, I'm not," he fought back. "It just feels kinda off. I don't know."

Devon gave him a half-hearted shove. "Of course it feels off. It's a spooky old cave! But it's *fine*. Don't be such a *pussy*."

The word twisted in his gut, curling around his already tight chest. "All right. Let's go." He pushed past Devon into the darkness.

The first thing that hit them was the overwhelming smell, like old leather and gasoline and mothballs rolled into one. Construction equipment, rusted and useless, created a semi-circle that made Jake feel like he was being judged. Long-dead gods left to rot in the dark. The floors were covered in trash that increased in density the further they went, propagating like weeds.

"It's so quiet in here," Devon admitted. Silence had fallen over them, an unconscious need to be stealthy taking over. A bubble of light and noise that moved through the shadows.

"No birds, bugs, or bats," Jake parroted from his father's tangents. "Just a wet hole." He didn't speak the last part. *A wet hole, waiting to be fucked.* Awakened by laughter, Jake had wandered into the kitchen and saw "the lads" as they called them, the group of work friends that gathered weekly to knock brews back and commiserate. They had the decency to quiet down once they saw the bedhead and nightgown. One shot a leering wink toward Jake before his mother ushered him back to bed, to pretend the whole thing was a dream before next Saturday repeated the cycle.

Soon the space in front of them opened up to reveal a dried-out fountain, the centerpiece of an empty plaza. Benches and empty store shelves created a maze of metal, dumped before they reached their final destination. From here, the mall branched off in four directions. A tattered sign over one hallway noted that it led to the Food Court, a modern hieroglyphic of a burger with an arrow pointing.

"******, are you ready to do another take?"

Hearing his deadname was a gut punch. Jake stopped dead in his tracks, hands clenching and unclenching. The weight on his chest grew like chainmail. Devon kept walking, phone first. Oblivious. He didn't even turn to see if his friend was following. Everyone fucks up at the beginning, he told himself. It's fine.

Instead, Jake circled the decrepit pond. Thick green algae stuck to the bottom, so at least, for a moment in time, water ran through it. Something about that made him sad. He was overcome with the urge to toss a coin in, although he had none.

A sharp pain in his chest caused him to falter, bracing a hand on the fountain edge. *Warm.* He knew they had underground heating systems in Europe and roads that melted snow as soon as it touched the ground. Maybe this was something similar, something natural. Maybe that's why they chose this mountain in the first place. Strange his Dad had never mentioned it.

"Hey! Check it out—a generator. I wonder if it works." Devon was across the plaza, leaning over the box, cords zigzagging outward. He'd placed the flashlight down, and the beam shot straight to the cave ceiling. Soft brown ripples sweaty with condensation splayed as far as Jake could see. It looked like he could sink a hand into it and press until the imprint stuck. He zoned out, the lack of oxygen starting to get to him. A drop of water fell, and the cave roof appeared to billow. He blinked and finally looked away. Took a long, deep breath—as much as he could at least. His binder was soaked in sweat, but slightly rigid, like papier maché.

A set of quick, deep rumbles brought him back as the generator struggled back to life before settling into a steady rhythm, cutting through the silence of the cavern. Devon cheered and Jake offered a thumbs up. A slow, static hum joined the noise and they watched as old signs and lights blinked back on for the first time in decades.

DEAR —SHOPPERS,

Jake froze. The announcement was so loud it made his head rattle. He glanced over at Devon, who looked elated. He'd started recording again, panning the camera to capture the plaza. The voice was strange, fluttery and booming. Like several people were talking at once.

He sat on the edge of a bench and dug both hands underneath his shirt, fingers wiggling under the hardening material to coax some space for his lungs to expand.

The cavern seemed to shift again, reacting to the broadcast. The generator sputtered and died but the lights stayed firmly on. Was the backup power kicking in? He struggled to remain upright as mounted signs swayed, some falling over completely. The ground shook beneath his feet, the same waviness from the ceiling reverberating. Jake remembered the earthquake drills from school, and how his teachers warned of multiple shockwaves, signs a big one was coming. "Something's wrong," he rasped, voice thin from straining.

WE ASK THAT— YOU FINALIZE YOUR PURCHASES— AND MAKE YOUR WAY TO THE CHECKOUTS. THE. GRAND POINT —MALL WILL BE CLOSING IN—KZZT—30 MINUTES.

"Wild that some of this shit still works!" Devon yelled. Neither voice carried beyond the plaza, despite their volume—the air itself seemed to absorb everything.

Stumbling, Jake made his way over and frantically put his hand on his friend's shoulder. "Don't you feel that? I don't think we should be here anymore!"

"What, are they gonna lock us in here?" Devon laughed heartily at his joke. "Let's check out the food court."

Jake didn't have the strength to argue. After weaving slowly through the labyrinth of shelves, hands alternating on the cool metal for balance, he finally looked up from his feet and bumped hard into Devon.

"Hey," his friend asked, ignoring his hasty apologies. "What language is this? It's not . . . English, right?"

Jake stepped out beside him and looked around. The storefronts *seemed* right, with swooping fonts and familiar shapes. But when he squinted, he realized they were all written in a bizarre, lopsided alphabet, with some letters massive compared to others. It was like a child imitating what they saw during an outing, a memory, an idea.

A display sat outside one shop, a table covered in wooden blocks and a yellow, mushy substance. He wondered if it was rotten food, somehow preserved in the contained environment.

A piercing, metallic crash rang out from behind them. Jake grabbed Devon by the arm and pulled him away just as the shelves began to collapse, bolts whizzing past like bullets before the metal structures clattered to the ground. If Jake thought the announcement was loud, this was unbearable. Shrill scraping etched itself into his ears. Mumbling *oh shit, oh fuck*, the pair watched as their only path to the outside was completely blocked off.

ATT—ENSHION SHOPPERS. THE —BRRZT— MALL WILL —CLOSE. IN 20 MINUTES. PLEASE MAKE YO—YOUR WAY TO. THE CHECKOUT COUNTER.

They struggled for several minutes to pry the bars loose to no avail. Devon screamed in frustration and kicked one.

"Fuck!" he yelled, hands running through his hair. A pause, and then he was digging through his pockets, frantic. "Where's my phone!?"

Jake clutched his chest, the wheezing growing worse. A barking cough forced its way out of his throat, and he wrestled against the sting, hands braced on his knees. His foot slipped a few inches on the rough ground, his shoe snagging something.

"No . . ." he whispered, crouching down to pick up the completely smashed device, a spiderweb of cracks from edge to edge. "It's—it's OK, we still have mine," talking to himself more than anything, self-soothing. Pressed the unlock button before coming to a horrible realization: no bars.

"We couldn't use walkies down there either." His father's words echoed in his head, and Jake felt bile rise in his throat. "That's another thing they don't tell you, signals have trouble carrying underground."

"We are completely *FUCKED*!" Devon screamed. His voice didn't carry beyond their tiny bubble, but the dome above them seemed to undulate in response.

"Devon, it's OK. We can find another way out. Let's just. Keep going—maybe there's a secret back exit."

Devon grabbed Jake by the shoulders and shook him, spit flying. "How do you know? Did your Dad tell you something!?"

"No, I just—"

He stopped and gave Jake a curious look up and down. "Wait, what's wrong with you?"

Jake put up his hands defensively, trying to steady his breathing. "N-nothing! It's just hot down here!" To illustrate his point he wiped across his forehead, visible droplets flinging to the ground.

—*THE M. A LLLLL WILL CLOSE. IN 15 MINUTESsssss.*

The voice was becoming more distorted, the words slurred together, fading in and out.

"Where the fuck is that coming from?" Devon yelled over it, lightly jogging past the shops around them. Jake watched him gradually fade from sight, the words to call him back caught in the cage of his chest.

The cave grew silent.

As the seconds grew to minutes, he felt more and more uneasy. He grabbed a metal bar for support and dragging himself onward. There was only one direction to go.

Deeper into the mall.

Each shop grew more bizarre, soft clay formations that grew from the canopy above to form muddy stalactites, dripping putty into half-formed structures with paint splotches spreading throughout like mold. Each sagged more than the last. It smelled fetid, of road-kill and vomit, hot and moist, clinging to Jake's throat.

The smell was coming from the mounds.

Curiosity overtook nausea. Jake pulled his sweat-soaked shirt upward, holding the damp material over his nose as he stepped closer to the mass. It was unsurprisingly warm to the touch, and solid despite its mushy appearance. Imagination sated, he pushed down, intending to regain his balance before setting off again. Instead, his hand went through the mound like cracked porcelain. He yelped and fruitlessly attempted to pull back before slipping, fingers grasping for purchase before sinking now, finally, into something soft.

Jake's body reacted before his mind did, pulling out and away, ass landing hard on the ground. The foul stench blasted his nostrils, so strong he felt dangerously close to passing out completely. His fingers were now covered in a viscous, dark liquid that refused to come off no matter how hard he wiped on his pant leg. With his clean hand, Jake blindly struggled to turn the flashlight on his phone and aim it at the cracked shell.

Beams of light danced over the shape, a familiar configuration of holes lining up. A decomposing corpse, mouth hanging open as the tissue had dripped off the bones, a tomb inside a tomb. He glimpsed a once white puffy jacket, now stained dark with blood and fluid as it dangled off the shoulders, knowing if the carapace completely broke, he'd gaze upon the rest of what was once human.

He felt another deep rumbling and turned as quickly as his body would allow. The path behind him was dissolving, the stores losing their shapes and melding into a solid wall, the same texture as the dome, jagged lines like stretch marks weaving the pieces back together. Like it was meant to be like this. Jake knew if he reached out and touched it his hand would come away hot like the fountain in the plaza, a warmth from something alive.

The phone in his hand dropped to the ground with a soft *pumph*, the sound absorbed completely, sucked into the mush surrounding Jake's feet like quicksand. He scrambled like a crab, away from the encroaching wave of mud.

"Jake."

Devon's voice was strange, muffled somehow. Jake crawled toward it and around another mound, a cluster of standing coffins. His friend lay slumped against the wall of an optometrist's office—at least, that's what he thought it was meant to be, with the oversized eyeglass design above the storefront, but like everything else, it had begun to melt into the same viscous slop. Devon's leg was twisted, hands braced over the knee like that would hold him together.

TEN. TEEEEEEnn. MINUTES wewillclosein TEN minutes.

"What . . . what do you think happens when the mall closes?" Devon sounded so small. Tears stained his dirt-covered cheeks. Jake drew himself up so they were sitting shoulder to shoulder, staring at the mass of earth as it stretched toward them. He thought he should say something, anything, but his voice was completely gone.

The oddest thing was how loud it was becoming—Jake had grown so used to the silence, the stillness of the cave. The sound of ragged breathing and strange gurgles spurring the avalanche onward was nearly deafening.

THANK YOU FOR SHOPPING WITH USss TODAY. THE MALL IS NOW CLOSED.

Jake put his arm out, desperately pushing against the assault of clay, and felt the bones in his arm give out with a sickening *snap* as the wall closed in completely.

the philosophical quandaries of meeting your doppelgänger in moonshine city

angela liu

Moonshine City still had that new building stink.

Aya stared at the white lines in the parking lot as rain dotted the asphalt. These lines were the only traces left of MAPITA Mall, that charmingly run-down shopping center that had stood here for two decades before. Aya could practically hear the crackling carnival tune of the old crane game machines outside the pharmacy upstairs where she and Keisuke used to play for counterfeit Pokémon plush dolls.

"'Shop happiness.'" Kayo pointed to Moonshine City's towering logo on the front entrance like a second sun. The same slogan was printed on the hundreds of banner flags hanging along the auto-walk from one atrium to the next.

The new mall was the centerpiece of Hitobashi City's "Town Revival" push. With three hundred customizable coworking spaces, two food courts (one for local cuisine, the other for international), six VR escape rooms, a Showa-style shooting arcade, and a boutique for every fashion period and fetish you can imagine, there's a little nook for everybody. Nevermind the phone calls to the head of the town committee at 3 a.m., or the faceless mannequins sent to Fujiwara Co., the architects in charge of the construction. The dazzling new mall had been featured in the latest issues of *Popeye* and *Men's No-Non*, with a special live TV tour of the space featuring the idol sensation Magical Girls Deluxe in mini moon skirts and blouses to match the mall's logo. Even adventurous weekenders board hour-long trains from Tokyo just to visit the city-within-a-city.

Moonshine City has something for everybody.

"Do you think they take Mastercard?" Aya asked as she followed Kayo in.

↑ ↓

Aya sat at one of the cafeteria-style tables, watching a cartoon dumpling sing about the seasonal menu on the screen bolted to the wall. "Watermelon bubble tea! Kagawa-style cold udon with a mountain of summer veggies! Smoked eel bowls! Locally sourced!"

"If you stare at the screen long enough, they say the dumpling will tell you the secret of life," Kayo said, putting down the tray with a paper boat of takoyaki slathered in sauce and green onions.

The two girls halved wooden takeout chopsticks and turned on their cellphones at the same time, both clicking to their favorite mobile game, *Demon Cats*. The Dynamic Duo—that's what people had been calling them since middle school because you'd never see one without the other close by. Kayo, the tall and loud one, the leader, and Aya, "the other one." Freshman year of high school, Kayo tried to start an occult detective club at school, spurred by her summerlong marathoning of *Doctor Who* and *Death Note* episodes, but Aya was the only person she could recruit.

"Did you hear about Aki?" Kayo asked, not looking up from her phone.

"That he got kicked out of Ueno Zoo for trying to climb into the panda pen?"

"No, no." Kayo glanced around the crowded food court to see if there were any familiar faces. "His sister said he uploaded a video of himself wandering around some abandoned mall a few stops away. Like talking to the mannequins and laughing at nothing. It was creepy as hell, but the weirdest shit is that no one's been able to reach him since."

"Like he turned off his phone?"

"Like he vanished off the planet."

Brown sauce dripped onto Kayo's new *Demon Cats* x UNIQLO t-shirt.

"Fuck." She clicked her tongue. "This shit better come out."

Aya watched her friend rush off to the bathroom, dodging strollers, chairs, and giggling couples like a star quarterback hurtling through a zombie apocalypse. Just as she was about to pick up another octopus ball, a faint ring cut through the food court cacophony. Aya winced, putting down her chopsticks. The ring seemed to chime through her whole body like a massive tuning fork. *What the hell is that?* She swallowed hard to clear her eardrums. Her ears popped, saliva sliding down her throat. The ringing finally stopped.

"Project Happy Station. Coming soon to a mall near you!!"

Aya looked up at the screen. The singing dumpling was gone. A new commercial was playing with 8-bit fanfare. On the screen, faceless mannequins shambled around a dark hall until they fell into a large hole in the ground. The hole fed into a chute that dropped them down into a giant aluminum vat several floors below. Some fell directly into incinerators. The remaining mannequins basked in the vat of sticky golden liquid until they were expelled from an opening in the bottom. Crawling back to their feet, they now had faces, hats, clothes, shoes, but their mouths were abnormally large, an impossibly wide line of teeth.

The screen glitched.

This time, Aya's face appeared. Except paler, hair longer and shinier, bigger eyes.

"You're pretty hot," her doppelgänger said.

Aya looked around, but no one else in the food court was paying them any attention.

"They don't get you. When're you going to figure that out?" her doppelgänger sighed.

"Who's 'they'?" Aya said, feeling stupid for responding to a screen. It was the same feeling she had when Kayo made her try one of those love simulation games and her phone would ring with fake calls from her virtual boyfriend each night. "How are you today?" Kei, Boyfriend Option #2, would ask in that lush familiar voice actor voice during his 10 p.m. call, the time she'd set for their daily "check-in." She'd picked Kei, the two-dimensional bespectacled student body president, purely for his name and thick glasses.

"You know that better than I do, don't you?" Her doppelgänger smiled the way Aya wished she could. Perfect teeth and pimple-free skin, clump-free sky-high lashes. The way Keisuke's new girlfriend probably did. "You don't need them. I've already taken care of everything."

"Everything?"

The doppelgänger unbuttoned the top of her blouse and the camera zoomed in on a skin-colored fastener at the base of her neck. She tilted her head and smiled, raising her hand to her neck, pulling ever-so-gently on the fastener, the first clip of flesh . . .

Kayo returned, wiping her hands with a *Demon Cats* hand towel from her purse. There was still a faded wet brown stain on her shirt.

"The dumpling tell you its secrets?" she asked, following Aya's nervous look to the screen.

The cartoon dumpling was dancing around with anthropomorphized discount tags and plates again.

"Yeah, two-for-one sale on the secrets of the universe," Aya said, unbuttoning the top button of her shirt, patting the skin just to be sure there was nothing there. "Too bad I'm broke."

Kayo laughed, still dabbing at the stain. She motioned toward the screen with her chin. "Then just use that last-minute discount to ask it how to make Keisuke fall in love with you."

↑ ↓

The first time Aya met Keisuke, he was organizing his Pokémon cards on a bench outside the discount supermarket in MAPITA Mall.

"My mom said Pokémon is too violent," Aya said, standing over him with a pack of cigarettes her father had sent her to buy. She remembered the boy from the neighboring class, always reading alone at his desk during breaks.

Keisuke looked up at her over the rim of his thick glasses, blinking. Without a word, he flipped through his cards and pulled out two cards—one with an orange dragon, the other with a blue one.

"Fire beats water, BUT—" He pulled out a third card with a rhinoceros-looking creature. "Ground beats fire."

"And water beats ground," Aya finished, looking at his cards so she didn't need to look at him. She'd spent hours studying the different characters on her hand-me-down phone as her parents argued in the kitchen.

A woman toting a screaming toddler in one hand and a Baskin-Robbins cake in the other walked past them like a siren.

"It's not about violence," Keisuke said, sliding the card back into his deck. "It's about strategy. It's about figuring out weaknesses and strengths. It's about how to train your Pokémon to bring out the best in them."

Aya could only nod. There was something mesmerizing about a boy who could speak about cards like gods. The only thing she could speak so confidently about were the designated times she was supposed to get her mother's pills ready.

"Where's your mom?" she sputtered when he went back to organizing his cards.

"Waiting for them to put the discount stickers on the ready-to-eat food," Keisuke answered, not looking up. "It usually takes a while."

"Yo, Aya."

Keisuke walked past the vending machines with his tailored blue Oxford shirt and his posse of followers with cockroach-like durability for his verbal abuse. He might as well have been a classic Greek statue in a soy sauce-stained high school uniform.

Aya swallowed back the urge to vomit, mustering the last of her nerves to wave nonchalantly at him as his posse watched. How long had it been like this? A wall of strangers between them?

"Yo. Here for shopping?" she asked, amazed at how calm she sounded. She motioned at his Muji paper bag with her chin.

"Something like that. Do you know where the Zoff is?" He glanced at Kayo, flinching slightly like someone catching sight of an abnormally large rodent, before turning back to Aya. "I need new glasses."

"It's on the fourth floor. Past the tentacle cat Hello Kitty statue and next to the Ghibli Store."

He made a sound from the back of his throat. Aya knew he had always been bad with directions, though she doubted the rest of his posse knew.

"It's a little confusing, but uh—"

"She could totally show you the way," Kayo interrupted with a grin.

Keisuke's minions perked up like raccoons at fresh garbage.

"Yeah, sure, if you don't mind," their king answered.

↑ ↓

Three things Aya had never told anyone:

(1) She hated Barbie—an aunt bought her a My-Size Barbie during first year of elementary school, telling her she could dress up the plastic-eyed doll in her own clothes and accessories. Aya was convinced the doll would wake up in the middle of the night and murder her to steal her identity.

(2) She had been in love with Keisuke Harada since the fourth grade when he beat all the other kids at dodgeball, huffing like an asthmatic Mad Max in thick glasses and a Pokémon t-shirt.

(3) Her doppelgänger hid in mirrors, screens, and night-time windows. She wanted to be friends.

↑ ↓

The elevator smelled like artificial strawberry flavor. Keisuke's posse felt miles away, sipping on fountain drinks in the food court. Hikaru Utada's throaty new song scratched over the speakers above the number pad.

Aya tried not to breathe too loudly.

She fought the urge to bring up the dodgeball game, how it sometimes played in her head like a favorite bookmarked video on YouTube. *Stalkers bring up the past where they're nothing but invisible characters,* she thought. And Aya wasn't a stalker.

"When did you start wearing contacts?" she asked instead, pressing 4. The elevator doors closed, and her mind automatically swept over to a reel of smooth hotel elevator doors, rotating beds, and neon spotlights.

"I have swimming practice after class now so it's easier that way,"

Keisuke answered, eyes on the numbers above the door. He'd grown more than ten inches since the fourth grade, the envy of all the other boys in their class. She barely recognized him the summer after his mother remarried. He hadn't come to MAPITA Mall for weeks, no message or anything, and then she saw him at the train station the day before classes started. He was dressed in all name-brand clothes with a neat new haircut like someone going to a wedding.

"I liked your glasses," Aya murmured.

"A lot of the other kids used to make fun of me because of how thick they were. Even my stepdad did."

She knew that, but she never had. She missed those glasses.

The elevator doors opened. The floor was lit up with neon emergency lights, an emerald sea of little running stick-men. Mannequins lined the walls with big smiling mouths, an eyeless audience. Aya's blood ran cold.

"I think this is the wrong floor," she said, tapping on the elevator's close button.

"Looks like the right floor," Keisuke said, staring at the large red 4 on the LED panel.

"The Zoff isn't here." Aya frantically tapped the other floors on the number pad, but the doors still didn't move.

"Let's just take the stairs," Keisuke said, getting off the elevator like someone disembarking from a burning boat. The emergency lights buzzed along the walls as they stepped through the dim-lit hall. The mannequins watched them—their wide mouths seemed to be moving, undulating, but it was too dark to be sure.

"Do you have an appointment with the Viewmaster?"
An eyeless mannequin in a blue tuxedo stepped out of line.

Keisuke glanced at Aya as if she might, as if she were acquainted with the monster. She shook her head. Themed escape rooms had gotten popular, and maybe they'd simply stumbled in on one of the new ones during a soft opening. A fellow part-timer at the convenience store where Aya worked had dressed up as a mannequin for Halloween the year before and had gotten yelled at by the manager for scaring customers.

"The Viewmaster's expecting us," Keisuke lied the way Aya's mother sometimes had when the bank called about unpaid credit card bills. Aya was both terrified and impressed.

"Come this way," the mannequin directed.

↑ ↓

The two followed the mannequin through a pair of metal doors into a hall of familiar-looking stores and stands: novelty shops selling cat-shaped mug cups and glittery notebooks, bag shops with walls of colorful backpacks and leather purses, escape rooms with advertisements of other mannequins battling dragons and deadly mannequin-eating plants.

Each shop was filled with mannequins walking around, chatting, and shopping. None paid Keisuke or Aya any attention.

The three stopped in front of a giant neon sign that read "The Viewmaster." A frenzy of sound spilled from the arched entrance. Coin chimes, hyper-cute kiddie voices singing invitations, frenetic Vocaloid music. Neon pink and blue lights speared across the ceiling. Arcade games flanked one side, pachinko machines the other, and at the far end was a line of crane games, each machine filled with plush dolls.

Screens along the wall played a documentary-style video featuring mannequin factory workers, glossy body parts stacked in giant vats, rolling red conveyor belts, crematorium-sized towers puffing smoke, bodies boxed and taped. At the end, an eyeless mannequin girl opened a delivery box and was soon hugging her new girl-shaped plush doll.

"A New Body. A New You."

"Something for everybody."

Keisuke and Aya turned around, but their escort had blended back into the crowd of mannequins outside.

Keisuke walked up to the change machine and took out his wallet. He slid a 1000 yen bill into the slot and three black coins tumbled out of the opening.

"Might as well try it out. They're probably beta testing some new indoor horror theme park or escape room. They might be taking videos and will upload them onto YouTube later. Wasn't Aki in one, looking like a weirdo?" he said, heading over to one of the crane game machines.

Keisuke never used to call anyone a weirdo. "Yeah, that makes sense," Aya said, feeling like a miserable parrot. She reluctantly took out the only 1000 yen bill in her wallet, the one she hid inside a good luck amulet so her mom wouldn't find it when the older woman went through her things, looking for Aya's part-time job money.

Goodbye dinner. She sighed, sliding the bill into the change machine and picking up the three shiny black coins that came out.

"Hey again, pretty girl."

The mannequin girl in the screen above the crane game machine had turned into her doppelgänger.

"It's dangerous here. But you know that, don't you? Or did you want him to like you that much?"

Keisuke was already playing one of the crane game machines, leaning over the panel to get a better look at the position of the claw. There was a giddiness to his face that hadn't been there earlier. He'd always been the one who liked playing these games, while Aya liked to watch him.

"Do you like the shape of his collarbones? Or are your eyes just stuck?" her doppelgänger asked.

Aya couldn't stand the way her doppelgänger grinned at her, like the girl already knew all the ugly thoughts in her head. Instead, she glanced over to the crane game machine next to the screen. It was filled with plush dolls, fluffy bead-eyed girls all wearing outfits eerily similar to the ones Kayo had. Some wore glasses, others sported miniskirts or pink wigs like the one Kayo wore during a holiday play in middle school. One was wearing the same brown-stained *Demon Cats* x UNIQLO t-shirt.

"Want to play a game?" her doppelgänger asked, waving to her on the screen. The Vocaloid pop music crescendoed in the background in a vibrating flurry of synthesizers, so loud that Aya could barely hear the doppelgänger's next words: "A body is just a place-holder. You outgrow it. You find one that fits better. So why not take yours off? Try on a new one?"

"My body?"

The plush dolls in the machine seemed to wave at her now too. Little felt and cotton creatures. Little skin and organ creatures.

"'What is essential is invisible to the eye,'" the doppelgänger recited from Aya's favorite childhood book. Her grin darkened, reaching for the base of her own throat, to the skin-colored zipper. "But everything else can be sewed on."

Aya felt hands on her face, even though she couldn't see them. They seemed to be kneading her skin.

"I know you better than anyone else. I know what you want. So let me help you."

Aya watched her doppelgänger pull on the zipper, her neck opening. Wider and wider until she could see something in the cavern of her throat—another face.

"A winner! A winner! We have a winner!"

The manic voice pulled Aya out of her trance. She turned toward the flashing lights of the crane game machine behind her.

"Hey look, this is so trippy," Keisuke said, holding a plush doll of himself wearing a Pokémon t-shirt and glasses. He took out his phone with his other hand and held the doll up to the glass to take a photo.

That's when Aya saw it, poking out of the top of his blue Oxford shirt. The skin-colored fastener on the base of his neck.

"Did you get one too?" Keisuke asked, walking over to show her the plush doll. "Creepy as hell, but kinda cool too."

The clothes on the doll were stitched in perfect lines, down to the lightning-striped sneakers he used to wear every day of fourth grade. For a moment, she thought of those summer days at MAPITA Mall, how they'd sometimes go to the food court and buy neon green melon soda floats from First Kitchen, and he'd show her his cards or the latest manga he was reading. How long had it been since he'd shown her something without an audience? Without his posse hovering a few feet away?

Aya looked at the fastener on his throat again.

"No. It's harder than it looks," Aya lied, squeezing the three coins in her pocket.

"Want me to get you one?" he asked, glancing into the crane game machine with a gambler's high. There were so many little Ayas, ones with bleached blond hair, ones in frilly dresses that would embarrass her to wear in real life, ones with sunflower eyes and blue-painted lips. Which one would he like best? "Like old times."

On the screen, Aya's doppelgänger winked at her with her gaping eye holes.

"Would you?" Aya asked, trying to sound the way she imagined Keisuke's girlfriend sounded. She'd never seen her, only heard the rumors about the pretty girl he'd met at his part-time job at the dentist's office near the station. She was on the track and field team at her school, but still made time to take care of her sick aunt. *A real beauty with a heart.* Aya wanted to inspect the girl's teeth too, pluck out each one with the pliers from her mother's toolbox. If she slotted those teeth into her own mouth, would that give her the same smile?

Keisuke handed her his mini-me plush doll the way he used to with the Pokémon and shiba dog plushies and slotted one of his black coins into the machine. "Just watch me," he said, eyes brimming with confidence. The metal claw moved right, swinging above the wide-eyed dolls like the claws of a god. Which one would be the winner?

I know you better than anyone else. I know what you want. So let me help you.

Aya raised her hand to the fastener on his neck, taking hold of it carefully, like a surgical knife. It was warm in her fingers, like living skin. Gently, she pulled the zipper down, the flesh opening neatly until she could see his spine and the narrow cavity inside his chest. Where his heart should have been, there was a small cage, and inside it, a half-rotted doll in a button-down shirt, its face already unrecognizable. He was exhausted, wasn't he? She opened the cage door. The doll fell out and crumbled to dust on the floor. With her other hand, she slotted in Keisuke's plush doll and closed the door again.

"A winner! A winner! We have a winner!"

Mannequins had gathered by the entrance of the Viewmaster with their shopping bags and oversized fountain drinks, giant mouths open but silent. They were watching.

The crane game machine flashed its lights. Keisuke didn't move. Aya's doppelgänger was gone from the screen. Instead, Aya felt a faint pulsing in her throat, a warmth in her chest. Her mouth widened into a grin. She pressed her face into Keisuke's back, breathing in the smell of him, the smell of the old mall. It had been so long.

↑ ↓

"Hey, did you hear about Aki?" Kayo said as they rode the autowalk toward the food court. The summer "Shop Happiness" banners hanging from the ceiling had already been replaced by an autumn theme with happy jack o'lanterns and red foliage. "His sister said he came back. Just went on some trip to 'find himself' with a girl he met online. Apparently neither of them really knew how much it costs to find yourself, so they ended up coming home."

Aya made a noise in the back of her throat as she messaged someone on her phone.

"Hey, did you hear me?"

"Yeah, yeah," Aya said, looking up to give her friend a big grin before returning to her messages.

Kayo had never seen her friend so busy, so upbeat. It was hard enough getting her to come out on weekends now that she was seeing Keisuke every day. She didn't even pick up the phone at night anymore. It almost felt like her friend was making a whole new life without her. Was Keisuke leading Aya on? Kayo had mentioned that possibility several times, but she'd been brushed off like a nagging insect. Kayo didn't want to admit that it hurt her feelings, how her best friend didn't seem to trust or listen to anything she said anymore. What happened to the Dynamic Duo?

"I'm meeting Keisuke later at the new First Kitchen that just opened downstairs," Aya said, finally putting her phone back into her pocket. She ran her tongue over her teeth to make sure there was nothing stuck between them. "So, I don't think I can do the *Demon Cats* raid tonight. But I'm sure there'll be a ton of other people there anyway, right?"

"Yeah, no big deal," Kayo said, squeezing her *Demon Cats* bag. *Who cares about playing a dumb game together anyway?* "I guess that talking dumpling really did know all the secrets of life?"

"Something like that. You can figure out a lot just by looking."

What the hell does that even mean? Pretentious. So fucking pretentious. "Yeah, I guess I just gotta keep looking," Kayo said, feeling a scratch in her throat.

As they entered the food court, a dancing dumpling hawked the latest seasonal menu items from chestnut tarts to grilled Pacific saury.

It danced and watched, knowing there was something for everybody.

one last time

derek des anges

The Walter Gropius Memorial Mall was not built in the Bauhaus style. Perhaps that was what had resulted in its condemnation, instead of its salvation: nothing about it really memorialized the architect whose name it had taken, aside from a large Expressionist sculpture in the main atrium, a copy of *Monument to the March Dead* without any indication of what that monument had ever meant. Its slow decline had begun almost immediately, when the more conveniently located Billy Backwars Mall had opened on the other side of town.

The cost of detonating the graffiti-covered, beer can-filled, piss-stained corpse of the mall, with its final patinated pennies corroded to the bottom of the fountains, its spectacular molds creeping up the locked bathrooms, and its arterial pathways still presided over by *Final Sale* signs in lurid orange, far exceeded what the land developers had wanted to sink into the site.

And so, like a cat with a decaying bird to which it fully intends to return, they buried it.

Under rubble, slag, and infill left over from the demolition of a branch railway line, Walter Gropius Memorial Mall became a raised burial mound, supported by concrete columns. Its foundations were to be repurposed as the base of a luxury apartment block.

Under the blackened windows, even the snake plants, forgotten in their pots, withered and died, their lightless cave a tomb to the last hangers-on, a haven for cockroaches, a breeding-ground for foraging rats.

There are, however, things that grow in the dark.

The Walter Gropius Memorial Mall had been the scene of no small number of dramas in its lifetime: before its terminal illness, lovelorn teenagers had squabbled, and two had suicided, hanging themselves after hours from its tall atrium; one would-be ATM thief had been tased by a mall cop, gone into seizure, and died abruptly on the polished floors, passing out of life between the rubber-soled work shoes of the suddenly contrite security guard. Following the final closure, three separate and unrelated shootings, two overdoses, and one sex-related killing had taken place in various locations around its sprawling, unloved shape. From the air, it was reminiscent of an asterisk or a pentacle.

Despite the inevitable rumors, the Walter Gropius Memorial Hall remained stubbornly and almost ludicrously unhaunted by any human ghost.

Pre-burial, one amateur web series, investigating haunted sites in the underexamined rash of towns in the county, had been forced to conclude that the "ghostly howling" observed by one drunken informant was actually the local pack of stray dogs; that the creaks and groans were the unsafe settling of old joists under strain; and that the unnatural glow was a combination of ambient street light refracting from the ever-present clouds above the town with the admittedly eerie light of phosphorescent fungi growing in the darker recesses of the building.

They were fined $500 for trespassing on an unsafe site on the release of the episode.

The Walter Gropius Memorial Mall's burial came and went. In the near-total darkness, the carcasses of stray dogs which had not escaped in time provided final, fulsome meals for sleepy rats. The deceased rats in their turn fed the fungi, which flourished, putting up callow green glowing umbrellas with no one to see them.

And the soul of the building twisted uneasily, since being fed into wakefulness with human and animal life, worshipped with misery and discounted sports shoes, spilled gasoline, broken hearts, heroin, and Claire's unhygienic ear piercings every Saturday and Wednesday. It writhed, and ached, beneath its soil coffin.

In the dark soil, the rubble, and decay, the soft white filaments of luminescent fungus embraced the body of the Walter Gropius Memorial Mall, and the soul of the Walter Gropius Memorial Mall said: *I don't want to be luxury apartment buildings.*

The fungal embrace in the stygian depths said: *There's no light anymore. No life. Even I need a little of that to keep going.*

The Walter Gropius Memorial Mall murmured: *You're not going to leave, are you?*

The clasping, reaching branches of microscopic hyphae did not reply, and the soul of the Walter Gropius Memorial Mall returned to the contemplation of its sad demise, brooding in the dark about the Billy Backwars Mall, the town bypass, the indignity of Spirit Halloween stores, and the faint vibrations of construction boards being driven into the ground above to shield the works from trespassers.

↑ ↓

At 7 a.m. on the first Friday of construction, when the ground has been broken, James Rossiter finds something under his boot.

There is all sorts of crap on any given empty lot, of course. People throw things in there. The blue-painted construction hoardings don't offer much of a shield, only a challenge to intrepid graffiti artists and urban explorers; also there's that one guy who likes to break into places so he can masturbate in them. James Rossiter has been warned about Jerkin' Joe.

When he raises his insulated workboot and finds a thick white paste-like substance directly beneath it, his first thought is *ew, that goddamn pervert*; but it is not semen. He knows full well what that looks like, and this is not that.

His second thought is that it's a thick cobweb, a big spider's nest, which is actually even worse, and he'd have kept on thinking that too, only now he sees there's a tiny little white mushroom head sticking out of the foamy-looking mess, and when he squints...

The whole mass is almost invisibly small mushroom heads.

"Huh," says James, and once he's back in the cab of his vehicle, out of the line of sight of Craig Denison, the foreman, he calls his union rep. "Tracy," he says, "Tracy. What's the law like around disturbing protected species and stuff? Who gets blamed for that if we bulldoze some fancy ecology and upset the Left?"

Tracy makes a sucking noise. There's typing. "Owners. Supposed to do a survey. If they've messed that up, they're on the hook. You don't get hit with shit." She emphasizes the word *shit* at length.

"Thanks," James says, and ends the call. He shrugs. Bluewater Prospect probably haven't done a survey, but that's not his problem: that's *their* problem. Legally.

Now that he's seen it, he can't un-notice it, however, and wherever he looks there are small patches of bleach-white haunting the broken soil, creeping up wherever the passage of heavy vehicles and men's boots has turned wasteland weeds into churned mud. They look like vitiligo, or more like thrush on the back of his throat from that one time he'd gotten sick with it. Sins of the father, or more accurately mother, in his case.

Obviously it can't be that rare if it's everywhere here.

Probably not even a real problem.

James waits for someone to radio and let him know to start. Coordination is key; positioning is important. Apparently there's something under here that may make the ground unstable. Caves or something. And digging in the wrong spot could send one perfectly good 320 GC excavator and, more importantly, one imperfectly insured James Rossiter crashing into a hole, and he can't afford time off for serious injuries. Besides, it'd foul up the order of work.

So he waits for the earpiece to tell him when; and in the meantime—

He takes his phone out and looks at the lock screen. There are three preview messages from an app he'd told Laurie he'd deleted.

And outside the window, just below the cab of the 320 GC, there's a spiderweb of lacy white slowly oozing over the mud.

"Hey," asks the earpiece, abruptly, without any indication of who's supposed to be answering—they're all linked to the same broadcaster, everyone hears everyone's conversations, he's complained before but no one gives a damn—"Hey, who was meant to be clearing the central quadrant? There's roof tiles *everywhere*."

"Not it," James says, pressing the call button. His ear briefly fills with an unlovely chorus of his temporary colleagues all disavowing responsibility, until only two are left, insisting that they *did* clear central quadrant and they didn't see no damn tiles.

"They're all *fuzzy*," says the first voice. "Denison, did you see this? There's fuzzy tiles all over the central quadrant."

"Are they just scattered or overlapping?" asks someone who definitely isn't Denison.

"What the hell does it matter?" asks the first voice, and then a moment later, adds, "Overlapping. They're laid out like someone's trying to build a roof out here on the mud. Except they're *fuzzy*."

"Fuzzy how?"

James patches himself back in. "White and fuzzy like threads are on it?"

"Yeah man, is this some practical joke you pulled?"

James shakes his head to the empty cab. "I, uh, I think we should maybe call the survey team again."

↑ ↓

By noon no one has done a lick of work and Denison is so livid that he's turned an interesting shade of red, so red he's almost purple with rage, looking even more like an overloaded close-to-coming white man's glans than normal; this is not an observation James Rossiter makes to anyone else beyond *damn, that man looks like a dick*. He doesn't need anyone asking why he's so familiar with the sight and why it pops into his head so easily. After all, he told Laurie he deleted that app and as far as all her little gossip crew are concerned that's the end of it.

No one cares about James's similes today anyhow. They've got a roof to worry about.

The roof is knee-height now. No one's actually seen it growing, but every time they look at it, it's taller than it was. The guys have taken to measuring it with the laser levels. It is 609.7 mm tall currently.

"Just knock it down already," Denison shouts, into the earpiece.

James, like everyone else, ignores him. The roof now extends across most of the site. They've backed the vehicles into what feels now like the parking lot: the guys are having a smoke and vape break, again, except for James, who quit two years ago, and Fuyum, who says he's not smoking during Ramadan and looks like he regrets the choice.

The roof, tracing several hundred yards, is completely enmeshed in soft white strands. Here and there James can see little tiny white mushroom heads.

He's not sure anyone's noticed them. He doesn't want to be the one to point them out. He *definitely* doesn't want to be the one to point out that they look like tiny little penises.

Manuel is filming it on his phone.

"Everyone's going to think you faked it," Fuyum says, glaring with nicotine-addicted envy at the prerolled cigarette behind Manny's ear. "You can't put that on YouTube, they'll just say you faked it. People can fake anything."

"I'm not putting it on YouTube," Manny says, squinting through the screen. "I'm sending it to Carla."

James peers down at the ground where the top of the building, in its cocoon of white, silk-like thread, is emerging from the dirt. The dirt falls easily from the stuff. He can't quite see it moving, but he thinks it's growing even while he's looking at it: rising out of the ground. It looks like long, bored Saturdays hanging out in front of the game store. It looks like cheap milkshakes. It looks like a fountain with a security guard next to it. It looks like a mall.

"What kind of seed does a mall grow from?" he asks, under his breath.

"You know there was a mall here before," Fuyum says, catching only half of what he's said. "They didn't even demolish it."

"You think it's the same one?"

"I didn't say that," says Fuyum, with the deliberate precision of someone who is hangry and determined to make everyone else suffer with him. "I don't think they cotton-wrapped the last one."

Halfway through the afternoon, no one's done a damn thing aside from film the increasingly tall mall from a variety of angles and lament that they didn't pull the bags of construction sand off the roof before it got to head height. Denison is pulling his hair out; Tracy has told James to stop calling with questions about OSHA and "ghost malls"; Fuyum is on the verge of giving up on giving up on smoking—and still the silk-husked mall is growing.

"We're contracted to break ground, lay foundations, and insert the plant framework," says Beemer, a lifer who has taken up the post of official spokesperson for the nonworking workers, while Denison has a nervous breakdown. "We haven't been contracted to demolish an art installation."

"It's not a *fucking* art installation," Denison hisses. "And even if it *was*, it's an unauthorized one. This lot was auctioned to Crassar and Crewe Developments legally!"

"And we're not contracted to do a demolition," James puts in, beginning to enjoy himself, "art installation or not."

"We're willing to negotiate an amended contract," Beemer says, brushing down his high-visibility vest for imaginary specks of dirt. "But until that contract is negotiated, no demolition. And until demolition, we can't feasibly provide any labor on this site. And since that's a problem with the *site*, Crassar and Crewe still owe us our hourly rate."

"Says who?" Denison barks.

Beemer produces his phone. "Section 82b II of the county labor code clearly states—"

↑ ↓

The Walter Gropius Memorial Mall tastes the familiar, exhaust-fumed air of its rightful home as it rises, slowly propelled back toward the empty gray-white skies of the backwater town by its fungal partner.

Rise again, rise again, the Walter Gropius Memorial Mall sings to itself, pulling up still-connected electricity cables with such force that lights all over town start to blink out. *Rise again, rise again.*

The infill peels back from its walls as if it knows it shouldn't be there. The truth of it is, of course, that the thin white body of the ever-expanding night-fungus has infiltrated the dirt hereabouts and can move it as it wishes, and so the wrecked corpse of the Walter

Gropius Memorial Mall arises like the head of a midnight mushroom, thrust up through the rocks of its untimely burial, ready to spread the biggest, juiciest load of spores the town has ever seen.

The feed pipe for the dead fountains rips and shudders. The foundations of the mall pop out of their grave like rotten teeth from a suppurating socket. The Walter Gropius Memorial Mall returns from the depths.

Standing in what is now definitely the parking lot, James Rossiter and his colleagues wait until dusk, when the roof of the mall is over the height of their heads, and the mall still hasn't stopped coming; they wait, and, with one last argument with Denison, they go back to their own cars and they drive home.

Only the night watchman remains, his post by the entrance to the lot untouched by much except the blackout. He shines his flashlight over the white-wrapped form of the Walter Gropius Memorial Mall, recalling younger days spent trying to steal pennies from the atrium fountains; recalling the ugly replica statue within; recalling the vain attempts of his high-school teacher to tie in the mall with the history of the Weimar Republic.

He wipes mud off his boots on the rim of his booth, takes out his phone, and goes back to reading about the flat earth conspiracy.

Above him, the reborn mall's smashed-open windows call silently to the animals of the night.

And the Walter Gropius Memorial Mall lives one last time.

layaway

rick hollon

As a kid you learned the rules that keep you safe: Always step on tiles the long way. Never look down the service corridor. Santa isn't real but still wields ancient powers, best left unexamined. Never touch the poinsettias, no matter how they tower there in the center of the mall, no matter how inviting their leaves.

Your mother couldn't explain layaway to you, though you asked.

Mikey Gibbs, two grades ahead of you, slipped into the red and greenery of the poinsettias the second day of December and no one ever talked about him again, as if he had never thrown a rock at you on the playground two weeks before, as if he had never spilled Coke across the cafeteria, as if the floor weren't still sticky there under everyone's sneakers. You touched the bruise hidden by your hair and you counted your steps across the tiles, head down. You didn't look at Santa, though you heard him laughing.

You learned the rules that help people like you as a teen: Wear black but not so much that you become a poser. Feign an interest in this band, this actress, this girl. Keep your shoes clean so they seem new. Never open the door to your secret thoughts. Don't notice the curve of Benji Jackson's lips, the curl of his fingers, the way you hear him breathe in the dark of the theater even when the speakers rumble through a car chase. Be Pierce Brosnan, steely behind the wheel. Shoplift small things, but only small things: Tic Tacs and shoelaces and a Pantera button from Hot Topic. Anything bigger would get your ass hauled into the service corridor. Don't go into the service corridor.

Jennifer Calvin slipped an Aqua CD into her bag two weeks before Christmas and no one ever talked about her again, as if her white-out graffiti didn't still spell out exactly what you were on the bricks of the eighth grade hallway, as if your cuticles hadn't split from flaking away each letter, as if her empty desk didn't collect dust beside yours. As if you couldn't still smell her Dr. Pepper lip gloss from when she leaned in close and sing-songed into your ear, "What if I told *Aaron* you're a little fruit? What if he got you *alone* in the bathroom? Would you *like* that, freak?"

Your fingers brushed Benji Jackson's reaching for the Junior Mints box in his lap. He scooted away in his seat, eyed you in the dark. You couldn't hear his breath anymore. You never hung out with him again. Jennifer Calvin's desk was gone when you returned from winter break. No one else noticed.

Do you remember what you'd said, what you'd wished, long ago, your small hand cupped against Santa's ear? He sat enthroned in a mountain of poinsettia, idols of Rudolph and Frosty and light-up candy canes arrayed around him. A camera flashed but it was miles away. His belly was padded, a dry rustling sound beneath your elbows, beneath your heart. He had no pulse; the pulse you felt came from somewhere deeper. Underground. You thought he would smell of shortbread and eggnog, or maybe, like your father, he would reek of automotive grease and Jack Daniel's and Irish Spring. Instead, he smelled like winter air, like frost on a fallen leaf, like your nose against the glass. His eyes flashed green in the lights, flashed red.

No one gave you any rules as an adult. Your mother only in-canted: Get a degree. Don't be like your piece-of-shit father. Get a girlfriend. *Amount* to something. But you scrubbed out of second semester chem and didn't see much point sticking to it after that. So you wound up counting the tiles (your boots were too big to fit on one tile, but you still did it) and the tiles brought you to the CD store down the JCPenney wing. It was a shit job, but better than some. You showed up to each shift halfway baked, which helped. Bruce the Juice, who hopped between registers in the food court, sold decent weed and gave all his fellow retail martyrs a discount. You told him your secrets, once, when you were blitzed out together in the back of his Chevy S-10. "I figured," Bruce drawled, but you knew he'd only heard half of it. The other half was too big to share even if you tried. Buried too deep in the heart of everything else.

You still wore black, though you didn't pretend to listen to Pantera anymore. You added color again, discreetly, a button here and there, a streak bleached pink in your hair. You looked at yourself in the mirror one night, still living in your mom's house, fresh from the closing shift. You laid it all out on the bathroom counter: eyeliner and lipstick and blush and foundation. You'd smuggled it in under your coat the way others might bring home drugs. You ran the sink so she wouldn't hear, wouldn't ask, would think you were masturbating. But it wasn't that. It wasn't anything, right? It just *was*. You breathed hard. Then you buried it deep in the trash, all of it, and walked back to your room. You bit your cuticles until they bled again.

One time Jennifer Calvin's father shuffled through your store to purchase a Blu-ray of *The Dark Knight*. The ghost of her outlined his cheekbones. A question caught in the root of his throat, as if he'd just caught the scent of a lip gloss no one made anymore. He swallowed it down again. He left without his card, never came back for it. You brought the card home and cut it into tiny pieces in the trash. It seemed the proper thing to do.

Sometimes, in the parking lot, you made out with a department manager from Sears, or you would hotbox with the new hire at Yankee Candle, but it never went anywhere. That also seemed proper. None of you were going anywhere.

Two days before Christmas you saw Benji Jackson, back in town for some godforsaken reason. He was different. He called himself by his middle name now. He wore tailored pants. He had an earring, another ring through his lip. Your eyes widened when you recognized what change he'd made, what door he'd opened.

Sickly holiday music pumped down from the ceiling. You rang him up for his gift cards and took your break and walked with him past Santa, the Santa who was always the same, who scowled deep in his yellowed beard. Angry, or a warning. A rule broken, or something happening too soon.

Past the poinsettias to the hallway where no one went anymore, because the Elder-Beerman had shuttered and no one wanted what was in all the knickknack stores, all the screen repair kiosks, all the plain little dreams someone else dreamed before they bubbled away again into nothing. You didn't see any of it anymore. He told you about art, about basement shows, about German Village in the city. He was big into Basquiat and Leyendecker. He swam regularly.

You mentioned Klimt, whom you only knew thanks to a calendar you stocked for the holiday rush. He smiled patiently. You watched his lips, eyed the elegance of his trapezius above his collar. You wanted to bite his lip ring. He touched your chin, hesitated. His wrist smelled of cinnamon and olive leaves. "Great catching up," he said. He left.

He drove back to his family, back to his visit, armed with gift cards from five stores. He never came back. You didn't get his number. Why would you? You were 35 and still wore a Radiohead t-shirt, the one with the bear crying into its hands.

God. You were never told how this works, how any of this works.

It should have been the Christmas Eve rush the next day. Weeds sprouted in the cracks of the tiles now, dead, barbed. You stumbled, laces caught in thorns. Darkness yawned from empty storefronts, dancing shadows outlined in red and green. How many years had it been this way, tucked just out of sight? Your boots shuffled across the perpendicular tiles. You didn't count any of them. You didn't care.

Santa beckoned from the heart of the poinsettias. They were wilted, unwatered. The lights of his temple had dimmed. You looked around and wondered how this dying mall could still afford to build its pyramid of poinsettias, there at the crossroads at the heart of it all. Santa's eyes were dark, reflected the holiday lights, went dark again. You remembered the shape in the dark, the vast green form, and you put the question away.

One unspoken rule you learned once you grew up: no one can tell you the truth.

Santa's teeth glinted in his beard.

You turned left instead, toward the service corridor.

Leaves crunched underfoot. Something scurried past your boots. A mouse, a broken bird, some child's lost bear. You thought to count tiles again, but you couldn't see them anymore. Wet snow sifted down from a broken skylight, settled in your hair, trickled under your collar.

"Layaway doesn't last forever," Santa had growled to you, once. He had warned you. Far away, Dean Martin crooned through some perennial Christmas standard. Rudolph's nose swelled with light. "Everything in the mall gets paid for, someday. It comes due."

Now Mikey Gibbs stood waxen under a feebly lit candy cane, blood like cherry syrup frozen at his temple. His eyes had faded but you recognized him. You recognized him better than his own mother would: a boy now only as tall as your chest, slowly mummifying in the embrace of poinsettias. It soured the pit of your stomach to see how small he was. How small *you* had been when he'd thrown that rock. The process, the cuckoo-bird act of socialization, pushing out those who weren't the proper kind, started so early.

Now you reached the security office and found Jennifer Calvin drying into the wall, painted into place across the bricks. Poinsettias birdbone-pale cuffed her wrists, twining around her. You didn't want to see this. You wanted to look away. The Christmas lights illuminated nothing else. Her teeth were hidden beneath a slack white tongue. Somewhere tinny speakers scratched and skipped through Aqua's "Happy Boys & Girls." The grass beneath your boots crackled like cellophane.

You found a broken CD at her feet. You picked it up, nicked the pad of your finger on its edge. The drop was black against the silver.

One more door remained in the service corridor: Management. Light jumped and shimmered beneath the crack. You could hear Dean Martin again, crooning on a loop, crooning through a canned eternity. Your grandparents had danced to this song.

Santa stopped you, hand against your chest. Poinsettia leaves poked through his collar, ruffled through the hem of his coat. His belly was rumpled, swollen, a shirt packed with leaves. He tried to speak to you, but vines clotted out between his teeth. You closed your eyes, pushed past him. He rustled and collapsed into a pile of old clothes.

"Layaway is, well," your mother had attempted, tugging you away from the one-quarter capsule machines, tugging you away from the three-quarter race car rides, "layaway is when you can't pay for something now, so they set it aside for you. They lay it away."

You didn't understand anything she meant, then. You didn't learn the important lessons from her anyway, or from dad, whenever he bothered to show up on his weekends. You learned the important things in the mall.

You took a breath. Your feet kicked out from the briars, traced the shape of tiles. You knew this mall inside and out. You knew where the tiles were, how their pattern repeated. You counted them. Three steps forward, carefully placing your boots on the longways tiles. Nothing perpendicular.

You clutched the broken CD and rested your fingertips on the door handle. It crumbled to dust, sifted down in ash and bits of gravel, its component ores unraveling. The wood of the door cracked, bloomed toadstools, guttered into humus. The plaster showered down with the snow. You felt it waiting for you, the holly king, the holy thing, as everything crumbled. You felt its heartbeat push waves of heat against your cheeks, your eyes. Your tongue dried in your mouth. You looked up, up again, forever up.

It was a bound colossus, groaning under the weight of pavement, cracking the ribs of steel and copper that had wound around it all these years. Rudolph and Frosty and countless strings of lights blinked a hundred colors in time to the wash of its heart, scattered along its arms, its legs. Its antlers were strewn with knots of Cadillacs, hefted husks of Winnebagos. Trees that must have grown here before the mall broke ground, sycamores and field oaks and ash, stretched skeletally from its chin. English ivy and feral rose and poinsettia pulled its hands and hooves into the earth. Its cunts and cocks swelled and withered in time, dozens of them, battened down with stop signs and grand opening tape and final clearance signs, trailing garlands of holly and tinsel when the holly king strained to rise.

The gale was thick with its musk. It filled you, distended you. You lost control of your mouth, drooled onto the snow.

You wanted to say something cool, maybe something literary that Benji could have appreciated, or even something smooth like Pierce Brosnan. But all you could do was stumble forward, beaten by that heartbeat like waves, in and out, hot and cold. Flushed and gasping for air, nauseous and throbbing with need. You held onto the broken CD. You fell to your knees. You crawled forward.

Your debt is due, the beast rumbled, everywhere, in your head, inside your pelvis, the root of your spine. Your pith shuddered with it. Dead poinsettia leaves swirled in the snow, wrapped around your face, whipped aside again. *Pay it to me*, and its voice was all you had ever known, the lean throb of your neurons, the weight of your marrow, the need inside you. The colossus, even felled, rose higher than you could imagine.

The CD shard was such a silly thing in your hand. You bled in the snow, in the roar of the wind, in the stink. You didn't notice. You rose, crunched through the ruins of the theater, the sticky popcorn, the glass of the atrium, the broken crockery of a thousand poinsettia pots. You staggered to your feet. You cut the first vine you found. The poinsettia snapped away, withered. Next the English ivy, thick as a hawser. Maybe Benji would have liked that word. That one tore the skin from three knuckles as it parted.

You cut a band of cellophane, and it was enough.

It is paid, it said through your jaws, and you barely felt the ache it left in your teeth, the way your gums bled. Snow gritted your eyes. When you could see again, you stood in the parking lot with bloody hands. Everything pulsed, deep down, too numb for pain. Beyond a cyclone fence you saw the mall, what was left of it, already half demolished. A signboard promised new delights, new enticements, outdoor shopping, new places to spend your money.

But you knew the mall was dead.

You had never thought to learn what would happen from here. Who were you, without it?

let's go and sit by the pool

wan phing lim

It was their usual routine to take the bus from Green Lane to Gurney Plaza on Fridays after school. Shilin and Akid proudly wore their uniforms throughout the ride, she wearing two metal badges—a squarish one of her school with a big bright star, and a yellow rectangular one of her name in black—adorning her left chest like scout badges, he showing off the blue and white striped tie.

The wind blew in their faces, the engine roaring and subsiding, the conductor's single-hole puncher knocking the metal railing above after every stop. Shilin and Akid would have to shout to talk to each other, so mostly they kept quiet inside the blue KGN Hin bus, looking out at the State Mosque on their left, at the angsana trees along Scotland Road, at the turf club's wide green fields, and at Mr. Konishi's marble mansion-castle in the distance. In the afternoon heat, it was easy to fall asleep. But not for Shilin and Akid, who didn't hold hands, but let their thighs touch on the seats, flesh hidden beneath the bright blue cotton of her long skirt and the dark green of his trousers.

Once at the mall, Akid removed his tie and Shilin her badges, especially her name tag, so as not to bring shame to their school or to themselves, if ever the occasion arose. They crossed Kelawei Road, not holding hands, and the air conditioning welcomed them as the sliding doors glided open.

Today, Shilin carried her Pendidikan Seni art portfolio in her hands, not wanting to leave it in her school locker over the weekend. Inside were her four wayang kulit puppets, watercolor on manila card—instead of real goat's hide—stuck to wooden satay sticks. She held the folio over her chest like a shield, an armor. The art teacher, Mrs. Hubbard, had given her a four out of ten for her puppets. That amounted to a D, and Shilin wanted to go home to rework it, and submit it again if she could.

Akid was languid and laid back. He wore a spiral coil hair band over his longish hair, and he walked with an ease. He had a quiet charm and confidence. Shilin did not have those qualities, and she wanted desperately for them to rub off on her.

Today, Akid brought a helmet along, in case she wanted to ride home with him. His motorcycle was parked near an uncle's house on Medan Maktab. But girls didn't like helmets—they messed up their hair. Besides, Shilin could imagine her mother's face if she ever came home on a motorbike, clinging onto Akid! Already she had been warned about wearing the baju kurung uniform for Muslim girls, which was more see-through without the blue pinafore. It was inappropriate for Chinese girls, her mother had said, and it would attract the "wrong" type of boys. But Shilin did not care. She loved Akid and she worried about him.

In Kedah, the state next to theirs, the religious teachers had been frisking Malay girls for marks of Satan on their bodies. This morning, it happened at her school. The black metal purge had arrived in Penang, the ustaz and ustazas witch-hunting for worshippers of the devil and the mark of Iblis. Upside-down crosses, five-pronged necklaces, free sex, and goat sacrifices. Shilin and Akid laughed. It was so absurd. Now any dark-skinned teenager who loved metal music and dressed in black was trouble.

In the basement of Gurney Plaza, they grabbed a brown paper bag each, a cheeseburger and small fries for her, a Big Mac with large fries and a large Coke for him. A chocolate sundae to share. They went up to the ground floor of the shiny new mall, where Lancôme, Shiseido, Biotherm, Kanebo, and Kosé counters gleamed with perfume bottles and eyeshadow palettes. Shilin and Akid slid along a narrow lane toward the toilet that led to a cargo lift. Inside, graffiti covered the doors and elevator walls: *Fauzi Kote. Kepala buto. Fizwan Babi. Ma Puki. Love iz everything. 0164048896 hisap kote call. Tetek tembikai. Body montok.*

Shilin giggled and Akid sniggered. He unzipped his backpack for a black marker. "Akid love Shilin" he scrawled, the big heart-shape looking like a housefly instead. Shilin laughed, slapping his backpack. The triple-panel doors opened on the seventh floor, and they took the emergency staircase, past the Bilik AHU, and there was their rooftop spot, shielded from the afternoon sun by a large water tank and an air conditioning compressor, with a huge bladed fan and a churning pool of water inside, covered by a metal grill.

Lunch, finally. In this hot, hot weather. Hutan hujan tropika. Hutan hujan khatulistiwa. But there was nowhere else they could go, for lunch followed by a kiss, and maybe more. A light breeze was coming from the shoreline, where the mainland and Kedah loomed in the distance.

They put their backpacks down and slumped against the black water tank. Akid's helmet carried their doggy bags, and they tucked into lunch eagerly.

"Sepultura has a new album," he said, chewing his Big Mac.

"Oh yeah?" Shilin said, noticing a large cardboard box at the corner, a dumpster filled with plastic ropes and placards made of styrofoam. A broken mannequin's leg stuck out, white and bare. "Any good?"

"I love it. Heavy, catharsis."

"Ca what?"

Akid laughed. Sepultura, Slipknot, System of a Down. Akid's favorite bands, and Shilin had memorized them like she memorized her History textbook dates, Perang Dunia Pertama, 1914 to 1918. Perang Dunia Kedua, 1939 to 1945. She used acronyms and categorized the bands by geographical origin. From the US: Slayer, Pantera, Megadeth. SPM. From Scandinavia: Meshuggah, Emperor, and Nifelheim. MEN. From Malaysia: Blackfire, Punisher, Nemesis. BPN. Gejala black metal, replacing the gejala bohsia. Always a social ill for every generation, and this happened to be theirs.

Shilin finished her cheeseburger and folded the wrapper. Akid crumpled his, tossing it at her playfully.

"Eww!" She tossed it back. "There's cheese on my hair!"

"Up here we don't have to hide," he said, and leaned forward to kiss her, the taste of onions in his mouth. Shilin laughed and ewwed. But he was right, and it felt right, and she let him. All the while, from the corner of her eye, she watched the big fan blade underneath the grill, churning and churning, like a helicopter's rotor blades, the water roaring beneath it.

↑ ↓

They left their bags by the water tank. It was safe and surely there was no one to touch them. Who would want to steal a bunch of high school textbooks? Even the cleaners wouldn't want them, couldn't read them. Akid left his helmet too, a round blue orb looking like a bowling ball. They took their wallets with them.

Shilin wore a scrunchie on her right wrist and with that hand, held Akid's left. Together they bounced two floors down along the emergency staircase to the sixth floor, where Magic City waited for them.

Shilin rushed to Daytona USA, grabbing a seat and getting onto her red Gallop Hornet. Next to her, a boy was already racing a purple Gallop, and she recognized him immediately. It was the Fernandez boy, Gregory Fernandez, from the same street, in the same school uniform as Akid's. Akid hated him because he was always coming round to her place. Now what was he doing here? Was he here to spy on them? That snake! Shilin ignored him. Perhaps she could outrace him instead. Insert Coin, Press Start Button, and her car got going.

Akid was at his usual Aerosmith shooting game, Revolution X. Brainless, mindless, gunfire on helicopter metal. Then, with four Magic Tokens left, they moved onto their usual game of air hockey, the *plop plop pling* sound always sending a thrill through his spine. Next, to the foosball table, where Fernandez joined Shilin as Akid went to the counter to buy more tokens.

"Hello, girlie," Fernandez said.

"Hi, Fernandez," Shilin said.

"Tried to outrace me, hey? What are you doing here?"

"Um, playing. With Akid."

"A kid?"

Shilin narrowed her eyes. "You know who."

"Orkid?"

"Shut up, Fernandez. He hates your guts, so go away."

Too late: Akid was coming back. His jaw tightened when he saw Fernandez.

"Joining us for a game, Fez?"

"Why not," Fernandez said, standing next to Shilin.

Akid slotted four tokens into a silver tray and pushed. The balls rolled out into the open drawers. For Fez, playing foosball was like tackling a girl. Concentrate, let the ball slide and swish around, and then, when the opponent wasn't looking, when there was an opening, shoot and score!

Shilin sensed the tension and moved away from the table.

"No, you stay here," Fez said, grabbing her arm tight.

"Hey," she said.

"Hey, don't touch her," Akid said.

Fez raised his hands. "Sorry, bro."

The game began. Steel rods, like metal satay sticks, flying but in place. The toy football men slid up and down the table and somersaulted back to front. Guarding, blocking, shooting, scoring. If the table wasn't so heavy, the boys would've flipped it over.

Shilin had had enough. The Daytona jingle blared in the background, and the white noise of gunfire and explosions gave her a headache. She went to the air hockey table and played with the pusher. She glided it along the smooth, gleaming surface, pretending to strike. The LED lights made the table look like a spaceship with a neon glow, a warm and safe feeling she loved.

She went back to the foosball table, standing by Akid's side, one hand on a rod to help him win the game. He made a move to score, but grabbed her wrist and twisted it instead.

"Ouch!" she said.

"Don't stand here, please!" Akid said.

The ball went in the goal. Fernandez had won. Akid slammed his hands on the table side, then regretted it. It hurt.

"I was only trying to help!" she said.

Akid looked at her.

"It's only a game, bro," Fez said, wearing a victory smirk.

Shilin looked at Fez, hot tears forming. She hurried upstairs to the water tank.

↑ ↓

The chocolate sundae had melted into a puddle of Milo-ish cream. They had forgotten to eat it. Shilin cursed, looking for a place to throw it. She remembered the dumpster and walked toward it.

The mannequin's arm was now sticking out. Inside were decorations from last year's Hari Raya, Deepavali, and Christmas celebrations from the grand foyer downstairs. Nylon strings, ribbons, and styrofoam bits. Snowflakes, ketupats, and oil lamps. But the poor poor mannequin, with its brown eyes open and eyelashes painted on, a leg detached, a right arm swung backward in an awkward angle.

Shilin could not throw the sundae puddle into the box, and she went back to the water tank instead. It was still humid and the breeze was strong from the shoreline. Bayu laut and bayu darat. Bayu laut was the daytime breeze, when air is hotter on land, and wind rushes in. Bayu darat was the night-time breeze, when air is hotter on water, and wind rushes out. Shilin had memorized the diagrams for the final school exams. She remembered the arrows, the moon, the sun, the simple beachfront, the curly waters and a coconut tree. "Darat," she memorized, alliterates with "day" but happened at night. Therefore, "darat" does not happen during the day. And if she knew one, she would know the other. The exams were easy like that.

Rushing footsteps disturbed her thoughts. It was Akid, face scowling but eyes worried.

"Shi, I'm sorry," he said, pulling her close. "I lost my temper."

They hugged. Then he removed the scrunchie from her wrist to look at the crusty red lines she had kept hidden from everyone, except him. Shilin winced. The wound was still raw, made only yesterday with an orange penknife, the same cutter she had used to carve out her wayang kulit puppets. And how had Akid known? He had watched her do it. The wayang kulit and the wrist. A crescent moon, a jagged lightning, an upside-down cross, a rose, a five-prong star.

It was noisy up here, too, Shilin thought. After-work traffic had begun, and the birds were going home for the evening. The hum of the air conditioning compressor, only white noise before, was suddenly loud and maddening.

More footsteps followed. It was Fernandez.

"Oh, a love nest!" he said, eyeing their school bags by the tank.

"Hey, you followed me!" Akid said.

"This place isn't a secret, Kid. Or should I say Orkid?"

Akid's jaw clenched. The sun was low in the sky and it blinded him. *Do not let the sun go down while you are still angry.* His hands trembled and he let go of Shilin. *Anger comes from Satan, Satan was created from fire, and fire is extinguished only with water; so when one of you becomes angry, he should perform ablution.*

"A lot of people have been up here," Fez continued, kicking gravel with his school shoe, white but smudged, a lace loose and come undone.

"Go away, Fez," Shilin said, her voice pleading. "Why can't people just leave us alone?"

"Do you know what 'people' in school are calling him?" Fez said. "Anak Syaitan. The devil's child."

"Oh, shut up," Shilin said. "You're all being so mean."

"Maybe I should strip you and look for tattoos."

"Hey!" Akid said.

"That's what the ustads are saying in our school. Black metal girlfriends."

"What?" Shilin said. "Girls don't listen to black metal."

"Oh, but their boyfriends do. And you know how easily influenced they are. The next thing you know, you're the human sacrifice. No more goats."

"Are you the moral police now? We're not even in the same school, so why bother me?" Shilin said.

"No, but your mum asked me to look out for you. And my mum too. You're being blinded by a Satan worshipper. And a Muslim."

"What the—"

Akid brought the helmet down on Fernandez's face. The boy winced and crouched, hands over his nose. Akid struck again, crashing the helmet on his back. *Careful not to smash his head, lest he go into a coma,* Akid thought. *Or break that beautiful nose on his Eurasian face. Now what would the girls think? Ha!*

"Stop!" Shilin cried. "You'll kill him."

All negative words uttered can be pummelled back into a person's body. But Akid did not hear her. He only heard the words: bapuk, pondan, faggot. Blinding rage, fist of fury, all the words Fernandez had said, going back, going back into his body. Words can wound, but helmets do the job better!

"Stop!" Shilin cried again.

Fernandez got up and charged at Akid. *I'll break his legs,* Fez thought. *The soldiers therefore came and broke the legs of the first man who had been crucified with Jesus, and then those of the other.* The two boys crashed onto the grill with the rotor blades and churning water.

"No!" Shilin screamed. The blue helmet was now coated in red, and it rolled toward her like a bloody bowling ball. She ran toward the dumpster and picked up the mannequin's leg. Fernandez's tie was hanging low—she did not want it getting caught in the fan blades. Akid's coil headband had come undone too, and both their school shirts were now stained crimson, like a girl's period soaking through her skirt. Period all over their chests.

Shilin swung the leg on Fernandez's back and the grill caved a notch. She screamed, and the boys screamed too. "Get off, get off the grill!" she called. The boys clambered off, the fan blowing their shirts and hair in all directions.

They continued. Akid picked up his helmet again and whacked Fernandez's shoulderblade. Polycarbonate plastic on bones, crack, crack, crack. Fernandez was now in a ball, in a fetal position. Shilin held the leg high again to attack and to defend.

"Enough, Akid. Stop!" she cried.

But Akid did not stop, so she swung the mannequin leg on his head. Akid winced and turned to lunge at her. The leg dropped. He was so much stronger. *Animals, animals, animals,* she thought. *For him to turn on me like that. Love, hate, pain, pleasure; I'm a human sacrifice.*

All he needed was to grab her scrunchie, and as she thought so, he did. She crumpled in pain.

On the ground, by their school bags, she saw the melted chocolate sundae. She opened the plastic cap and sloshed it on his face. Akid spat and Shilin grunted, an animal's grunt. She smeared the ice cream on his face, like making papier mâché. Up here, we don't have to hide, Akid had said. *So we can all be animals*, she thought. Fernandez groaned.

Suddenly the mannequin leg moved. Shilin froze. It walked back to the box, slow and languid, upright, like a real woman walking. It climbed into the box and emerged carefully with its torso, arms and head, as though whole and awoken. It now walked back toward them, a full woman. The boys saw it too and they froze. Was this a dream? Some sick, sick, dream? Had they hit their heads too hard?

The mannequin came toward Shilin and stopped. It held out its right hand. It was tall and slender, shapely and naked. It had no hair and its face held no emotion. Shilin's head only reached its breasts—smooth with no nipples.

Let's go and sit by the pool, it said.

"You can talk?" Shilin said.

Yes. I've been watching you. From my box. Go and pick up your portfolio.

Shilin obeyed, ignoring the boys, Fernandez on the ground in pain, Akid silent and dazed. She smoothed down her hair, matted with blood, sweat, and ice cream and came back with her folio across her chest.

The mannequin held her by the scrunchie hand and guided her toward the compressor pool. It bent down and removed the grill, unimaginably strong, the blades now exposed and in full view. The artificial wind rushed at Shilin's face and long hair. Like a circular jacuzzi, the water bubbled and churned, the rotor blades longer and taller even than the mannequin.

Watch, it said, getting into the pool. The blades turned but did not touch its legs. The mannequin beckoned. *Just a little dip*, it said, still holding Shilin's hand.

Shilin tucked the portfolio under her arm and bit her lip.

It's OK, it's not going to hurt.

She took off her school shoes and socks.

Don't have to strip, it said.

"I want to. I hate getting my shoes and socks wet."

Shilin lifted her uniform skirt and stepped in slowly. The blades were invisible, or she was invincible. The fan was still there, she knew, metal cutting flesh, metal hitting bones. But she felt nothing, only the wind. No bumps, no cuts.

The mannequin sat on the edge, its body angled and upright. Shilin followed, the water warm up to her knees.

It's clean, it said. *The water is clean*. The mannequin held her portfolio and opened it, leafing through the pages. It told her what it liked on every page. Still life, oranges and apples on a table. Landscape, a day out by the beach. *Berkelah di tepi pantai*, it described.

"You speak Malay, too?" Shilin asked.

I speak the language you want to hear.

A portrait of hands, sketched in pencil. Tender, fisted, relaxed, twisted. A palm outstretched, a wrist with veins. The mannequin nodded, an appraisal, a praise. An approval, approved.

Then came the wayang kulit puppets. Four figures on satay sticks, with long, black limbs, fingers and toes like skeletons. Four puppets, to represent the four types of wayang kulit in Malaysia—Javanese, Kelantanese, Purwa, and Gedek. But the puppets had no human faces. The first was replaced by a goat skull, the second a coiled serpent, the third a large dark flower, and the fourth a white oval face, much like the mannequin's. Fauna, fauna, flora, and femme divina. All four wore intricate headgear and costumes of Siamese, Kelantanese, and Javanese royalty, as traditional wayang kulit characters did.

The mannequin paused. *You foresaw this?*

"Maybe. But I wouldn't know—until it's happened."

How did you make the holes so intricate? A mallet?

"No, a math compass," she said. "And a pen knife."

Interesting, it said, running its fingers across the puppets' heads. *Show me your wrist.*

Shilin hesitated. Did it know about her wrist? But she extended her hand, making sure the scrunchie was in place. It was light blue with small white flowers. The mannequin lifted the hair tie for a peek.

Does it hurt?

"A little."

Want me to use the mallet instead?

Shilin laughed. "No."

Do you see the fan blades around us?

"Yes."

But do you feel them?

"Not at all."

Good. You are not goat's hide.

It held onto her, and together, it plunged both their hands into the compressor pool. The water continued to bubble, and the blades did not touch them. No bumps. No pain, no hurt.

When her hand emerged, her scrunchie was soaked and the scars had disappeared. The mannequin removed the scrunchie and tied Shilin's hair into a ponytail. Then it gave her a kiss on the head. *Ten out of ten*, it said.

jude deluca

Dedicated to Rick Mays, Gail Simone, Adam Warren, Talent Caldwell, Carlo Barberi, and Sunny Lee

STORY THUS FAR: Five college students were the sole survivors of inhuman experiments at the now destroyed Area 52. Alice Vane, Gina Vivaldi, Salli-Ann Maza, Maximillion Thibodeaux, and Bridger Warren were shocked to discover they'd been killed and resurrected via alien technology. Now wielding extraordinary powers, these five banded together as GENERATION DEAD.

Operating out of a small Nevada state university under the watchful eye of their alien-cyborg housemother, POSE, RAINBOW, WINTER, AIRGUN, and SEATTLE are navigating the start of their 20s while fighting to save the world from the otherworldly horrors bent on controlling or destroying the Earth.

Or they might kill each other. It wouldn't be the first time!

From the diary of Alice "Pose" Vane, May 1997

I believed the sooner we put the Secretary's Day Massacre behind us, the better. Though I still wonder why a college would hold a dance for Secretary's Day. At the very least, Professor Edward Scott Ellis would no longer victimize any other innocent secretaries. My team made certain of that. **(EDITOR: See the previous issue, folks!)**

Unfortunately, what started as a day of relaxation after the bloody social gathering blossomed into a nauseating event that almost doomed the world.

What else is new?

It was the week after the dance that Gina proposed we take a mental health day at the recently reopened Roswell Falls Shopping Plaza. Ever the mall rat, our beloved Rainbow seemed to have the right idea to brighten our moods. A harmless dose of old-fashioned consumerism was just what we needed. Even dour Salli-Ann looked more relaxed than I'd seen in ages.

None of us expected that our next battle would begin with a seemingly innocent journey to the food court.

"Check out this crowd," Gina said of the large gathering of people assembled at the entrance to the dining area. The food court had been undergoing reconstruction since December and it was finally ready to reopen. We saw some reporters and photographers for the local paper; I recognized the Channel 8 news logo. Mugging for the cameras was our illustrious Mayor Blanche Hannigan. Her signature blonde beehive was hard to miss from any distance.

"Leave it to Hannigan to use something as petty as a new food court for publicity," Salli-Ann said with her usual disdain for the mayor. "And our taxes pay that woman."

"*We* don't pay taxes," I pointed out.

"Place sure looks fancier now," Max noted, reading a list of advertised eateries helpfully placed next to Hannigan. "Got some high brand places. Rosenbloom's Bakery, Stoker's Kitchen, Joey B.'s, Aunt Sue's Hot Dogs. They got Falzone's Pizza! I ain't been to one of them in ages."

"Count me out," Bridger announced, eyeing the food court with disdain. "Sorry, but my body's a temple."

Max scoffed. "Dude, I've seen you inhale a deluxe cheeseburger ranch extra-large pie by yourself."

"Yeah, from Mama Simone's! You wanna break her poor pizza-making heart, Max?" Bridger solemnly placed a hand on his chest. "I'd *never* betray the trust between me and the local pizzeria by indulging from a *chain* pizza place. Where's the love? The heart?"

"Your devotion to Mama Simone is noted and appreciated, Bridger," I giggled.

"Welcome, everyone!" Mayor Hannigan motioned for the reporters and cameras to give her their full attention. "I'm so happy you could join me for this momentous occasion at the Roswell Falls Plaza. It's been a tough several months while the cornerstone of our fair community underwent renovations, but I swear to my constituents the Plaza is back and better than ever." A dark look suddenly formed on Hannigan's face as she added, "I'll again remind the public the rumors of the Plaza being shut down because an army of swastika-adorned 'elves' ransacked the building are JUST rumors, and ludicrous ones I might add."

Remembering that horrible holiday season made me shudder. Gina nervously twirled a strand of her multi-colored hair, Bridger buried his face in a newly purchased comic, Max lowered his signature Stetson over his face, and Salli-Ann was inconspicuously whistling.

(EDITOR'S NOTE: See *Generation Dead: I'm Dreading of a Nazi Christmas* for more details)

"I admit," Hannigan continued, "the closing was a blessing in disguise. As you can see, the Plaza's food court has been made over on the heels of the new millennium. Nothing but high-quality establishments offering delicious meals made from the finest, organic ingredients AND at low prices. Don't take my word for it—here's the endorsement from our special celebrity guest!"

Salli-Ann nudged me with her shoulder. "Check out the 'celebrity guest.'"

"Oh my God!" Gina's face lit up. "It's Bobby Metcalf!"

"Bobby Metcalf?" I echoed the name. "I remember him! He was in all the Invisible Grandma movies. My parents took me to see *Invisible Grandma Goes Hawaiian* on my twelfth birthday."

"Did you *like* it?" Salli-Ann inquired.

"...it had its moments," I tactfully admitted, seeing how happy Gina was watching Bobby Metcalf wave to the crowd. Looking back, it was surprising to see him so much older than he appeared in those movies. He acted like his presence was a bigger hit with everyone than it was. Only a few people were clapping—and politely at that—but Gina clapped hard enough for everyone in the mall. At least Bobby had one devoted fan.

"Who cares about *Invisible Grandma*? He was Trevor, TREVOR, in *My So-Called Family*!" Gina reminded us. "Don't you guys remember Trevor? 'Don't Sweat It Sis?' He was hilarious and a total hottie! Oh, I had a HUGE crush on him."

"That show went downhill when they brought in the talking otter," Max added.

"What was wrong with Uncle Salty?" Gina asked. "I had a doll of him."

"Nah man, the road trip season killed it," Bridger explained. "They had Bigfoot in three episodes back-to-back and he delivered a baby."

"Why would he be here of all places?" I openly wondered.

"Who, Bigfoot?" Bridger asked, looking around to catch sight of the fabled apeman, earning an eyeroll from Salli-Ann.

Gina enthusiastically waved at Bobby hoping to catch his attention. "You think he's signing autographs? How's my hair look? My nose ring OK?"

Bridger asked, "Didn't Metcalf do time for shooting up a gas station in Los Angeles? I heard Zsa Zsa Gabor slapped him into submission until the cops arrived. She's hardcore."

"Uh-uh, he joined a cult since he couldn't get any acting gigs." Max laughed. "Or became a Born Again Christian. Same diff."

Miffed, Gina got up in the boys' faces. "Bobby Metcalf did NOT do time and he did NOT join a cult! He's a great actor! He's . . . between roles."

I asked Salli-Ann, "What do you think about the mysterious Mr. Metcalf?"

Salli-Ann scoffed. "Like I care about a washed-up child star who played a one-note character. All he did was make boob jokes. So juvenile."

"*Really?*" Gina reached into one of Salli-Ann's shopping bags and pulled something out. "With that in mind, I wonder who you bought this copy of *Lovely Waitress Fights Uncut and Untamed* for?"

Stammering, Salli-Ann angrily made a grab for the video game Gina held behind her back, shouting, "GET YOUR HANDS OFF MY FIRST EDITION IMPORT!"

To defuse the situation, I jumped in. "Gina look! There's already a line for autographs!"

"*Holy shit!*" Gina shoved the game back into Salli-Ann's hands and ran through the crowd toward the former child star as he chatted with several older women.

"Should we stop for lunch?" I asked.

"Nah, Al." Bridger shook his scruffy head. "Like I said, corporate fast food's poison." Hopping on his skateboard, he added, "You guys pig out. I'll go by the arcade, see if I can beat my high scores."

"You're oddly picky for someone with a known habit of treating an entire box of individually wrapped snack cakes as dinner," Salli-Ann mused as she inspected her 18+ game. "I swear if Gina bent this . . ."

"That's *junk* food, not *fast* food. Major difference, Miss Winterberry Pie."

"Always an important distinction to make." I couldn't help but add.

"See? Alice gets it. That's why she's the leader." And with that he rode off.

"C'mon Salli-Ann." Max offered her his arm. "I'll buy lunch so you can tell me all about your forbidden video game desires."

"Keep dreaming," Salli-Ann huffed before smirking and pulling him by the collar of his flannel shirt. "But you can buy me lunch anyway."

"Of course," Max said, eagerly letting himself be led. "So, how's things going with Mizz Sarah on the relationship front?"

"Good," she replied. "How are things with Mr. Robert?" As Salli-Ann and Max discussed their significant others, Gina waited to be photographed with her primetime childhood crush. She gleefully pointed at Bobby, mouthing, "Oh my God." I smiled and gave her a thumbs up.

All around me people enjoyed themselves, eagerly converging at the various stands or chatting over their meals. Mayor Hannigan was right: the food court looked completely different. Bigger, neater, cleaner. I heard loudspeakers playing "Wannabe" by the Spice Girls as I scoped out the various offerings.

I realized we really needed today. I know it's self-indulgent and a bit awkward to talk about it, but the five of us do deal with a lot of horrible things most people couldn't imagine. I mean, we *died*. We died and they rebuilt us. That's been our lives. We didn't often have days to ourselves. I wanted to take it all in and enjoy where I was with my friends.

I should've guessed it wouldn't be that simple.

At the very heart of the food court was a majestic marble fountain. The water poured from jars held by intricately carved angels and cherubs, sparkling in the sunlight streaming from the huge windows overlooking the court. I had to admit, it clashed with the more ultramodern surroundings. As I looked at my reflection in the blue water, people tossed coins in, creating ripples on the surface and dispelling my appearance. The coins steadily sank below. Upon closer inspection I saw that the fountain was deeper than it appeared. I couldn't see any coins hitting the bottom before disappearing.

Shoppers raved about the food, eating with gusto. Many were seated and digging into their meals, while others walked and ate. Some talked about cheating on their diets or going back for seconds. Those still in line discussed how hungry they were. Every stand had a smiling, pimply-faced teenager taking orders and handing out food. I felt bad for the workers being overwhelmed on the first day and made a mental note to generously tip when I bought lunch.

There were so many different stands to choose from, so many delicious scents sailing toward me. I noticed at the very end of the court a stand that didn't have many customers. Upon closer inspection I saw it was the Falzone's Pizza Max had mentioned. Placed behind a protective clear barrier were artisanal pizzas, much fancier than I would've expected to find in a mall food court.

"It all looks so good," I said to myself, before my gaze zeroed in on a pie labeled fig and goat cheese. The sight of it made me feel famished. "I've always wondered what goat cheese tastes—OH!"

I immediately took a step back when I looked up and saw the server standing in front of me. He'd been leaning over the glass, right near my head. I practically brushed against his forehead as I looked up. Where did he come from? He was dressed in a neat, clean white chef's outfit with a name tag that said "CAMPBELL." His black hair was slicked back with gel. His face, though. This will sound bad and you're free to admonish me on it, but his face and forehead were covered in painful-looking zits and pustules.

"Sorry for shouting," I said. "I didn't see you standing there."

The server said nothing, vacantly staring at me.

"Um, 'Campbell,' is it?" I nervously laughed. "I'd like to place an order if that's OK. It all looks tasty, but I'll try the goat cheese and fig for now." Remaining silent, he kept staring at me as he raised his left hand toward his face. Thinking that he was going to scratch his acne, I said, "You shouldn't pick at that. You could give yourself permanent..."

The words slowly died as Campbell placed his thumb and index finger around the largest zit on his cheek and squeezed. The swollen pimple jostled against the pressure. My eyes darted from the zit to Campbell's eyes as he squeezed harder. Harder. I couldn't look away. His expression never changed, and he kept his eyes directly on me.

"Stop it! You're hurting your—!"

As his nails broke the surface of the protrusion, I realized there was an... *outline* pressed against the inside of the zit. That's when it exploded in a shower of blood and pus. Onto the pizzas. Onto the counter. Onto Campbell's white uniform. I couldn't say anything. Couldn't find the words. What *could* I say as he stood there, his expression blank as blood and oil and something else spilled from his cheek. I was vaguely aware of some ooze splattered on my blouse. Campbell shoved his fingers *inside his cheek*... and pulled something out.

I'm in a lab as rough hands hold me and make me watch as they bring a body out on a metal slab. The body's more like a pile of boils and sores, to the point I wonder if it was ever human.

When the overhead lights flash on, I make out the shape of what was a head and recognize a pair of empty, gray-green eyes once full of life.

"Amy? Amy?!" I'm screaming, trying to break free. No matter how strong I am, my captors are stronger. They've taken measures against someone like me. I don't know at the time, but they hadn't thought of everything, which is why my friends and I escaped, but Amy didn't. There's nothing left of her except her eyes.

A tray of nasty-looking surgical tools is rolled out next to what was once my best friend. They glint in the light, polished metal shining so bright it almost hurts my vision.

"Find out what went wrong," the voice demands. "Too many from this batch were unsuitable. Salvage what you can. Start with the eyes."

I hear myself screaming and begging them to stop but they ignore me.

After they've removed Amy's beautiful eyes, taken what was left of her, I'm forced to watch as they go inside and see what's there.

(Editor's Note: For more of the tragic story of Pose and her dead friend, read *Generation Dead: Origin*, now in deluxe trade edition)

"—ice? Alice? Earth to Alice, come in Alice!"

"What's wrong with her?"

"Maybe she needs something to eat."

Freed from my memories by familiar voices, I shook my head and saw I was still in the food court.

I heard Max say, "Welcome home, Miss Vane."

Salli-Ann observed, "You look like you saw a ghost."

Gina added, "She looks like she peeked underneath Bridger's bed."

"It—" I struggled to find my voice again. "Pizza. His face. H-he went inside—"

"You found Falzone's!" Max cheered. "I was looking all over for it. Let's eat!"

"*NO!*" I screamed, turning around to face my friends. I felt the color drain out of me once I saw what they were doing.

"Yeah, Max," Salli-Ann said. "Finish your hot dog then we'll get pizza."

Eating. All of them, eating. Devouring, really. Max held a foot-long hot dog covered in almost every condiment known to man.

Salli-Ann worked on three big scoops of ice cream, drenched in chocolate sauce and sprinkles, in a waffle cone she grasped with both hands. Gina, dear, sweet Gina, was engrossed in a Boston cream donut bigger than her fist.

Something rose in the back of my throat as I watched them stuff their faces without a care in the world.

"Mmm! Aunt Sue knows how to make a good dog." Max laughed as he voraciously took another bite out of the processed sausage, bits of onion and relish on his goatee.

"There is *nothing* in this world better than cherry vanilla," Salli-Ann moaned as she ran her tongue up and down the cone.

"Y'know what makes this sweeter?" Gina asked, frosting and filling smeared around her lips. "Bobby Metcalf paid for it after I got to take a picture with him! I will remember this donut for the rest of my life."

As my friends ate, all I heard was their jaws moving, chewing, as if they'd never eaten before. They practically shoved the food into their faces. All around me, people ate. They ate, and ate, and ate. No talking, laughing, not even breathing. The conversations were dead, replaced by primal hunger. I swore even the loudspeakers broadcasted the sounds of people eating. Of animal flesh being ripped apart. Biting, swallowing, belching, moaning—everywhere. It was deafening. A gluttonous cacophony. Was the world itself being devoured around me?

"So Al," Max asked. "What kinda pizza you want? Salli-Ann's paying."

The thought of pizza brought forth the image of an eruption of bloody pus in my mind and the—the *thing* I saw in Campbell's face.

The empty gaze.

Amy's empty gaze.

The inside.

Going inside.

I didn't realize at the time that I was running. I ran as fast as my genetically enhanced legs could take me from the sounds of all that eating, until I finally found a garbage can and became violently ill.

"Alice?!"

Gasping for air, I realized Bridger was heading toward me on his board as I stood hunched over the waste receptacle.

"Easy, easy, fearless leader." Bridger helped me to a bench next to a candle store. I held on, sobbing, nauseous and as distraught as I'd been in Area 52. The experiments and torture felt like yesterday, although I knew it happened four years ago. I was vaguely aware of shoppers staring at us, and Bridger growled, "The fuck you losers looking at?!" The gawkers quickly dispersed; his expression softened as I cried on his shoulder.

When I had no more tears left, Bridger departed and returned with a cold can of ginger ale from a nearby vending machine. The thought of consumption still left me mortified, but the soda helped my stomach.

In between slow sips, I asked, "Weren't you at the arcade?"

"Closed early," Bridger explained. "Some chucklefuck had a problem with a blonde in a private school uniform for whooping his ass at a fighting game. She shoved him headfirst into the claw machine. Owner kicked us out. I was heading back when I saw you tossing up breakfast."

I quickly recounted what I'd seen at the pizza stand, everyone eating in a frenzy and remembering poor Amy. "It exploded on his face, Bridger. It went everywhere. Look, look at my clothes." I gestured to my stained blouse.

"He pulled something outta his *zit*? What was it?"

"I didn't get a good look. He dug his fingers inside then suddenly I was reliving four years ago before Max snapped me out of it." I finished the remaining soda in one gulp. "I think that boy *wanted* me to see it."

"Did you tell the guys?"

"No, I—oh," I stood up. "What was I thinking?! I ran off when someone needed help! What kind of superhero am I?!"

"Al, you were *triggered*," Bridger said. "It happens."

"We need to get back!" I urgently picked Bridger up. "Max and the girls were going to eat at that place! We have to stop them!"

The sudden sounds of screaming coming from the other end of the mall told me we were too late.

Bridger and I hurried back to the food court only to find, in the brief time since my departure, everything had taken a 180-degree turn straight into Hell.

The sounds of people stuffing their faces were replaced by frightened yelling. Innocent shoppers ran for their lives from moaning, pustule-riddled figures. I recognized people I'd seen eating with friends or waiting to order food, transformed into monsters. Around me, snarling figures leapt on all fours, faces blooming with zits.

Near a mall directory, an elderly woman in pink sweats was tackled by her grandchildren. She screamed while the kids held her down and pried open her mouth. The biggest of the three had something in his pockmarked hand. A donut, like the one Gina ate.

Snapping into action, I grabbed a potted palm tree by the entrance and swung it at the donut-armed grandchild as he tried to shove the pastry into his grandmother's mouth. The boy went flying, and I feared I might've overdone it when his siblings saw me, shrieked, and lunged with their hands curled into claws. As they got closer, I could make out squirming figures nestled within their growing blemishes.

A torrent of water drenched both boys and sent them through the front window of a nearby music store.

Bridger, his hands manifesting twin geysers of water, asked, "Were those little kids?"

"We'll worry about that later!" I picked up the dazed and injured old woman and looked around. I saw a small group of people huddled in a nearby alcove on the second floor. One of them was a Channel 8 cameraman, recording everything live. I jumped, landed on the second-floor balcony, and sprinted toward the unaffected individuals. Mayor Hannigan huddled in a corner, sobbing and pulling at her hairdo. So much for our community leaders.

"Here," I said, laying the woman down, "I don't know how badly she's hurt. Stay hidden until this is over and for God's sake don't eat anything!"

I reconvened with Bridger, dodging more of the afflicted as they ran toward me. Some had food in their hands, others were armed with plastic trays or heavy shopping bags. A shrieking prep from

Joey B.'s came at me wielding butcher knives. The blades shattered against my indestructible skin. Taking advantage of the cook's surprise, I grabbed his arms and swung him in an arc as a makeshift battering ram. The zombies seemed more durable in their possessed state, so I wasn't too worried about injuries. The three kids who had assaulted their grandmother were rushing toward me when I threw the cook their way.

Bridger unleashed his hydrokinetic abilities to force zombies into a clothing store called Change for the Strange, but more were coming. I knew we couldn't fight them off forever, but I didn't want to think of what might happen if they escaped the mall in their current state. Focusing on submission and detainment, I shoved my hands into the ground and proceeded to pull up the floor, tossing off the oncoming frenzy.

"Seattle! Destroy the food!" I ordered. "That's what's causing this! Destroy the food so there's less of them to worry about!"

"Gotcha boss!" Seattle turned his powers on the rows of food stands, hopefully destroying the contagion's source. I made it my job to fight off attackers going after him when I dodged a razor-sharp beam of multicolored light. Seattle was distracted and didn't see the barrage of icicles hurtling toward him. I tackled him before he got skewered, and we crashed into a Chinese food stand.

"Oh no," I said, having found the rest of my team. Rainbow, Winter, and Airgun stood in front of the fountain, which now spewed putrid-looking oil. All three were covered in some of the nastiest looking blemishes I'd ever seen. Their eyes were dull and empty as their skin became more pockmarked. Rainbow and Winter kept their sights on me and Seattle. Airgun coldly summoned and fired bullets of compressed air to take down fleeing shoppers who hadn't been turned, letting them be swarmed by the possessed.

"I was barely gone *five minutes!*" I shouted at the ridiculousness of the situation. "Did you even finish eating before this started?"

"Don't sweat it, sis," a voice assured me. I watched as Bobby Metcalf, his smiling face acne free, stepped out from behind the fountain. Gesturing around him, he asked, "Can you blame me for taking advantage of a good opportunity?"

"Pfft. There's a big shock," Seattle muttered as I glared at the former child star. "It's always the celebrity guest."

"The plan *was* for them to take root for a few weeks before moving forward," Bobby said. "Let them settle in. Since I snagged *three* members of Generation Dead on opening day, I moved up the timetable." I gasped. "Like you guys have secret identities. You don't even wear masks!"

"You wouldn't be so smug if Zsa Zsa Gabor was here!" Seattle shot back.

"*DON'T FUCKING TALK TO ME ABOUT ZSA ZSA FUCKING GABOR!*" Bobby screamed, his face bright red. "That bitch is why I've been stuck living off store openings and comic conventions!"

"Right, because you won so many Oscars for *Invisible Grandma in the White House*," I deadpanned.

"ANYway," Bobby continued as he maneuvered himself between Winter and Rainbow. "I might've snagged your friends, but I'd prefer to have the complete set to show her."

"Her who?" I demanded.

"Mother, of course." Bobby fondly smiled. "My loving Mother who gave me my new supporting role. I found her at my lowest, and she gave me direction. She's my ticket back to stardom. Here, say hi to my new family!"

"Oh *Jesus*," Seattle groaned as Bobby showed us what was under his shirt.

"Aren't they cute?" Bobby caressed one of the pulsating fetuses growing on his chest. "I help Mother Dearest find homes for her little darlings. Those with higher ranks like me keep our minds while we foster the cuties. Hurts like Hell at first but once you're used to it, it's kinda nice when they pop out, ready to show the world what they're made of. I can even accelerate the growth, as you might've noticed. The rest become incubators. Normally they get used up and tossed aside, though sometimes Mother has a use for special people. Don't take my word for it. Oh, Mother dear!"

The ground rumbled and the mall shook. Looking around, Seattle and I saw the rest of Mother's thralls were silent, their dull eyes turned toward the fountain. Bobby's grin grew wider as something HUGE shot up out of the oil, ascending toward the ceiling.

"Whoa," Seattle gaped. "That is one bad mother—"

"Shut your mouth! Look! Look, Mother!" Bobby held his arms out, waving toward the gargantuan creature gazing down at us with a dozen eyes. "Mother of Gluttony! See what your favorite son brought you!" He pushed Airgun, Rainbow, and Winter to the fountain's edge. "With their powers we don't have to hide! And I have more!" He pointed toward me. "That one, Pose, she's a powerhouse of raw strength! Indestructible, beautiful skin! Perfection!"

"I'm pretty too!" Seattle seethed.

"We'll show the world what we can do," Bobby joyously screamed. "It all starts here!"

The sounds Mother made indicated she wasn't happy in the slightest, as Bobby quickly picked up. He fretfully asked "W-what's wrong? Aren't you pleased?! I brought you *power!*"

"You completely exposed her operation *on the first day and on live TV!*" I shouted.

"And now people who can stop her KNOW TO STOP HER, numbnuts!" Seattle added.

"SHUT UP!" Bobby shouted at us, but Mother was louder. "Don't listen to them! Mother, it's still good!" Bobby pleaded as Mother glared at him, bearing rows of sharp teeth. "No one outside the mall knows what's happened! I-I got too excited! I overstepped my boundaries but it's OK! I-it's all good! I wanted to show my love for you, Mother!" Every single eye narrowed, and Mother shrieked and dove forward, jaws wide open. "*MOTHER NOOOOOOOOOOOOOO*—!"

CHOMP!

Watching the outline of Bobby Metcalf slide down Mother's throat, I stood up.

"Seattle, deal with our friends." I cracked my knuckles, my patience fully evaporated. "I want to talk with Mother."

All at once, my three zombified friends and the eyes of Mother zeroed in on us. Seattle blasted Rainbow and Airgun across the food court. Winter darted ahead, beams of cold shooting from her fingertips. Jagged ice gauntlets slashed at my midsection as I somersaulted over her. She attempted to backhand me as I dodged in time for Seattle's geysers to send her through the counter of Rosenbloom's bakery.

Seattle kept our friends occupied, avoiding air bullets and deadly rainbows. Mother towered over us and roared again as she shot toward me. As her oil-soaked teeth came at me, I pulled my right fist back and delivered an uppercut with all my strength and rage. Her lower jaw went into the roof of her mouth, fangs shattering. Mother screamed and landed on her side, eyes spinning.

"One day," I said. "We only wanted one. Fucking. DAY!"

Not waiting for Mother to get her bearings, I grabbed the biggest fang I could find and with both hands I rammed it all the way into Mother's head.

I ran down Mother's side, dragging the fang through her skin, slicing her open down to her base. I screamed. Mother screamed. The possessed screamed as the embryos on their skin exploded amidst Mother's death throes. Mother's babies were stillborn, her victims collapsing to the floor.

Entrails and unrecognizable organs spilled from Mother's body along with Bobby Metcalf. The semi-digested actor stood, skin melting, deliriously laughing, and lunged at me. I smacked Bobby's head off. It soared through the mall windows.

I heard Seattle whistle as he helped our groaning friends get their bearings. "Damn, Zsa Zsa Gabor's got nothing on you, Pose."

As Metcalf's body fell, I gazed into Mother's eyes.

There was nothing inside.

I helped my friends.

I thought of Amy.

(NEXT ISSUE: BIGFOOT AT THE BEACH HOUSE!)

cherry cola lips

j.a.w. mccarthy

My mother's full of the kind of energy that makes her sizzle like water on a hot stove. As we drive down Main Street, she's pointing out the new Panera, the Starbucks, the Walmart, where endless acres of farmland used to be. In profile, her cheeks are plump. Her jaw is tight and sharp, but not in that weird shiny-stretched plastic surgery way. There's no longer the loose droop she used to drag around, no more curled hands and locked joints, no more heavy sighs as she laments age and motherhood and all the things that weren't really her choice.

The last time I saw her—three years ago—she was still out East putting color-coded stickers on her antiques so I'd know which ones not to undersell after her death. Now that she's back in Hellensville, it's like she got her spine cracked into place. Some magic elixir spilled through her veins, and she's a new woman with a varnished grin I've only seen in old photos, driving too fast, one hand on the wheel, sparking with a joyful mania that I wish would sizzle to vapor.

As annoying as it is, it's also kind of nice. When my father died, the burdens of a mortgage and bills and raising a child alone carved lines in her face, broke her back so that we survived on fumes and stubbornness. My mother became a seventy-year-old woman over-night.

Whatever she's on today—whatever's made her young again—I can't argue with that.

"You won't believe it," she says, a smooth, unknotted hand flying off the wheel. "Remember all the time you used to spend at the mall? There wasn't even a movie theater—I didn't know what the hell you and that Kristen did all afternoon."

I don't like thinking about Kristen. I can't even say her name anymore without having to scrape bitter residue from my tongue. "There wasn't anything else to do in this town," I say quietly.

Mom pats my thigh and the car swerves. "Well, you won't recognize it now, Lainey. I can't wait to show you."

I've never seen anyone this excited to go to the mall.

The building is the same as it was twenty-five years ago, a stocky one-story sprawl anchored on one end by the now-defunct discount department store, Trenwell's—a big deal at the time, the first national chain to make a footprint in Hellensville—and the windowless food court on the other end. Even the "Everything Must Go" signs are still plastered over the department store's double doors and windows, caution yellow faded to diluted piss.

As we get out of the car I can see broken mannequins inside, sooty with dust and age. Kristen and I used to topple those mannequins because the distraction bought us more time alone in the dressing room.

"Don't be mad, but I have a surprise for you," my mother says, linking her arm with mine. She's never done that before.

"Why would I be mad?"

She shrugs, eyes straight ahead as she leads me to the mall's main entrance. "I know you don't want to be here, that you think I'm crazy."

She's not wrong. I must've used that word at least a dozen times when she announced that she'd sold the house and was moving across the country, back to the farm town where we'd lived my senior year. We'd both run screaming from Hellensville after I graduated, me to the city and her to a job opportunity out East. Though I've been living only seventy miles north of Hellensville, this is the first time I've been back since college. It's always been a single exit on the highway, one I sped past while I struggled to keep those thoughts of Kristen at bay. Until my mother insisted I come here to see her new condo and how the town has changed and why she plans to spend the rest of her life here.

So far, this mall is not convincing me.

It's the same on the inside: scuffed pink and gray tile leading to a row of narrow storefronts that were once Farley's Fashions, Shoe Addict, Generous Gems, Praise Be Books. Those stores are gone now, though, nothing beyond the metal roll-up doors besides empty display cases and stripped shelving. As we make our way toward the food court, I count one occupied storefront for every three that are closed. I'd hated it back then, how all we had were these local shops that reflected the hick-ness of the town, making it impossible to find the clothes I admired in magazines. My mom's been talking for days about how Hellensville has been revitalized, but the mall has been left to molder in inadequacy and disappointment, a time capsule of my regrets and a reflection of my current failures. If it wasn't so apt, it might be funny.

"The way you were talking, I thought it was going to be remodeled," I say.

Mom shrugs. "It's nice to have something familiar. The way it used to be."

Even the skylight is still dirty, clouded with soot and bird shit. A hothouse without the plants, just a few mall-walkers who look too young for that kind of thing, and a handful of people my own age stagnating in front of what used to be Heritage Yarn. No families with little kids, no teens, even though it's a Saturday. As we make our way toward the food court, I pick up a strange industrial smell, rubber and something bitter, metallic. Mechanical blood rooting through earth that's turned to concrete dust.

"Where are all the kids?" I ask.

"Oh, they don't need this place," Mom says briskly.

She drops my arm and sprints ahead the minute we round the corner into the food court. Blue-speckled formica tables and mismatched folding chairs gather like a skeletal audience around the Snack Shack, same as it was all those years ago. I spent almost every minute between last bell and dinnertime here, sucking on a fountain soda as I watched Kristen microwave bagels and corndogs, love-drunk under her thrall. Then, finally, she'd put the little "Back in 10" sign up and electricity shot straight up my spine as her eyes met mine and that dimpled grin opened up her face. Kristen called and I followed, wiping Coke cup condensation onto my jeans.

How dopey I must've looked. There's that same puppy eagerness on my mother's face now, except it's not Kristen she's running to.

The guy behind the counter is boyishly handsome and half my age. Pity pings in my chest because he should be in college or Hollywood or anywhere except making change in the Hellensville Mall food court. My mother beelines to him, and I hurry behind, like I should catch her arm and pull her back before she makes a fool of herself in her enthusiasm for microwaved nachos or whatever her stupid surprise is. But she's fast, elbows on the counter, him leaning down so they're face to face, both grinning. As they chat, she fidgets with a lock of hair, which all my life had been a respectable bob, black cotton candy laced with gray. Now it's a long pour of lacquered black, impossibly thick and shiny and . . . youthful. Like her stance, her giggle, her fingers that creep across the counter to meet his.

I'm standing in the Hellensville Mall, and my seventy-year-old mother is kissing a food court guy young enough to be her grandson.

She turns and waves me over while he nuzzles her ear. But I can't move. I'm staring at the letter board sign (only the prices have changed), the stack of generic Jazz soda cups, the shriveled hot dogs slowly rolling in their case.

Kristen should be standing here, tongs flailing as she tells me about how many bagels the Shoe Addict pervert had today. She should be here with me now, speculating about the pod person invasion that has surely claimed my mother. Instead, she's been gone from this place longer than I have, a runaway according to the police, kidnapped according to her parents, bones beneath the strawberry farm as I sometimes speculated. I'm tasting her cherry cola lip balm again, but it's a bitter memory on my tongue.

Kristen spread a thick layer of cream cheese on an everything bagel while the guy from Shoe Addict leered. I didn't like the way he leaned over the counter to get a better view of her ass. Catching my gaze, she rolled her eyes, and I snickered into my Coke. Though Shoe Addict got a bagel or a hotdog at least three times during every one of her shifts, Kristen assured me he was the harmless kind of creep. She served him with her usual smile, the one that made her dimples emerge.

"So, if you're looking for more hours, I could use some help in my stockroom," he said as she handed him his bagel.

I jumped from my seat and strode to the Snack Shack. "Hey, could I get some nachos?"

Shoe Addict widened the spread of his arms on the counter, edging me away. "What do you make here? I can pay you more."

"Sorry, got a customer," Kristen said.

"Her? She's not a customer. She's——"

"Customer," she insisted, turning her smile to me. Shoe Addict lingered, finally leaving with a huff as Kristen methodically layered tortilla chips into a paper boat.

"Fucking creep," I said.

Kristen tipped the chips back into the bag. "Definitely. He thinks I'm gonna hook up with him or something? He's like forty and sells shoes to my grandmother."

"All the old guys want you. Why are they such gross hornballs?"

"It's my youth and beauty," she said, grinning. She reached under the counter and placed the "Back in 10" sign between us. "Ready?"

Arms linked, we raced to the opposite end of the mall, passing crotchety old coffee enthusiasts and junior high kids loitering in front of Local Gifts. We didn't care for the clothes in Trenwell's, but we still flipped through the racks as fast as we could, grabbing the few things that didn't repulse us: baggy camisoles from Lingerie, mom jeans from Clearance. All that mattered was that we had something we could take into the dressing rooms.

The attendant handed us each a plastic disc and we hung them outside of the adjoining stalls at the end of the labyrinth. After making sure no one else was around, I slipped into Kristen's stall with my handful of clothes.

"Yay or nay?" she asked, her hair a bolt of gold satin swinging with her movements. The dew-kissed meadow scent of her Herbal

Essences shampoo filled the cloistered space. She had already stripped down to her underwear, slipping on a black cami that barely skimmed her hips.

"Go up a size and you could do fishnets," I said, wriggling out of my t-shirt. I shimmied into the largest cami I'd selected and stood next to her, surveying myself in the mirror. "See, like this one's long enough that you could—"

Before I could finish, Kristen grabbed me around the waist and pulled me close, lips latching onto my still open mouth. Our tongues slid over each other's, hungry and wet and almost too fast, as if we might get caught at any moment. That was her thrill, but I didn't like the fear. I longed to linger, cup her jaw the way I'd seen in movies, twist all those long blonde strands around my fingers, relish that first taste of cherry cola lip balm on her mouth. As she pulled away, my teeth caught on the invisible rough spot on the center of her lower lip. I loved watching her swipe lip balm over it again and again, outlining that peculiar little anomaly only I knew about.

"I gotta get back."

Had it been ten minutes already?

Our first kiss had been between the dumpsters behind the mall, a quick but full-contact peck on the lips after she called me "cute" for accompanying her as she took out the garbage. I didn't know what it meant until she pulled me into the Trenwell's dressing room and kissed me there, breathing this life into me I'd never felt before. I'd already spent my first two weeks in Hellensville sitting in the food court, pretending to read a book while working up the nerve to talk to her. She was cloaked in a late summer haze that made her features a soft focus blur, glistening pink and gold, her teeth bright white starbursts as she made conversation with customers. I wanted to be on the receiving end of that smile. So when she came over to my table offering a soda and asked me all about myself, I felt an immediate relief, the possibility that once school started I wouldn't be spending lunch alone in the library. Her admirers watched us, silently waiting while I held her attention. Me. I never would've guessed we'd end up more than friends, even though she reminded me that whatever this was had to stay between us.

"Don't be mad," she'd say when the dressing rooms got crowded and she insisted I wait five minutes after her before leaving. "It's just this town."

Giggling, we got our clothes back on and dashed out of the dressing room, tossing our unwanted garments at the attendant. I headed toward the exit into the mall, but Kristen grabbed my hand and led me to an unmarked door near the women's restroom.

"It's faster," she said, pulling me into a fluorescent-lit hallway lined with gray doors. I was surprised as she clutched my hand, lifting it with hers to point out the employee entrances to Farley's Fashions and Generous Gems. Her skin was cool and dry against my own clammy palm. I wanted to rub my sweat on my jeans but didn't dare let go. She dropped my hand when we reached the back door that led into the food court.

Her boss, Tony, was already behind the counter, waiting for her.

"One ten minute break per shift," he barked, slamming the cash register drawer shut as we approached. "Not two, not three, one."

"This was my one break," Kristen said, sliding behind the counter.

"It's your second."

"How would you know?"

Tony planted his hands on his hips, completing the middle-aged dad look. With his tucked-in t-shirt and khakis, he was as bland as this town, the dark bags under his eyes and droopy jawline a muppet-like contrast against his aggressively receding hairline. Kristen said he'd been handsome once, a track star in the seventies; his picture hung in the trophy case at school, all bright blue eyes and juicy lips and shaggy brown hair curling over his collar, "like John Travolta in *Carrie*," as she described it. I guessed that was what she pictured when she was flirting with him.

"Maybe your friend here would like this job," he said, tipping his head toward me.

Kristen scooted closer to him, hip out, one hand twirling a lock of shiny blonde hair. "Aw, come on, Tony. I had to go to the bathroom. You want me to get a UTI?"

"Jesus." Blushing, he shook his head. "Just finish your shift, OK?"

She patted his elbow. "Yes, sir!"

Once Tony was gone, she poured me a Coke. I knew I shouldn't, but I couldn't resist letting my fingers linger atop hers as she handed me the cup.

"Summer's almost over," she said, sighing heavily as she brushed my hand from hers. She glanced around the empty food court. "Things will be different when school starts."

↑ ↓

"This is my daughter, Lainey," my mom says. Food Court guy holds his hand out to me and we shake. "I've told him all about you, baby."

"But you didn't tell me about him," I say.

Mom laughs. I guess she saves the giggles for her new boyfriend. "Because he's the surprise. Can you believe it? Tony and I have been dating for three months now!"

I squint. Bright blue eyes, a full head of shaggy brown hair, lips as juicy as a frothy Orange Julius. No one gets out of Hellensville, not for long anyway.

"Oh, I knew your dad," I say. "This was his stand back when I was in high school, right?"

Tony gives me a quizzical look before those full lips stretch into a rubbery smile. "Oh yeah, my dad."

"Family business, huh?"

He nods dumbly, glancing at my mom. "Yeah, it's nice."

Mom grabs his hand and turns it over on the counter, sliding her fingers between his. "I was just showing Lainey how much Hellensville has changed. We're a city now. Maybe she'll want to move back someday."

I'm too old for a "fuck the suburbs" diatribe, but I'm tempted anyway. My mother thinks that because I haven't dated anyone since the divorce, that means the city is cruel and a town like Hellensville will welcome me with desires fulfilled and new love, as it seems to have done for her. I slipped once, complained to her that I'm at the age now where I'm invisible to men and a mother figure to women, so I guess I had this coming.

"I gotta work, babe," Tony says as a couple of women approach the stand. "Tonight?"

"Definitely," my mother agrees, stretching up on tiptoes for another kiss.

Back at the condo, Mom spends the rest of the afternoon getting ready for her date with Tony. We eat an early dinner, her jumping up from the table between bites to show me her new python ear climber and a selection of shiny body-con dresses. It's all so strange and inappropriate, me suppressing the urge to lecture her about how short the skirt is or how she's too old for Forever 21. But I know I'm being judgmental and bitter, so I keep my mouth shut and nod along with her excitement. Maybe it's my insecurity about my own age rearing its many ugly heads.

After my mother leaves, I wander around, searching for her secrets, for whatever flipped the switch in her. On her bedroom vanity I find various serums and creams, the kinds of products that promise skin-plumping and wrinkle-erasure but can't deliver more than basic hydration. Nothing unusual, nothing that looks like it was brewed by an alchemist in exchange for her soul.

I scrutinize my face in the mirror, crow's feet surfacing like spiteful bookends, lines deepening on my forehead, a new one taking up residence for every fight I had with my ex. I know I've been sleepwalking these last few years, letting time drape its heavy weight over my face and body. Soon, I'll look older than my own mother. I rub a little La Mer into my frown lines and hope her magic is this simple.

As I'm leaving, something else on her vanity catches my eye: a familiar tube of lip balm.

Cherry. I pick it up, bracing for the "Cola" on the label, but it's just cherry. I need to get out of here.

It's not a nostalgia trip, but muscle memory takes me to the mall. I park in front of Trenwell's. The windows are dark, only a dull backroom glow highlighting the toppled mannequins. The last time Kristen and I kissed inside Trenwell's dressing room, she crushed my heart, my fantasies, any hope I had of acceptance in this town. Then I simply stopped existing to her at all.

Six months later she stopped existing too, at least in Hellensville. Her parents kept putting up posters, even though the police said she was eighteen and all our teachers claimed she talked of going to New York after graduation. Funny how she never told me about that.

Now, sitting here in this parking lot, staring into this frozen relic of first love, all I see is a sealed coffin. Kristen is gone and I never really knew her. I feel rudderless. Old. As left behind as this place.

But there's movement.

As neon-hazy as a synth-pop album cover, a man and woman appear hand in hand. They move past the empty racks, past the overturned mannequins, pausing briefly as they skim the doors. I strain for a better view between the faded "Everything Must Go!" banners. Long black hair, silver tube dress . . .

The couple stops for a kiss, grinning at each other, giggling. It's my mother and Tony running through the abandoned Trenwell's like a couple of teens looking for a secret place to smoke or fuck on a Saturday night.

I laugh, hard enough to make my stomach cramp. It's Hellensville in the nineties all over again, still aimless and boring and offering nothing else to do, except it's my mother making out with her twenty-two year old boyfriend in the mall while I'm out here, middle-aged and irritated like a parent waiting to pick up their kid. I start the engine right as more forms appear inside the abandoned department store.

All middle-aged and slightly younger, like the mall walkers I saw earlier today. They're spinning racks, poking each other with disembodied mannequin arms, doing the things I would've done at seventeen if I'd had friends, things I might be doing now if I still had Kristen. Mom and Tony lead the way and all the others follow toward the back of the store, into the women's dressing rooms.

↑ ↓

Things were different once school started, as Kristen had promised.

She folded me into her friend group, saved me a seat at their cafeteria table, but I became one of many. A constant ring of admirers held open doors, noted her opinions on clothes and music, inflated themselves with stories of trips to London or shoplifting in the city, breaths held for her response. It wasn't just the kids either. Teachers volunteered homework extensions, the lunch ladies gave her extra french fries, the cheerleading coach guaranteed acceptance. I'd never been in the orbit of someone so beloved.

There were rules at school. When our fingers brushed in the hall, she was quick to pull back. When I stood too close, she wedged another friend between us. When other girls talked about which guys they wanted to hook up with, Kristen's voice was the lustiest and the loudest. It stung at first, but the secret thrill of our fingers meeting under the cafeteria table was a reassurance, her pinky hooking mine as she discussed pervy gym teachers and weekend plans. Even as she denied me in public, I knew we had something special, something no one else had.

I was the only one who accompanied her to the mall for every one of her shifts. I was the only one she put the "Back in 10" sign out for.

When we were at the mall, it was summer again. Kristen made smoothies and bagel sandwiches, shooting me sly grins and eye rolls while I pretended to do my homework. All we had to worry about was Tony and the Trenwell's dressing room attendant.

"We are so gonna get caught," Kristen murmured one afternoon as I traced her neck with pinprick kisses. She slumped against the stall's carpeted partition, sighing under my touch. I loved how her collarbone slid so smoothly between my lips, how her hair tickled my nose so that my every inhale was a dewy meadow. "Seriously, we have to——"

"But we're so quiet," I whispered, nipping my way back up to her earlobe.

She pulled away abruptly. "Brandy saw us."

"Brandy?"

"Brandy Blackwell. She was in one of the dressing rooms last week and she saw us go in together. I told her I was helping you zip up your dress, but you know how she is. She's been dying for some dirt on me."

"We were in a dressing room together. So what?"

This time Kristen's sigh was barbed, irritated. "You don't get it." She adjusted the neckline of her shirt, covering where I'd turned her collarbone rosy with my kisses. "This——" she swung her arms outward as if she was trying to sweep all of the tiny dressing room into her embrace. "If this gets out, it's over. I'm not like you, Lainey."

I reached for her, hoping to calm her, hoping to feel that silky blonde hair slide between my fingers. "No one knows, OK? We're careful. And really, would it be so bad if people knew I was your girlfriend?"

Kristen backed away from me, crossing her arms tightly over her chest. "Is that what you think this is? This was just a summer thing—an experiment. I'm not gay, OK?"

There was a finality to her statement, the bright puncture of "gay" rupturing the air between us like an accusation, bloated and ominous and refusing to fade with the rest of her words. A finger pointing at me. I was suddenly ashamed, the kinship I'd found with her a mirage, a fallacy, a joke I'd been too dumb to recognize.

I waited the requisite five minutes after she left, staring at the pile of strappy tanks she'd abandoned, thinking about how I'd have to hand them back to the attendant as the tears bullied my eyes.

All the things I wanted to say—should've said—flooded my mind:

You're the one who kissed me first.

It feels good because you love me like I love you.

Please don't tell anyone I'm gay.

Empty-handed, I raced out of the dressing rooms. I knew there wouldn't be a seat at the lunch table for me tomorrow, but I was more afraid that Kristen would tell everyone that I was some lascivious lesbo who'd misinterpreted her kindness, got aggressive and jealous when she tried to let me down gently. Everybody wanted her, but it was the creepy new girl who went too far, followed her into the Trenwell's dressing room, tried to cop a feel.

The tears were starting, but I'd left my bag in the Snack Shack. Wiping my sleeve roughly over my eyes, I marched into the food court, focused straight ahead, picturing myself swiping my bag from behind the counter without ever looking at her.

But Kristen wasn't alone. Tony was with her, standing close, one hand casually cupping her waist. They were both smiling, laughing as she twirled a lock of perfect blonde hair. Then, just as I made it to the stall, she reached up with her other hand and ran her long, slender fingers over Tony's wet, gaping lips.

↑ ↓

Helium giggles and tinny voices prick the air, leading to the labyrinth of the Trenwell's dressing rooms. It's like a freshly unsealed tomb here, the air swollen with the musk of released breaths spread atop cold mildew. I step around fallen shelving and "Price Buster" signs. Naked clothing racks wheeze at my approach. Threaded throughout, that strange metallic tang I noticed upon first stepping into the mall with my mother this afternoon. Steaming raw meat in a metal refrigerator.

The earthy, coppery odor intensifies with my every step. Voices tamp down, giggles evaporate, words still unintelligible but now thick and wet, a smear of slurps and sighs. I imagine couples like my mom and Tony in the changing stalls, vigorously making out like some teenage thrill. What am I doing? I should get in my car and head back to the city. My mother's already shown me everything I need to see.

Then, in the largest stall in the back, I see it: feet. Pairs upon pairs of feet.

Before I can turn around, a man pokes his head out and spots me, then they're all streaming out—six, seven, eight people, eyes wide, mouths and hands coated in red. Blood. They could be Shoe Addict, the Generous Gems guy, all the other business owners from twenty-five years ago who are magically young again like Tony. Like my mom.

The swinging stall door fans that raw meat tang in waves as everyone races past me and out into the store. I'm stampede-pressed against another stall door, trapped, wishing I'd paid more attention to all the secret exits Kristen had led me through twenty-five years ago. Tony pushes past me, leaving one pair of feet in the stall.

My mother.

"Lainey . . ."

She stands outside the changing stall now, her palms fervently wiping her mouth, smearing blood down her chin, across her cheeks, turning her crystal smile wet pink. More bright red spatters her slinky silver dress. As I approach, I expect her to tell me it's not what it looks like, that I should leave, but instead, she stands back and holds the door open for me.

Atop a narrow metal gurney lies a woman, a sheet draped over her body. Spots of blood soak the white fabric, some fresh rich blooms, others crusted rusty brown. Her body beneath seems disconcertingly thin, deflated—all rigid lines and knobby points, flat where hands and feet should be. Only the woman's face is clean, unmarred. Pink, fresh. Dimples hint in the shadows beneath high cheekbones; satiny blonde hair fans out around her head, all blurred in a late summer haze under the harsh fluorescents.

Kristen. Exactly as I remember her, exactly as she was twenty-five years ago.

"I wanted to show you, but I didn't know if you'd understand," my mother says, her voice soft, hesitant. "I thought if you stayed here longer, you'd see how good things are. This is a miracle, Lainey. Kristen has given us the ultimate gift."

It takes everything I have in me to rip the sheet off. I'm not surprised by what I see, but it's still shocking: exposed muscle and bone, arms and legs that end in tattered stumps, her ribcage split open to reveal a cornucopia of organs, purple and red and gray, picked to scraps, drying in the fetid air. Small loose bones are scattered on the table, picked clean except for knobs of gristle. Toothmarks stipple the few swaths of intact flesh like bites into overripe fruit. Some exposed bones bear nicks as well, and I picture my mother's mouth there, ravenous, lost in the frenzy. All those mouths—all those teeth—sucking life and beauty and energy from Kristen's marrow, slurping her up in a grand feast of excess and pursuit of eternal youth. Did they preserve her face out of some sort of respect, a tragic beauty queen as their deity? My heart aches at the sight of the collarbones I loved to kiss, still pristine, intact. All those lips that aren't mine on them, taking more than I ever would.

I step back and feel my mother's hands on my shoulders.

"Tony knew she was special. He kept her here for us. He showed us how to feed on her, share her gifts. He—she—saved this whole town."

"So you're . . . eating people? Is this why you came back?"

My mom's hands slide down my arms. Her grip is firm, but not forceful. "Please, Lainey. You have to understand. I'm strong and healthy and young again—everyone here is. I've never felt happier, more alive. Don't you want that? For me, for yourself?"

There's a scream building in my throat, but it's knotted up with bile and the cold scrape of shock. I know what I should do—call the police, get out before my mother's friends come back and kill me, maybe eat me too. Flesh between their teeth, on their tongues, to be flossed away before they kiss their loved ones goodnight as if this is all so *normal*. How frightened Kristen must've been, her screams muffled in the back of Trenwell's while shoppers milled about, oblivious, all those years ago.

I approach the gurney again. She should look so small—there's only a quarter of her left—but she's still beautiful. Powerful. God, the power Kristen had over me at seventeen. My fingers trace her long dark lashes, her cheek.

Her lips part and I jump. Her chest heaves, sending a spray of dark, hot blood against my throat. Underneath all that blood and bile and burst organ viscera, her heart is a fist expanding and contracting. Beating.

"Lainey?" Kristen opens her eyes. Red streaks her blue irises like lightning. "Please. Lainey . . ."

She's just a head, neck, and shoulders fringed in shredded muscle and meat, but she's alive. I could scoop her up, take her to the hospital. Even if they can't save her, they can—

"Don't waste her sacrifice," my mother says.

I turn. Just a few feet away, her face still smeared with blood, my elderly mother looks barely fifty. After tonight's meal, will she wake up with the body and mind of a thirty-something? Tony's already looking and sounding twenty-two; when will he be young enough to stop? Can he stop? They all looked so happy, so free. Beautiful, weightless, no longer worn down by their pasts, their losses, their regrets.

"Lainey . . ." Kristen croaks.

She remembers me, after all these years.

She lifts her head and I lean down to meet her. She smiles weakly, those dimples deepening, and I'm enthralled again, wrapped in her summer haze. Maybe I'm her last happy memory, the hope she's clung to all these years. Maybe she has even more regrets than I do, like all those months she pretended not to know me.

Our lips meet. We're in the Trenwell's dressing room and we're seventeen again and the most beautiful girl in Hellensville is kissing me. That flat, rough spot on the center of her bottom lip catches on my teeth, thrusts toward my tongue, plumps with my saliva. The mineral stench of blood and chewed-up organs and the decay of this mall fall away, and all I taste is cherry cola lip balm. So heady, so sweet, even as I tear her lips from her face and work them between my teeth.

onitsha main, ochanja, the twins, nkpor, and the shadows of shoprite

somto ihezue

Onitsha Main

It started with the garri sellers. Basin by basin, the grains went gray with mold. Stall by stall, they all shut down. The small-scale carpenters down by the port were next. With soaring prices, they could not afford to transport their production materials into town. The Abada textile dealers packed up their bales of fabric and locked them in a warehouse. They planned to wait out the crisis. One morning, they woke up and found the warehouse razed, their fabrics with it. The Abada women wailed. The Abada women rent their clothes and rolled in the dirt. The flames roared higher.

This, this was how they knew. Onitsha Main Market, the largest market in West Africa, had gone missing.

The town of Onitsha had never faced a crisis of this scale. And it was not just Onitsha. Many bordering towns relied on Onitsha Main Market for trade and business. His siblings, the other major markets in the town—Ochanja, The Twins: Relief and Head Bridge, and the youngest of them, Nkpor—had looked everywhere. They looked in the Niger River, Onitsha Main was not there. They visited their cousin Ariaria in Aba, their brother was not there. They looked in anthills, on camel backs in the Sahara, in tomato baskets, and in every uttered word. It was like Onitsha Main had ceased to exist.

"I saw Onitsha Main in India haggling pepper prices," a spice caravan said.

"I saw Onitsha Main trudging through the Namibian desert," a cactus-turned-house plant said.

"I heard Onitsha Main dying." It was City-Tech Library.

Onitsha Main and City-Tech Library had been many things but friends. The government had seized a considerable portion of land from Onitsha Main. They had torn down the shops and drove out the traders. On the land, they erected the high-end Artificial Intelligence Library, City-Tech. It did not end there. The government went further to divert funding from The First Library of Ancient Arts & Histories. With City-Tech's ability to replicate original data and texts collected from The First Library, the latter was considered redundant. This led to its dilapidation and consequent shutdown. The First Library had been a dear companion to the markets, to Onitsha Main especially. Onitsha Main always visited. He liked to read about the histories of the markets, and how they came to be. This was how the texts described his own beginning: He had walked out of the Niger River, and when he offered Onitsha natives white sand in one palm and rice in the other, they welcomed him, offering him land in return. Onitsha Main loved the books in The First Library. They smelled of old dust and a time when everything was beautiful. Those days were long gone now with all the oil refineries and bunkers springing up everywhere. And with fancy libraries stealing his land. Of course, City-Tech did not pose a catastrophic threat to the environment, not like the refineries. But Onitsha Main was fine lumping them all together.

City-Tech never seemed to care. Nor did they acknowledge this profound enmity. They always had an air of superior nonchalance about them. With head raised high, eyes vacant; half closed, their hands were forever clasped behind their back. This enraged Onitsha Main even more. And whatever enraged Onitsha Main, the other markets were bound by brotherhood and duty to be equally enraged.

"What do you mean you heard him dying?" The Twins, Headbridge and Relief, asked in the same breath.

"My statement was self-elucidating." City-Tech went back to replicating terracotta motifs collected from the Igboukwu Museum.

"You are a liar!" The Twins burst forward. They were not known for subtlety. "Not surprising seeing as theft is your craft of choice," they scoffed at the terracotta replicas. "If anything happened to Onitsha Main, we would be the first to know!"

"I am built on land that once belonged to Onitsha Main—"

"Still belongs to Onitsha Main." The Twins did not let the library finish.

City-Tech blinked once. "If you insist."

Nkpor, fingers fidgeting, was going to say something.

"If you will excuse me, I have an encyclopedia to update," the library hushed the young market.

The markets did not know what to make of the things City-Tech had said. Onitsha Main was the strongest of them, the largest of them. He had been here since they laid the foundations of Onitsha. He was meant to be here long after those foundations were no more. How do you end a thing mighty?

"Where?" Ochanja joined the conversation. She had been silent since it started. "Where did you hear him dying?"

↑ ↓

Onitsha Shoprite Mall was shiny, new, and massive. It was the first mall the state had seen. People marched into it in the hundreds. The stores had the strangest things, things you only saw on Western television channels. Things like lasagna, a McDonald's, and orange-colored pumpkins. Word was it had everything. The day the mall opened to the public, the crowd had been immense and someone got trampled to death. Folks had come from neighboring towns, from Nnewi, Obosi, and Awka, all to get a glimpse of it. Even the state's governor had been there at Shoprite's unveiling. But like several other shiny and new establishments, Shoprite Mall never spoke.

Like City-Tech Library, Shoprite had also been built on Onitsha Main's land. The market had screamed and raved for months. When his siblings tried to calm him, he screamed even louder. He inflated the price of beans in retribution, but soon realized the people affected were people who could not afford to buy produce at

Shoprite. Onitsha Main readjusted the price. Then he caused the Niger River to overflow her banks, with hopes of flooding the mall. But the fishermen cried and wept as their livelihoods got swept away by the tides. The fishermen had never set foot in Shoprite either. The mall was not welcoming to folks like them. Again, Onitsha Main reconsidered. It was at this point the market decided to confront Shoprite Mall.

The Twins

Relief and Head Bridge. The rebels. Their rebellion evident in their names. They had completely taken on the names the colonizers brought with them, in a bid to rile up the older markets. It worked. Not one day went by when Onitsha Main did not remind them of their sacrilegious act. He pleaded with them to reconsider, to perhaps keep their native names, in addition to the foreign ones, just like he had done. The Twins were not known for heeding. Ochanja had taken more drastic actions. For decades, she cut all ties with them, refusing to trade or barter with them. Their wares were turned back along her routes and borders. Ochanja vendors caught trading with The Twins faced steep and harsh consequences. The Twins knew they had been partly forgiven when Ochanja's sanctions slowly eased. But the Twins had more rebelling in store. They interacted and did business with the smaller markets, employing trading systems only allowed among the five major markets. Dealings with the smaller markets had a guiding system, put in place by Onitsha Main to maintain order and their hierarchy. The Twins just relished seeing Onitsha Main spiral. Ochanja no longer bothered when it came to them. She had more important things to invest energy in, like brooding. Of course, they eventually got to her. Trading with sketchy offshore black market merchants and tanking the collective market value of the region's homegrown products was sure to enrage Ochanja. But all that was behind them now. All that mattered was finding Onitsha Main.

"What is the plan?" Nkpor asked, tightly hugging herself.

"We barge into that place, burn it to the ground, and bring Onitsha Main home!" The Twins let their voices boom, nodding in agreement with each other.

"Right," Ochanja sighed, shutting her eyes and massaging the bridge of her nose. They were giving her a headache. "That is not a plan."

"We do not have time to sit around for schematics and riddles." The Twins charged forward. "Terrible things could be happening to Onitsha Main while we sit here dilly dallying!"

A tad amused, Ochanja cocked her head to the side. "That is a big fancy word, even for the both of you."

"We are going with or without you!" The Twins proceeded to barge out of the meeting. Pausing in their tracks, they spun back around, their eyes wild and erratic. "You never liked Onitsha Main. You hated that he was the first of us, and not you. We are certain his predicament brings you joy!"

And silence met silence.

"There is one thing you still do not have." Ochanja rose, meeting their glare with a calmness. "A plan."

The Twins were visibly seething at this point. They were usually on the other end of exchanges like this, usually the ones provoking everyone else. A taste of their own medicine did not taste so good.

The Twins turned to Nkpor. "Are you coming with us?"

"I—I don't—" Nkpor fumbled for words, her nervous eyes darting from Ochanja to The Twins and back again.

"So that's a 'no'." The Twins stormed out of the meeting.

The Twins stood before Shoprite. It was fenced and gated all around. The markets had no gates. They had no walls. A wall was a cage. How do you cage a thing mighty?

The Twins stared down the establishment. They stood, they waited, until night gathered. They knew not what to expect, but they were going in anyway.

"It is OK to be afraid." Head Bridge took Relief's twitching hand in his. The Twins only spoke in two distinct voices when they were alone.

"We do not know what we're up against." Relief squeezed their brother's hand. "If they could hold Onitsha . . . what would they do to us?"

"There's two of us, and . . ." Head Bridge stopped. He was going to say "one of them." But no one knew what Shoprite Mall was, or if they were just one. No one had ever seen them. No one had ever heard them.

The Twins took their first step into the mall together.

"Can you feel that?" Head Bridge inhaled.

"It's Onitsha Main!" Relief exhaled.

But it wasn't, not entirely. Yes, Onitsha Main did exist in that feeling, but something was strange about it. Like an abhorrence of sorts. Like Onitsha Main was there and not there. And the feeling came from everywhere, shrouding The Twins.

"We should split up." Head Bridge let go of his sibling's hand.

"We've existed long enough to know that is a terrible idea." Relief tried to reach back for their brother.

"We need to cover more ground." Head Bridge started to jog away, down a hallway. "Meet back here when you find something." He waved Relief goodbye as he disappeared down the hall.

Relief disliked being away from their brother. Head Bridge felt the same way. Without one another, The Twins did not know how to . . . be. In the beginning, they had been one market. But far removed from Onitsha Main and Ochanja, they had been lonely. So they split themself in two, and have kept each other company ever since.

Relief walked down a fruit and vegetable aisle. The market could see the appeal. The food items were exceptionally plump and juicy, their colors radiant. Not that the markets didn't have aesthetically pleasing produce—Relief and their siblings just had a wider variety, ranging from the plump to the not-so-plump. The not-so-plump produce served a purpose. The masses found them affordable and readily available, especially during a food crisis, which was becoming a recurring theme. The mall clearly did not have the masses in mind.

Above all, the markets' food items smelled of earth. The potatoes had dirt in their ridges. The eggs had specks of feces. Some of the oranges still had their stalks and leaves. The corn still held their silk, the coconut their husks, and the meat their blood. On the mangoes, one could still smell the morning dew.

In Shoprite Mall, there was no dirt, no feces, no blood. There was no earth in this place.

Relief picked up a kiwi. The market had never seen such a fruit before. They gave it a whiff.

"Ugh!" Relief tossed it. It smelled of rubber.

"You should not litter."

It was Onitsha Main's voice. Relief had listened to it barrage themself and Head Bridge for decades, and would probably still hear the old market's voice long after they were dead. But the vessel that held the voice was formless, a thing unnatural. A weirdness. It had limbs where limbs should not be. It had eyes where eyes should not see. The voice came forth from where voices should not be heard. Not many things frighten a market. Their kind had seen wars come and go, plagues and pestilence, years burned over, people of all shades and creeds. But Relief had never seen a thing like this. It frightened them.

"Do not be afraid," the thing said.

"Bold of you to assume I am." Relief straightened up.

"I have heard of you," the thing went on. "Seen you, in Onitsha Main's memories." The weirdness paused. A long unusual pause, like it was searching for something within itself. "Relief, is it not? Should there not be two of you?" The thing looked around, but Relief was not sure which direction it was looking.

"Give us our brother, or this will end unfavorably for you." The market's hands balled into fists.

"The last great war you endured was the civil war of '76." The thing slithered forward. "I make you a promise . . . this you will not endure."

Relief did not intend to see that promise fulfilled. Kitchen knives materialized around them, like a giant halo. Their knives were known to cut deep and fast, the sharpest of all the markets. Though Ochanja would disagree. Relief sent the knives pouring down on the formless thing, like rain.

The thing did not step away. It did not hide. It did not find cover. It let the blades find all the corners of its distorted being. In some corners, the blades splintered, and the blades shattered. In other corners, the blades sabered through. Still, the thing stood, undaunted, a hundred knives jutting out of it.

Relief took many steps back.

"There is no running in this place." The weirdness stretched out all its hands, in every direction. "You are in my house."

The floor tiles of the aisle began to rumble. The thing pulled its hands inward, and the tiles rippled forward, yanking Relief along until the market's neck was clasped in the grip of the formless being.

It started to eat Relief. It started with their face, and the market understood what it meant to die screaming. This is how Relief would describe it: A child tearing at an overripe mango, skin and juice splattering all over. The thing gnawed at their ears, and Relief heard the roofs of their electrical appliance stores crumble and fall. It tore at their tongue and Relief tasted the fruits in their market farms fester and rot. It clawed at their eyes, and Relief saw fire, and fire, and fire. Relief thrashed, Relief tore, and the abhorrence ate on.

And Head Bridge came running, his body taking the form of his most purchased item: machine spare parts. He grabbed the weirdness and flung it. The thing went crashing from shelf to shelf.

"What was that?" Head Bridge ran to his twin, helping them up. "Is that Shoprite?"

Head Bridge searched Relief's face for answers, and what he found sent a coldness tingling across his skin. The market gasped, cupping his mouth.

"What?" The fright on Head Bridge's face found its way to Relief's voice. "What is it?" Relief grew tired of asking, and turned, looking into the glass pane of a fridge. Half their face was gone, eaten up.

"Did—did it do this to—to you?" Head Bridge reached for his sibling's face with quivering fingers.

Relief screamed, and all the glass panes in the aisle shattered to smithereens. "I am going to kill it!"

A scattering sound started behind The Twins. They both turned and from the pile of broken shelves, Shoprite Mall rose. And all the lights went out.

Ochanja

"Something is wrong!" Nkpor announced as she came to find Ochanja. The young market was frantic. "I can feel it."

Ochanja could feel it too. But being the rational voice of reason always fell to her.

"I am sure it is nothing. The Twins are most likely tearing down the place," she said, folding her braids into a bun. "I will go take a look, and drag them back if I have to."

"Maybe—maybe we should ask the other markets for assistance," Nkpor suggested. "We need all the help we can get."

"This is a family affair, and we fix our own problems." There was a finality in Ochanja's words. "The others come to us for assistance, not the other way around."

Nkpor did not push any further. "All right then, but I am coming with you."

"No, you are not." Ochanja gently shoved her sister back. "Some-one has to stay and hold down the fort."

"But—"

"It is not a request."

She was invoking her authority as the oldest market present. It would probably not have worked on The Twins, but Ochanja knew it would work on Nkpor. A little hypocritical considering that in times past, when Onitsha Main had invoked that authority over her, Ochanja had outright defied him. She did not like Onitsha Main, The Twins were right about that. She never tried to pretend either. The Twins defied everyone for the fun of it, but Ochanja defied Onitsha Main out of spite. She believed she deserved to be the first of the markets. Her goods were as authentic as her brother's, some would argue even better. Onitsha Main had the Niger River, but she had Upper Iweka where all the transport companies converged. It was Ochanja who granted access to the town of Onitsha. Her name opened all doors. But believing a thing did not make it true.

Onitsha Main was the first and forever would be—if he survived this ordeal. Still, it came as no surprise Ochanja would walk into the unknown for him. Disliking Onitsha Main did not mean she didn't care for him. She had the choice not to, and did not choose it. The two markets had been each other's first friends, having come into existence at nearly the same time. Decades had passed before The Twins and Nkpor came into the picture, followed by the up-shoot of the smaller markets, establishing the need for a lead figure. This was when the enmity set in. But Ochanja loved her brother still, and Onitsha Main loved her too.

Inside Shoprite Mall, Ochanja found a darkness. It was dense, like a mass of shadows clawing at her. Ochanja could not tell where her body began nor where it ended. One by one, the market sent lamps sailing to the ceiling. Like specks of dawn stilled in glass, the lamps gave light to the mall. Ochanja was one of the few markets that still sold lamps. Everyone else had upgraded to electric-powered bulbs and torchlight. Funny considering the country's power grid crashed every other Monday afternoon.

The lamps illuminating her path, Ochanja went from aisle to aisle until she found the weirdness. It was gulping Head Bridge whole. All that was left was Head Bridge's feet jutting out of its mouth. Ochanja barged forward. She grabbed the leg, and with all her might, pulled Head Bridge out of the thing's mouth. And as Head Bridge came out, he was holding onto Relief's hand, yanking his twin out with him. And when Relief came tearing out, they were equally holding onto another hand. All three siblings pulled and pulled, and at the end of that hand was Onitsha Main.

Enraged, bile and foam spattering all over, the thing charged at Ochanja.

"You will find I am difficult to swallow," the market said, as she grew in size, a giant, mighty. How do you swallow a thing mighty?

And the thing stretched all its formless mouths, and all its mouths ripped at the ends. Still, it was not enough. Worn and torn, it ebbed to the ground.

"There is no time!" Onitsha Main picked himself off the ground. "We have to kill it."

Getting eaten had taken quite a physical toll on the market. He was frail, his clavicle visible through thin stretched skin. His eyes and cheeks were sunken, and his head had many a bald spot. Despite it all, Onitsha Main found his feet, and he stood.

The Twins held the weirdness down, while Ochanja and Onitsha Main started a fire. Fueling it with cardboard papers and liquor, the fire burned fast, orange-green flames sweeping across the aisles, eating through the shelves and reducing the mall to ash and singed rubble. As more of the weirdness's wares went into the fire, the thing shrieked and flailed, but the markets held on tight. With the fire at its height, they brought the weirdness closer, intent on destroying it.

"Enough." It was City-Tech Library. They waded effortlessly through the blazing carnage.

"What are you doing here?" Ochanja asked while struggling to keep the thing down.

"What must be done."

"You treacherous little rat!" Onitsha Main spat. "They are in cahoots with this monstrosity! They aided it in capturing me!" he informed the other markets.

Ochanja left the weirdness to her siblings and rushed at the Library. But the market soon found her body unmoving. Like a pile of weathered rocks, she crumpled to the ground. The other markets came falling with her.

"What—what is happening?" Ochanja tried to writhe to her feet but found it impossible. Something was pinning her down. It was excruciating.

"Access to the legal records of government-owned establishments is a fascinating thing." City-Tech walked up to Ochanja. "The things one can do with such access, like sell off parts of your lands, change your names . . . have you temporarily shut down."

"We belong to no one!" Ochanja bellowed through the pain.

"That is not what the records say," City-Tech continued. "You belong to the public, and, in essence, the government."

"What—what did we ever do to you?" Onitsha Main strained.

City-Tech turned to the elder market. The library knelt, bringing their face closer to his.

"This town has the potential to be a modern high-end metropolis, but you and your ilk keep getting in the way."

The Library stood back up. The thing slowly slithered to them, curling up around their feet. The Library patted one of its many heads.

"You markets are not structured and the rules of organized society seldom apply to you. This city cannot thrive in such disorderliness."

The Library coaxed the thing forward, setting it loose on the markets.

"Not to worry, dozens of malls are already in the works, waiting to fill in the gap. This will be good for society, for Onitsha." City-Tech recoiled from mentioning the name of the town. "We will need to change that name to something more modern."

And Ochanja, powerless and sprawled on the mall floor, watched as Shoprite Mall ate her siblings. Then it came for her.

Nkpor

Nkpor knew what was coming for her. Her siblings were gone, and in their place, more and more malls went up. She should have gone with Ochanja that day. Perhaps things would have turned out differently. Or perhaps she'd have been eradicated alongside her siblings. Either way, she would have been with them. The smaller markets now looked to her for guidance, but Nkpor could barely guide herself out of the dark cloud looming over her. Hidden away in the depths of herself, past the okirika vendors, past the provision stores, past the men who blended cocoa, there did Nkpor remain. Her stalls were closing down with every passing day, traders were migrating, and sales were tanking.

"It is pathetic in here." It was Shoprite Mall sifting past into Nkpor's hidden places. This had been going on for a while, Shoprite finding and taunting the market. All in a bid to lure Nkpor out.

"You cannot harm me in here, and I am never coming out." This shred of resistance was all Nkpor had left.

"Of course, of course." Shoprite twirled.

The mall looked different now. They were no longer formless, no longer abhorrent. They shone. Nkpor could see bits and pieces of her siblings in the mall.

"But eventually though, maybe not today, but eventually." Shoprite let a smile gleam across their face.

They were right. Nkpor knew it. She could not stay hidden forever. Parts of her chipped away with each drifting moon. And the malls were growing in number, stronger, more massive. They would overwhelm her in time.

"I am barely even functional. Just let me be." A plea found Nkpor's voice.

"Oh, darling." Shoprite's cold fingers caressed the market's cheeks. The market pulled away. "As long as you exist, the small markets will flock to you. But if you fall," the mall tapped Nkpor's nose, "boop. So do they."

Nkpor inhaled, swallowing hard at the thought. But in that thought came another thought, and Nkpor held onto it.

"Plus I really want to eat you," Shoprite giggled. "You are so pretty, and I reckon you'd be more delicious than your siblings." The mall ran its fingers through the market's braids. Nkpor did not pull away. "And when I'm done, I would be the prettiest thing ever." Shoprite clapped with glee.

"Pretty is subjective."

The glee waned from the mall's face. Market and mall stared each other down. The glee quickly found its way back onto Shoprite.

"Oh well, until next time. Toodaloo!"

And the mall was gone, plunging Nkpor into a quietness. In that quietness, Nkpor opened the thought in her hands and knew what she needed to do. Onitsha Main would have called it madness. Ochanja would have been calm with rage. Relief and Head Bridge would have laughed and laughed and laughed. But they were not here. She was.

And for the first time in a long time, Nkpor stepped into the sun. She could feel them coming, the malls, from all corners, rushing at her. But they would not find her.

Nkpor gathered the small markets. She gathered them all:

Mkpologwu, Yam market, Books & Stationery market, Ogbo Tomato, Aluminum market, Ezinifite, Ose Okwodu, Plywood & Carpentry tools market, she gathered them all.

"Here, take my eyes." She folded them into Ezinifite's hands.

"Take my leg." The market handed one of her legs to the Plywood & Carpentry tools market.

"Here, it's a little heavy." Nkpor balanced the other leg in Ogbo Tomato's hands.

"And my hair . . ." She took folds of it and wrapped them around Yam market.

And when Shoprite and the other malls came looking, they found Nkpor was many. Scattered across the town of Onitsha. In all the small markets, in all the small places. Ten thousand strong. How do you end a thing mighty? A thing infinite.

T*wo anchor stores, both alike in dignity,*
In fair Verona Mall where we lay our scene…

Yeah, I gotta admit, I've never read Shakespeare.

Jules has, though. One of the perks of living on the side of the mall with the bookstore, I suppose.

The bookstore, the multiplex, Blockbuster…No wonder the people of JCPenney all seem so cultured. Brilliant. Elegant. Beautiful…

God, would you look at this girl? Absolutely radiant in her cropped sweater, lit by a beam of moonlight coming through the broken ceiling with her elbows resting on the plexiglass balcony.

And then there's me. Flannel and black t-shirt, hair chopped off so the zombies can't grab me, just a nobody scavenger from Macy's. I will never understand what she sees in me, why she would risk it all to be together, but I thank my lucky glow-in-the-dark stars for her every night.

"So what's the plan, gorgeous?" I say softly. Everyone seems to have turned in for the night, metal grates pulled down over all the storefronts, but the hatred between our families is even more dangerous than the apocalyptic world outside.

She startles, looking down into the shadowy atrium-turned-farmland, searching for me. She won't call out, not until she's sure; that mistake almost got us caught once.

I stamp my foot beneath the escalator that has been stairs since before either of us were born. The flashing lights on my sneaker draws Jules's attention, and she smiles.

"There you are," she says, and I cherish the sound of her voice in person, no static from our cobbled-together communication devices getting in the way. It isn't often I can risk sneaking over here.

"The plan?" I prompt, wanting to stay forever but knowing we need to keep our visits short, efficient. "You said we were going to play Romeo and Juliet. What does that mean?"

She doesn't answer right away, instead playing with her ring. "What color is yours?" she asks after a moment.

I look down. When the plague hit and our ancestors locked themselves away in this mall, they had to make do without proper medical equipment. One of their first developments was turning the surplus of mood rings in the jewelry stores into more accurate thermometers; the instant someone's temperature goes up, the ring changes color.

"Blue. All good." I look back up at her. Suddenly I don't want to ask what color hers is. I don't like any of this. "What are you planning, Jules?"

"Your people are working on a cure."

Their side got the culture, we got the Discovery Channel store and RadioShack, became more technologically minded. In the years since the end of the world, we've developed beepers that can transmit as well as receive messages, robotic pets that disable zombies by going after their Achilles tendons, and yeah. Possibly a cure, but it isn't ready yet.

"We still need a way to rapidly cool the mixture—"

"Like the ice cream freezer in our theaters," Jules says, like it's that simple, like my people would ever admit we might have a cure, like her people would ever help us.

I open my mouth to argue but she takes off her ring, tosses it to me.

It's still hot from her body, and bright red.

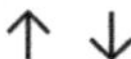

We've been sneaking around this mall for nearly a year. I know all the back entrances, all the broken skylights. Even with our families on high alert, it's easy for me to get up on the roof, cross over onto JCPenney's side, and drop down through the elevator shaft.

Getting back home with buckets of ice—that's another story entirely.

"They'll see us," Tio warns. As one of the few residents who has refused to take sides, he's the only person I could trust to help me.

Well, besides Jules, but she's in no condition for adventure. All the more reason we don't have time to waste.

Leaning over, I peek through the partially closed gate of the cinema. The war between JCPenney and Macy's never really ended, but we were on a break. Now the break is over: too many revelations, too many secrets and accusations and conspiracy theories. Our security systems have been bypassed by a couple of lovesick teenagers, my people have a cure, her people have been using me as a spy, we infected her on purpose . . .

The armies of JCPenney stand at attention, looking for any excuse to pull the trigger on their razor-winged Sky Dancers and corrosive water pistols. Same as back home, except we have robot attack dogs.

Yeah. They'll definitely see us. Question is, will they do anything about it? There's only so many times we can pass the tension back and forth before one of us has to declare a physical challenge and full out warfare.

"Do you want out?" I ask.

Tio shakes his head. "I'm just glad I talked you out of pushing the entire cooler. There's no way the extension cord would have reached."

I look at him. He's grinning. I shake my head, laughing and grateful for this last moment of peace.

And with that, we make a break for it.

We make it farther than I expect before someone sees us, almost to the food court that acts as the neutral zone between territories in this war about nothing.

I don't know who shouts first—her people realizing I'm stealing from them or mine thinking I'm working with the enemy. But after that, Verona Mall devolves into a chaos the likes of which it hasn't seen since that distant Christmas when people rioted over giggling Muppet dolls.

Sky Dancers zip past my head. Volleys of minuscule projectiles blast in from Macy's side, exploding on contact with the moisture on people's skin.

I drop one of my buckets, ice scattering everywhere. We don't go back for it; we don't have time. If we can just make it to the old Burger King in the food court, we have an ally in Lawrence, who was the fryer back before the world ended. He'll help us, he'll—

Tio screams next to me. I turn, telling myself that maybe his injury isn't severe, maybe—

Maybe, in the midst of worrying about each other, everybody forgot about the zombie that bit Jules.

For just a second, everything stops as we all stare at Tio, the gaping wound on his arm, and the undead ghoul with blood running from its mouth like a wild cherry Gusher.

I recognize the zombie, I realize distantly, my brain still trying to catch up. His face is distorted by death twice over, but I recognize him. Jules's cousin, I think.

I meet Tio's eyes, reach for him.

Could we both make it? If Lawrence could patch him up, could we make enough cure for him and Jules?

Everyone is still staring, but the world is starting to move again, people reaching for their weapons, murmuring in a slowly rising panic. The zombie lunges for me, and Tio pushes him away.

I feel a pain in my arm but I don't look. I don't want to know what caused it.

If I run now, I can definitely make it to Lawrence, but what kind of friend would I be—

Tio mouths a single word: "Go."

I don't wait for him to tell me again. There will be time to hate myself for it later, with Jules.

Maybe we were fools to think our love would be the thing that brought the yin and yang of our mall back together to form one BFFs necklace. To think they would see us sneaking around for fear of being discovered and realize that the war between our sides is more dangerous than any zombie apocalypse, and they would put aside their differences to celebrate our love as one big family.

Lawrence and I work late into the night, the kitchen of his former Burger King home illuminated only by glow sticks and the incandescent lightbulb of our oven. Someone must have taken out the power to the rest of the mall, trying to get an advantage over their enemies.

The battle rages, even here in the neutral zone. I try ignoring it, but how can you ignore the sounds of people you know dying in a war you helped start up again?

More than once, Lawrence has to shoot a zombie trying to crawl over the counter. Either people aren't properly dealing with the dead and people are turning, or someone is purposefully bringing the zombies in, using them as weapons.

But we keep going. We finish synthesizing the cure, our technology and their technology working as one to become something greater.

One dose. But if I can save her, that's all that matters.

↑ ↓

With the lights out, it's more dangerous, but I have nothing left to lose.

I run, every footstep blinking with LEDs and every heartbeat pushing more of the virus through my body. I run through the battles, ducking under projectiles and stepping over the fallen.

I run up the broken escalator, straight through the front entrance of the JCPenney anchor store.

That's when they stop me, twin laser sights of corrosive acid bazookas trained on my chest.

I hold up my arm, rolling up my sleeve to expose the bite.

"I'm already dead," I announce, wiggling the cool vial between my fingers. "But she doesn't have to be!"

There's no response.

"Are you really going to let her die rather than admit there might be one person from Macy's who isn't your enemy?"

Still nothing. I take a tentative step forward.

The PA system crackles overhead. "I'm sorry."

It's Francis. The guy Jules's family thought she would marry before she came out.

"Romy, I'm sorry—"

"Where is she?" I demand.

"It's . . . it's too late."

No.

No, no, he's wrong, he's got to be wrong.

I push past the guards, no one stops me, and I rush through enemy territory, overturning clothing racks and screaming her name until Francis takes pity on me and gives me directions to her bed.

She looks like she's sleeping, not that I would know how she sleeps. Our romance has been one of stolen moments and whispered promises, always looking over our shoulders.

She's not dead. Not yet—there's still the smallest rise and fall of her chest. But her ring is black.

So is mine, I realize, and I laugh deliriously. I've always wanted to have matching rings, I'd just hoped they would be wedding rings.

I go to her bed, sit on it because I'm too dizzy to stand. The virus moved through me quicker than it did her. Maybe that would be poetic if I cared anymore, the two of us dying together.

With the last of my strength, I open her mouth and pour in the cure. It never occurs to me that I could use it on myself.

I stare at her, waiting for those beautiful eyes to flutter open, but my own eyes are fluttering closed, and I have to rest my head on her shoulder.

Oh, we were definitely fools. Me, most of all, because I believed that I could save her.

I wake to a bittersweet taste and the morning sun streaming through the broken skylights above the neutral zone.

Someone moves beside me. Jules, half asleep and smiling brighter than the sun.

No, it's not real, it can't be. I'm delusional, she's a zombie, that must be it—

I touch her hair, her cheek, and she's warm. Alive. I take her hand, interlace our fingers. Our rings still match, but they're yellow; our fevers are going down.

"How?" I whisper.

Jules kisses me. I taste the same bittersweet on her lips.

"No friendly drop to help you after," she says, her voice so soft I almost don't hear it. "I will kiss thy lips. Some cure yet doth hang on them, to make you live with a restorative."

"I've still never read Shakespeare," I tell her, and look around. The carnage of battle still surrounds us, but it's peaceful for the moment. "Lawrence brought us here?"

She nods.

"Our families?"

"Talking." She reconsiders. "Shouting, cursing."

"But not fighting."

"Not fighting," Jules confirms.

Yeah, so maybe we were fools, but maybe sometimes that's exactly what the world needs. Fools, and a couple of store-crossed lovers.

anjum n. choudhury

Future City Mall stood on a platform sixteen steps high. Like the Parthenon. But without any of its majesty or craftsmanship. Obviously.

Sixteen steps. Four sets of four staggered by semi-wide landings.

The youngsters sweeping past Shondha were probably oblivious to how many steps there were—one of the many perks of youth. For Shondha, however, each step was a mountain in itself. She took them one at a time, stifling her whimpers as her thigh and shin bones pierced through decayed cartilage, scraped her kneecap like nails on a chalkboard, and shot jolts of pain up and down her leg.

She didn't venture out much because of her knee, yet it was this same knee that prompted her trip to the mall. Unsatisfied with the majority of clothes she bought online (she prided herself on being adept at online shopping), she'd decided that clothes were best bought in person. Compression tights, in particular, had to be inspected for their authenticity, fit, elasticity, and stitching along the inner seams.

Adjusting her orna across her shoulders, she drew herself up to her full height and marched through the entrance's metal detectors like her legs weren't ready to disintegrate. It was an overcast August morning, very muggy, and the cool air inside the atrium felt divine against her sweat-dampened skin. The ear-splitting blare of a fog machine being blasted somewhere in the eight-story building, on the other hand, not so much. Shondha knew the sound well, and also knew the acrid, medicinal smell that would follow. There was no escaping it these days. Dengue used to be a seasonal disease, but hospitalizations and deaths because of it now persisted all year round, and broke new records every day. Glossing over the root of the problem—bad waste management, and even worse drainage—authorities devoted their resources to spritzing larvae and fogging adult mosquitos with insecticide, poisoning the city's inhabitants in the process.

The smartphone and electronic gadget stores on the ground floor teemed with scrawny boys with what Shondha's daughter called douchebag haircuts, not a girl to be seen among them. The girls preferred to congregate by the waffle, juice, and ice cream kiosks, their hair sleek and immaculately straight despite the humidity, a few of them a tad too made-up for the mall. Shondha wondered what all of them were doing out of school or away from work at noon on a Wednesday. There were also a handful of mothers, struggling to secure their ornas and handbags to their shoulders with hands carrying numerous shopping bags, all while wrangling children inclined to wandering off. Shondha, as far as she could tell, was the only grandmother about.

Bouncing on the balls of her feet, she watched three escalator steps rise from the floor before thrusting herself onto the fourth and quickly grabbing hold of the handrail. The contraption's rhythmic whirr eased the constriction in her stomach. She hadn't tripped, or twisted an ankle, or gotten her orna caught in the escalator yet.

So far so good.

As if to say, "Think again," the lights in the atrium and the galleries overlooking it blacked out, and the escalator slowed to a halt.

Shondha pressed herself up against the balustrade to make way for the youngsters elbowing past her. Dim fluorescent lights powered by the mall's back-up generator flickered on, but the escalator steps remained still. The power was unlikely to return any time soon. Hour-long blackouts, usually three, sometimes five times a day, had become the norm ever since the government lost its ability to afford gas and coal imports for the power plants. Shondha resolved not to count how many steps she'd have to climb, one at a time, on this flight. Or the next. Or the one after that. Instead, she distracted herself by cursing politicians in her head and imagined delivering a rousing speech on how they wouldn't be here today if they'd pivoted to solar energy.

The back-up generator didn't power the mall's central air conditioning. Without its low and steady drone, fellow visitors' chatter and the fog machine's incessant blare seemed louder. More disquieting. The air grew warmer and wetter the higher Shondha climbed. The people bustling past her emitted more heat. Noxious fog clung to the still air, mingling with increasingly offensive body odor, blurring visibility, stinging the eyes, irritating the airways.

Through the haze, salespeople called out to passersby like frogs on a misty marsh:

"Leather bags, need leather bags?"

"Shoes, dressy shoes, flat shoes, shoes for every occasion."

"Cosmetics, madam, cosmetics. We've got all the international brands. American make-up, Korean skin-care."

"Do you need abayas? Hijabs? Accessories for abayas and hijabs?"

The prospect of resting her throbbing knee lured Shondha into a shop selling ethnic wear. Nothing caught her eye. Nothing seemed durable. Everything was unbreathable and scratchy to the touch. Prices were low, though, so shoppers had that. When she exited the shop, the escalator was gone, and the floor plan different. Deciding against retracing her steps through the shop—where the salespeople might mistake her for an unworldly grandmother—she decided to cut across another ethnic wear shop beside it selling near-identical clothes.

That led to a dead end.

The unstitched three-piece store next to it opened out to an entirely new floor plan.

Four more ethnic wear stores later—or perhaps it was two she happened upon twice—she found an escalator. It wasn't the same one she'd been climbing, but it led upstairs, which was all that mattered.

There were no pit stops this time. Blinkering against the tens of youngsters overtaking her, Shondha pushed herself to keep climbing. One flight, then two, then four. Until she made it to the seventh floor, where the western wear and sporting goods shops were housed. She gripped the gallery's handrail for dear life as she hobbled past several dimly lit shops that might've sold compression tights. She needed a moment, lest the marsh frogs heard the sob trapped under her grimace or saw the tears threatening to spring from her eyes.

On and on she hobbled in the muggy darkness, the fog machine's blare hammering her skull in tandem with the seismic pain radiating from her knee. At some point she let go of the handrail and lost sight of the escalator. The floor plan changed with every turn.

A bright emerald sign stopped her in her tracks. TIPI KO, its fluorescent white letters read, YOU MUST DROP BUY.

The shop windows underneath it, decorated with rows of animal and beverage plushies, looked into a busy, fully lighted store.

Shondha inched toward it in a daze. She knew about Tipi Ko, of course. Their ads were all over her Facebook feed. They sold everything from clothes and accessories to stationery to electronic gadgets and gadget accessories. And everything was designed to look either sleek and modern, or colorful and cute to cater to both manly men and girlie girls. Shondha didn't fall into either bracket, so she'd never felt the urge to visit.

Until now.

Bad leg dragging behind, she picked up her pace. A blanket of blissfully cool, clean air engulfed her as she pulled open the store's glass door.

"Here you go, ma'am." A smiling salesgirl in an emerald apron and matching cap over her hijab held out a green basket.

Teary-eyed with relief, Shondha accepted it as if it was a trophy.

"Please." The salesgirl motioned to a large bell hanging by the wall in front of a small sign containing what looked like instructions—likely the store's fire safety guidelines.

Confused, Shondha looked from the bell to the salesgirl and back. Then rang the bell with a flick to its clapper.

"Welcome to Tipi Ko!" every salesperson on the floor chanted cheerily.

"You must drop buy!" the salesgirl said in a saccharine, sing-song tone.

Shondha masked her judgment of the awkward tagline with a polite smile. It was, admittedly, a semi-clever spin on an English expression, but it didn't exactly convey a unique selling point. Then again, in a country where beauty salon ads claimed their makeovers helped dark-skinned women achieve "white supremacy," perhaps a well thought out tagline was too much to ask.

More shoppers streamed in behind her, rang the bell, and got a "Welcome to Tipi Ko!" from the staff, hustling Shondha deeper into the store. An aproned salesboy appeared at her shoulder to ask what she was looking for. His proximity, along with the clusters of youngsters taking selfies or filming themselves, made her acutely aware of how many people there were in the closed space, and how easy it'd be for everyone to contract an airborne disease if someone was infected.

She could've kicked herself for becoming so lax about COVID precautions in recent months. "Do you have masks?"

"Yes ma'am, this way," the salesboy said sunnily. He proceeded to lead her to the beauty section, and show her Tipi Ko's sheet mask line. "We also stock these in serum form."

"No, I mean cloth masks. Or surgical ones."

"Oh." His face grew grave. "Ma'am, thing is, we have those, but they're complimentary with customer purchases."

Clicking her tongue in disapproval, Shondha considered whether to buy something and get a mask or go someplace less crowded.

"Here"—the salesman held up what appeared to be a perfume bottle with several long, black reed sticks inserted—"try an aroma diffuser. This one's from our limited edition Four Seasons series."

"No, really, that's—"

He raised the sticks' tips to her nose "Autumn, see."

Shondha took an involuntary whiff as she jerked her head back, and froze. The cinnamon and oak aroma transported her to a place far away from the overcrowded, mosquito-infested, water- and garbage-logged streets of her home city—to a vast, open and untouched space where cool, dry winds caressed her skin and rustled fallen leaves, and where every painless step was accompanied by a clean, crisp crunch. It awakened in her a desire to go on a long trek through the woods. And when she caught a glimpse of herself in a nearby mirror, the notion didn't seem preposterous at all. For the woman staring back at her was neither shrunken nor enfeebled. Her eyes shined bright, her features were plump and smooth, her black hair lustrous, and her posture erect.

It was like a half-remembered dream, her reflection. Yet she felt as she looked: strong, energetic, agile.

Young.

She dropped the unopened aroma diffuser the salesboy handed her into her basket. Then a bunch of anti-aging sheet masks and serums, a special brush that infused the scalp with anti-graying properties, a hair tonic to go with it, and a weekly hair mask. She had second thoughts about getting a hair-drying cap, but the model on the packaging looked very chic, so she added it to her basket too.

She weaved past three sets of girls in the make-up section who were filming themselves trying on testers. They looked perfectly fine. But they had nothing on Shondha, whose reflection boasted dewier and tighter skin, thicker brows and lashes, and juicier lips the more testers she sampled. The salesboy supplied her with cleansing wipes so she could test more, and an unopened package of everything she liked went into her basket.

The salesboy offered to carry the basket for her as a bullet journal, a mason jar painted with daisies, a mug saying "Live, Laugh, Love," a deck of affirmation cards, a box of rose and raspberry tea for anxiety, a bunny rabbit hand towel, a watermelon floormat, and the Summer aroma diffuser from the Four Seasons line found their way into it.

Shondha rejoiced at being able to navigate the aisles with such ease. At the prospect of having so much new stuff! She was really accomplishing something here. Putting herself first. Becoming her best self. Living her best life.

In the clothing section, a maxi dress with a plunging neckline and cinched waist caught her eye. The salesboy stopped her from draping it over her arm, insisting she drop it in the basket instead. Past the jeans display (she liked wearing jeans, and couldn't quite remember why she'd stopped), she halted at a rack for tights. She knew she needed a pair, but couldn't remember why. Was it to go with an outfit, or was it to go running?

Why not buy for both?

Dropping one pair after the other into the basket, she heard a distant voice reminding her to try them on. Not only to make sure they fit, but to also make sure they gave her knee ample support.

The thought gave her pause. But she brushed it off and asked the salesboy to point her to the dressing rooms.

It was against store policy to let customers take more than one item inside. Shondha left her basket in the salesboy's safekeeping and locked herself in a dressing room with a pair of black and purple tights emblazoned with sequined skulls. She'd bent down to slip a foot through the elastic fabric when a hot huff brushed her cheek.

Skin breaking into gooseflesh, she snapped upright.

There was nothing on her cheek, though. Nor was anything amiss in the dressing room.

Bending down once more, she felt it again. Along with a dull discomfort in her knee. It came from a crack in the dressing room's wall. Shondha slapped a palm over it, fearing someone might be watching from the other side.

But the damp waft continued licking her. Peeling her palm away, she hesitantly pressed an eye to the crack. It was too fine to see out or in, thankfully. She let out a relieved sigh and inhaled the air slipping through. Then inhaled some more.

It wasn't clean, the air. It was thick and nauseating. It irritated her airways, flooded her tongue with a bitter, medicinal taste. She rested her forehead on the dressing room's wall, inhaling more and more, straining her ears until she heard the incessant and unpleasant blare of a fog machine somewhere in the distance.

The world is in shambles, she heard a faraway voice say.

An explosion of pain in her knee confirmed it.

"Ma'am?" came a knock at the door. "Is everything OK?"

Shondha stared at the sequined skull tights. What was she doing?

Pulling her salwar back on, she opened the door and bit back a yelp at the sight of the waiting salesboy. She hadn't really looked at him till now, but now that she did, there was something off about him. Like he was looking at her, but not with his own eyes.

More unsettling, though, was the sheer volume of garbage in the basket he was holding. Garbage she'd put there herself.

Unable to tear her disconcerted gaze from the basket, she held out the skull tights. "I think I'll go for the black ones."

"You must drop it into the basket, ma'am."

"O . . . kay . . ."

She complied dubiously, then locked herself into the dressing room with the black tights.

This wasn't like her, Shondha thought as she wriggled her hips into the tights. She'd never been a compulsive shopper.

The tights were a perfect fit. And as she admired how good her behind looked in them, and how painless her knee felt in them, she wondered if, perhaps, the other stuff in the basket was worth buying after all.

No, you stop that.

Sinking to her haunches despite her knee's protests, she took long, deep drags of the insecticide fumes seeping in. The things in the basket—they promised a fleeting escape. A hit of dopamine. A lie. She'd lived through war, famine, inflation and three—no, four— recessions, globalization, urbanization, earthquakes and cyclones, parenthood, grandparenthood, innumerable epidemics and a global pandemic. She didn't *need* an escape. She knew how to survive.

Breathing her fill of toxic fumes, she realized why the store didn't sell face masks. Those aroma diffusers were doing something funny to everyone's head.

Shondha's orna was made from sturdy cotton. She startled the salesboy when she stepped out with the lower half of her face wrapped in the lengthy garment. Pulling two more age-appropriate pairs of tights in the same size as the black from the basket, she turned to make a beeline for the checkout counter. "I won't be taking these," she said, motioning at the basket. "Thank you."

"Ma'am." Overtaking her with ease, he blocked her way, an unsettlingly obliging smile plastered across his face. "Sorry, ma'am, I didn't understand."

"I said I've got what I need," she said, loud and clear. "I won't be taking the rest."

"Ma'am, sorry, but that's against our 'You Must Drop Buy' policy."

"Your what?"

"Our 'You Must Drop Buy' policy. You must buy whatever you drop into your basket."

"What kind of a ridiculous policy is that?"

"It's posted by the entrance, ma'am." Oh, that patronizing tone grated on Shondha's nerves. "You consented to it when you rang the bell."

Shondha looked toward the entrance, equal parts mystified and furious. The sign behind the bell—the one she'd mistaken for fire safety guidelines—it was the store's deranged terms and conditions.

"Look, whatever it is, it's not legally binding, so I'm just going to buy what I need and go home, all right? Please step out of my way."

"Regrettably, ma'am, that won't be possible."

Shondha felt the rest of the sales staff's eyes on her, felt them surrounding and closing in on her.

"Our products guarantee 100% customer satisfaction. Customers simply can't help but buy everything they drop into their baskets." Bent from the waist up, as if paying her obeisance, the salesboy motioned to the nearest mirror. "You can have a look for yourself."

Rather than entice her this time, her reflection elicited a wistful sigh. Everything her orna didn't cover looked smoother, tighter, and more vivacious than it had been in years. But none of it was real.

And she didn't appreciate being manipulated.

"All right." Training a steely glare on the salesboy, she fished through the basket for the cosmetics she'd dropped in. 100% customer satisfaction, huh? Time to put the claim's veracity to the test. "Let's see if your beauty products are halal certified." She checked the packaging on a few of the items. "Nope. Seems like none of your make-up, hair, or skincare products are halal. Not ideal if you're selling in a Muslim country. And oh"—she raised her voice in feigned shock—"they're not cruelty-free either."

From the corner of her eye, Shondha saw the sales staff exchange nervous looks. There was a wobble, a trepidation in their voices the next time the bell by the entrance rang, and they had to sing, "Welcome to Tipi Ko!"

Shondha also felt others looking her way—the customers.

So this was enough to snap everyone out of their delirium.

"Do your products use post-consumer recycled materials?" Shondha demanded, crossing her arms over her chest. "It was Earth's overshoot day last week. Do you know what that means? We're using up Earth's resources faster than they're being replenished. An environmentally conscious business would've transitioned to responsible and sustainable production methods by now. Would you say Tipi Ko uses responsible and sustainable production methods?"

"Ma'am, please"—a salesgirl approached her—"we have some special offers you might be interested in."

The sales staff dispersed to frantically brandish aroma diffusers around the customers, more and more of whom were beginning to film the altercation.

"What about labor practices?" Shondha pressed, keeping the salesgirl at bay with an outstretched arm. "Do the factories manufacturing your products meet fire and safety regulations? Are the people making your products being paid fair wages, or is everything made in labor camps? What about you? How much are you paid per day? How many bathroom breaks are you allowed?"

Nodding in approval, the watching customers echoed her questions.

"So what you're telling me"—Shondha elbowed and wriggled toward the checkout counter—"is that not only is Tipi Ko insensitive to its customer base's religious beliefs, it's not environmentally conscious, and it doesn't pay its workers fair wages either. All so its shareholders can rake in millions in dividends."

Emerald green smoke erupted at the store's fringes with an ear-splitting *bang, bang, bang.* Panicked screams filled the air and bodies collided as it swept through the aisles, engulfing everything and everyone. Clamping her orna over her nose and mouth, squeezing the smoke's sting from her eyes, Shondha felt her way to the checkout counter.

Only to find it unattended.

She couldn't even leave the cursed store—the emerald fog was too thick to see which way the exit was.

The store grew deathly quiet. After what felt like an eternity, a figure emerged from the fog—a short, greasy-haired woman wearing an ill-fitted beige blazer over her saree and a KN95 mask.

"Good afternoon, ma'am, I'm the manager of this branch. I understand you're not 100% satisfied with Tipi Ko's products."

"I just want these tights."

"That's very regrettable, but please be advised, ma'am: compliance with our 'You Must Drop Buy' policy is preferable to the alternative."

"An alternative! Yes, good. Let's hear it."

"Ma'am, customers who wish to bypass our policy will be subject to a wisdom fine in addition to their total."

"You—" Shondha fought the urge to reach across the counter and strangle Miss Manager. "You're going to fine *me* for figuring out *your* scheme to drug us into buying more stuff..."

"Our *sales strategy*, ma'am. Yes."

Shondha should have left without buying anything on principle. But she didn't have the energy to try on more tights at another store, and these ones were so, so comfortable...

At least they were acknowledging that she was wise.

"How much is it?"

"That's decided on a customer basis at Tipi Ko's discretion."

"Of course." Rolling her eyes, she slid the tights over to the manager. "Just check these out."

"Are you sure, ma'am?"

"Yes, yes." Shondha was used to being extorted. It was impossible to get anything done these days without paying a "surcharge" or an outright bribe. And that was on top of all the taxes leeched from her savings, all so the country could continue hobbling along without power and its people could continue living in danger of contracting dengue.

Besides, if they asked for too much, she'd simply refuse to buy and start looking for the exit.

But when Miss Manager handed her her receipt, she found she'd only been charged for the three pairs of tights. The row labeled "Wisdom Fine" was blank.

It was a bluff. One last desperate attempt to coerce her into complying with their criminal policy.

Wise indeed.

Handing Shondha her shopping bag, the manager held open a glass door beside the counter for her.

Was that there the whole time?

"Thank you for shopping at Tipi Ko, ma'am," she said in that irritatingly cloying tone, as if Shondha hadn't just upended her store. "You must drop buy again soon!"

Unlikely.

The gallery past the door's threshold was now fully lighted and air conditioned. The mall had power again! And the fog machine's blare had, mercifully, stopped, too! The worst had passed. Just as Shondha knew it always would.

She'd done it. She'd survived. She'd extricated herself from yet another sticky situation by sheer force of will and wit.

But for some inexplicable reason, she felt like she still owed Tipi Ko something.

She was too exhausted, though, and in too much pain to continue pondering this . . . or where the door she'd just used had gone. She chose, instead, to focus on being grateful. Grateful she got her compression tights. Grateful her integrity and dignity had prevailed. Grateful she'd survived the day.

All the while unaware of the hard-earned piece of wisdom she'd now lost forever.

the intercessor

eirik gumeny

" —Find your mother's mother and shove *her* inside the horse, t—"

The door slammed shut, Lily's back pressed against the windowless steel. Her eyes were scrunched shut; she was breathing through her nose like a bull. Her manicured hands balled into fists against the small of her back.

"Oh," she started, fighting back tears. "Oh . . .*fuck* that guy."

"Wow," said Bern. "I didn't even know you knew that word."

Lily's hazel eyes opened, wide with surprise. Bern and Adi, her coworkers, weren't more than five feet in front of her, camped out in the back room, the overgrown closet that doubled as both storage and employee lounge. They were perched on boxes facing one another, knees pulled up like slacker gargoyles. Bern, rail-thin and tattooed, wearing a loose, pea soup-colored cardigan over his neon green uniform; Adi, shorter and heavyset, with Doc Martens worn down enough to expose the steel toes. The both of them apparently unbothered by the fact that the room smelled like an unwashed skunk.

"I didn't know you were in here," Lily said. She'd assumed they were both out on one of their many unsanctioned breaks, getting up to whatever it was that druggies and shoplifters got up to.

"Problem?" Adi asked, cocking an eyebrow.

"Oh, nothing," she answered, forcing a smile. "Just a customer being a customer."

Lily threw in a laugh, a trilling little giggle, for good measure, even as she heard the customer faintly swearing, still, on the other side of the door. Threatening Lily and her extended family in increasingly strange and zoologically impossible ways. He reminded her of Danny DeVito—short, bald, and quick to anger, wearing a rumpled and ill-fitting suit—only without the humor and the eventual heart of gold.

She never would have figured that people could be such raging b-holes during a Going Out of Business sale. And at Leonard's Laffs, no less. This place was a novelty store that had barely changed since the 1950s, the cheaper, less-funny cousin of Spencer's Gifts. Even *Lily* thought it was too tame sometimes.

But then she was still new, to Leonard's and the mall and New Jersey, and to being employed more generally. She'd been hired for the summer two days before they found out the store was closing. The Great Recession had finally caught up to Brookwillow—first the town and then the eponymous mall. The last two weeks had felt like ghost towns must have started, a silver mine drying up and every corporate headquarters at once realizing there was no reason to be there anymore.

The customer pounded against the door, sending Lily jumping.

"You in there, girlie?" His voice was muffled, but only barely. He must have been behind the counter, pressing his face against the door, shouting directly into the metal. "You think you can hide? You can't hide from me!" He pounded the door again. "I'm not leaving until you replace that Federal Booty Investigator glass I dropped getting into my car! That's on you! Whoever heard of glass breaking just 'cause a person dropped it? And then backed over it a little. This is your fault, honey!"

"Sounds like more than your regular, run-of-the-mill customer," Bern said.

"Yeah, I guess," Lily replied, unconsciously inserting herself between her coworkers. Putting distance and bodies between her and the customer thundering his meaty fists against the door. Then the smile again. "You would know! I'm sure he's just having a bad afternoon. Which one of you is pretending to be manager today?"

Technically, the Leonard's only had one supervisor, but Maria was stretched thin working overnights, counting inventory and closing up shop, figuring out what could be liquidated and where. Bern and Adi, by virtue of having been here since the 1990s, had been temporarily promoted. Even though Lily was pretty sure neither one of them had *ever* tucked in their polos the way they were supposed to.

"Rock, paper, scissors?" Adi asked.

"Honestly," Bern said, "this seems like it might be a job for the Intercessor."

"The Inter—you really think she's still around?"

"I mean, we are, right? She has to be."

"And you think Cindy Lou Who here is ready?"

"Everyone is sooner or later."

"What are you—" Lily started. "The mall has an intercessor? A prayer warrior?"

"Not like you're thinking," Adi said. "Less Christian, more capitalist."

"Consider her a customer relations specialist," Bern said.

"But only"—Adi shot Bern a look—"for the most *special* of cases."

Lily opened the door again. The customer had his back to them, was standing atop the laminate counter gesticulating wildly and inappropriately as he spoke, like the world's worst mime.

"—take *that* horse's head and stuff it up a giraffe's assho—"

"I'd like to think this qualifies," Lily said.

↑ ↓

The customer followed Lily through the mall like an obedient puppy, smiling and satisfied, rear end waggling, his world only as big as the five feet around him. The only possible future one that involved treats and belly rubs. Because here he was, *finally*, getting the attention and treatment he so rightly deserved. His complaint was being registered not only with a manager, but a manager, a *specialist*, of the *whole mall*. Lily was pretty sure she'd never been as happy as this toot-l-er was right now, and her parents had surprised her with a birthday party at Disney World once.

Of course, Lily wasn't so naïve as to forget that even good dogs could bite—and this customer certainly wasn't a *good* dog. There was no way that someone as entitled as this rampaging s-head wasn't eventually going to figure out they were lost.

Lily sighed. Lost in a mall. This was *exactly* what her parents had worried would happen when she started working here. The malls up north were so much bigger than the ones back home—and Brookwillow, especially, was *sprawling*, with floors and floors and floors, a carousel, a parking garage, an entire Rainforest Café! She would have loved to have seen it in its heyday, before all the shuttered storefronts and 70% Off signs. Would have loved to have shopped here, in this monument to money, just once—to have been able to take her time and take a seat and eat a pretzel and buy something nice and be a customer herself, be the one in charge *just once*, instead of always rushing through the east entrance, the closest door to the Leonard's, and then spending the next eight hours on her feet getting blamed for *everything*.

She'd probably get blamed for this, too, even though half the directions Bern had given her were for stores that weren't here anymore. Strangely, though, it wasn't the ones she would have *expected* to be closed that were closed. In fact . . .

Lily must have had some sense, subconsciously, that something was off, but, rushing to the railing and looking around now, she confirmed it: *only* the wrong stores were still open. Sam Goody. RadioShack. K.B. Toys. Kinney Shoes. No-name independents like Leonard's. The Borders was still holding up an entire wing. She was pretty sure she'd read an article saying the whole chain had gone bankrupt. Gimbels had been out of business since before Lily was born. But there it was, at the end of the corridor, clean and bright as it was in 1965.

Something about that creeped her out, even if she couldn't quite explain why.

The customer cleared his throat.

"We taking the scenic route or something?" he asked.

He was behind Lily, too close, practically leaning into her. She could feel the heat of him, the thick sweat of his aura; he smelled like salami. He wasn't touching her, but her skin crawled, reacted to each word as if it were a finger walking up her back.

"And here I am," he said, "without a camera."

Lily swallowed back bile. Each passing moment would only make things worse, she knew. She didn't like being this close to him, being alone with him, even if Bern and Adi had said she'd be fine. And she *really* didn't want to be on the receiving end of whatever rage—or whatever else—this d-bag had been saving up for the last ten minutes.

That's when Lily saw Erin Morgan stepping out from the Suncoast Motion Picture Company, a six-foot *Avatar* standee tucked clumsily under her arm. Lily had transferred to Brookwillow High pretty late in the year, hadn't made a lot of friends, but Erin, at least, despite being one of the popular kids, some kind of field hockey star, had always been nice to her.

"Hey, Erin!" she called, extricating herself from the customer and the railing. She started waving wildly, practically running toward the other girl.

"Oh, hey ... Lily, right?" Erin let the giant, blue, cardboard cat-man fall against the window, turning her full attention to Lily. Her black polo, at least a size too big, hung loose; her hair was braided into a messy crown. A knowing smirk pulled her lips sideways. "Brookwillow Mall finally got her claws in you too?"

"Can you help me? I'm looking for the, uh ... the Intercessor."

Lily winced as soon as she finished the sentence. Saying it out loud now, she realized how ridiculous the whole thing sounded. Customer service for *all* the stores? How would that even work? How would all the parent companies agree to terms? Bern and Adi were messing with her, they had to be. Taking advantage of the fact that they were in charge and that meant Lily had to trust them.

"I'm sorry," she said, shaking her head and smiling, "I, uh—I think this has been—"

She stopped. Erin's demeanor had dropped an octave.

"You're really doing it?" She nodded to the customer standing behind Lily. "This guy must be a monolithic dick to have pissed off Miss Southern Hospitality. The Intercessor is gonna have a field day with him." Erin's eyes flashed, something wild. "I didn't think you had it in you."

"What are you talking about?" Lily asked.

"You always seemed to straightlaced at school, so fragile, like a porcelain doll or something, like you might fall apart at any moment"—she leaned closer—"but I guess maybe you're a real girl after all."

"What? Of course I'm real. I don't—and soft is good, Erin. Kittens are soft, teddy bears are soft. Soft isn't a bad thing, I don't know why everyone—" Lily paused, took a deep breath, and reset herself. Straightened her meticulously tucked polo and smiled so hard her face hurt from the effort. "Can you, please, tell me where I can find the mall's Intercessor? I have a gentleman that needs to file a complaint."

"Uh, OK, sure." Erin pointed a thumb to her right. "Second fire door past the Waldenbooks." She paused for a moment, her face pinched in confusion. Then: "Word of advice, Lily? Make sure you're outside the splash zone. No one ever tells the new initiates that, it's like a hazing thing, but it's kind of a shit move if you ask me."

"Initiates? What do you mean, init—"

Inside the Suncoast, an entire display of *Star Trek* DVDs fell to the ground, the wire rack and the shrink-wrapped movies and the cardboard spaceship toppling and spilling and crunching at once. Both mall workers turned toward the sound, moving entirely on instinct. A customer near the display looked up, briefly locked eyes with them, and then began whistling, walking away quickly, deeper into the store.

"Son of a shitting bitch," Erin mumbled. She started back into the Suncoast, jogging as she got closer to the spilled DVDs and shouting toward her wayward customer. "Hey! I saw you! Help me pick this up, asshole!"

Lily's customer, meanwhile, was ready to start shouting, too.

"Hey," he roared from somewhere behind her, "if you two are done syncing your cycles, I got places to be and managers to talk to. Mall managers. The kinds of managers who can *fire* bubble-headed bimbos like you. So let's fuckin' go, all right?"

Lily closed her eyes and took another breath, tamping down the revulsion and anger.

"Of course, sir," she said, turning and smiling once more, "if you'll follow me."

The hallway behind the Employees Only door was darker than Lily had been expecting, poorly lit, the industrial gray of the mall easing into a dense midnight black. The stale air was suffused with cold and damp, worsening with each new step. The floor inclining slowly, subtly, down and down and down, a constant curve like a spiral staircase.

She was heading toward a basement.

Erin's word—*initiate*—repeated in Lily's head. She couldn't think of a single instance where that would possibly be a good thing. And coupled with *intercessor*? Even in her increasingly evangelical church, intercessors—people who prayed on behalf of everyone, for the sake of everything—were looked at as fanatical. She could only imagine what that meant here, for heathens in a half-dead mall. She'd never actually seen *Eyes Wide Shut*, but she assumed it would be something like that. Visions of pentagrams and candles and cloaked men in impeccable business suits flashed through her brain.

"—and she says, 'What are you doin' with that pickle?' and so he says—"

But then, getting murdered might actually be preferable to having to spend another f-ing second with this mother-f-ing customer.

An exit sign crackled to life in the dark, the outline of a fire door illuminated in the faint red glow. Lily rushed forward, then slowly, cautiously, she pushed open the door. Brilliant light flooded inward. Squinting and angling her head sideways, she lifted an arm to keep from being blinded and looked to the other side.

Lily was on the roof.

"Son of a—" the customer grumbled behind her. "What the hell are you up to, honey? This ain't no manager's office. This ain't no *anything*." He laughed, hard and derisive. "Did you get lost in the mall? I thought you ladies were supposed to have a sixth sense for shopping, the g-spot or whatever."

"Would you please shut up?"

"What's with the tone? This is *America*, girlie, and I can say whatever—"

Lily tuned him out.

Warped and dirty white polyvinyl tiling stretched along the length of the mall, from the fire door to the glass atrium to the parking garage beyond. An expanse of grungy nothing, spotted with vents and air-conditioning units—and what appeared to be an enormous pile of garbage, not more than twenty feet in front of Lily. The stench was awful, visceral, like vomit and old meat left rotting in the sun.

So this was a prank, after all, and Erin was in on it, too.

"Lily," she said to herself, "you really need to—"

She stopped.

Because the garbage pile wasn't a garbage pile.

Because the garbage pile was *moving*.

As Lily's eyes settled into the glare, as the shock of white light tapered into something more manageable, she realized she was looking at an animal, a creature, roosting atop the roof of the mall. An impossible creature. A monster.

A titanic, winged pig-thing sitting in a nest of its own filth.

The beast was the size of an upturned shuttle bus, bigger once, bloated once, but deflated now. Skin of rough and sun-bleached leather draping down, dragging across the rooftop like deflated hot air balloons. Wiry fur covered the thing's boar-like face, its six small eyes, its long snout. A dozen tusks jutted from and around its mouth, rising through half-rotted flesh. There were no arms, no appendages that Lily could see, but there was a seam along the thing's belly, more teeth—a second mouth. Everything beneath was lost in a knitted nidus of sticks and trash and shreds of fabric, blood and shit dripping through and staining the roof below.

Then Lily saw the bones, the skeletons hidden within the detritus.

"What the fuck is that?!" the customer shouted, rushing up to Lily's side and pointing past her, angling himself half behind her, using the girl in the green polo as a shield. "What am I even looking at? Why the fuck would you show a guy something like that?!"

Fear, and a complete and utter inability to process what she was looking at, paralyzed Lily. This was a monster, it had to be, but monsters weren't real. But this was—and this one—were Bern and Adi trying to—to *kill* her? Because she complained? Asked for help? Because she couldn't handle one shitty customer.

"Say hello to the Intercessor." Lily turned; Erin was marching her customer through the black hallway, his hands tied behind his back. "Or, as I like to call her," she continued, stepping beside Lily, "the Queen of the Mall. She may technically be an intermediary, but she's also judge, jury, and executioner, all in one."

Erin shoved her customer forward, toward the monster. Before anyone except Erin realized what was happening, thorned tendrils shot out from the nest of filth and bones and attached themselves to the display-dropper, gouging his skin, wrapping themselves tight. Before Lily could so much as blink, the tendrils retracted; the man's clothing, his skin, were ripped away. And then, before the flayed customer could scream, before the agony of a million raw nerve endings could even be felt, the monster's second mouth opened, a tongue erupted, and the man was pulled inside. The porcine stomach rumbled and undulated; bones crunched; blood seeped from the thing's haggard teeth.

"That should buy the Suncoast another couple months," Erin mumbled.

Lily spun to face her. "What did you just—"

"What? Isn't that what you came up here to do?"

"Kill a guy?! I'm not killing a guy."

"It's not—"

"It's murder," Lily said. "It's g-d *murder. You literally just murdered a guy.*" She gestured to the ground, her hands wild with adrenaline. Pointed with all her fingers to the deeply stained spot where the customer had, only moments before, been standing. "His *shucked skin* is *right there.*"

"The hawks will take care of that," Bern said, appearing and approaching from behind the monster. "There's a state park not too far from here; they love it." He paused at the hog-beast's side and began petting the folds of its fetid flesh. "And, for the record, Erin's right: this isn't murder. It's a ritual sacrifice to the corporeal incarnation of an eldritch chaos god. Completely different."

"Think of it," Erin said, "like feeding a mouse to a snake."

"Mouses aren't *people*," Lily countered.

"Neither are customers."

Lily turned back to Bern, to the monster, furrowing her brow.

"An eldritch chaos god controls . . . *retail*."

He shrugged. "Why else do you think money was invented?"

"How did you—"

"There's a ladder in the back of the back room. Straight shot to the roof." He nodded toward the customer kneeling and gibbering at Lily's side. "Very difficult to convince a customer to climb it, though. Ladders don't have the same cachet as a secret office."

Lily, shaking her head small, looked around again, hoping to see something that would help this make sense: a camera, a special effects team, Ashton Kutcher, *something*. Instead, she saw the bloodied husk of a varsity jacket crumpled against an HVAC unit, remembered a particularly unpleasant girl from her first day, causing a scene outside the Leonard's.

Bern saw her looking at it.

"Difficult," he repeated, "but not *impossible*."

"I thought—I thought she left. You told me you took care of her."

He shrugged again. "I did."

A sharp tug of her pant leg jolted Lily's attention to the customer at her feet.

"Please don't kill me," he blubbered, tears and snot blanketing the bottom of his face. "I'll go down on you. I'm really good, I swear. My wife's always saying at least my big mouth is good for something. Or, what, you a lesbo? I'll—I don't know, put on a wig or something. Tell me what you what me to do to you and I—"

"Oh my God," Lily said, kicking him off. "That's gross. You're gross."

"Hey, if that's what you want, that's what I'll—"

"Shut up!"

"You really want to make a moral stand about *this* fuckwit?" Erin asked.

"I mean . . ." The first inklings of doubt fluttered through Lily. "He's got a wife? That's got to mean something, right?"

"You're coming at this all wrong," Bern said, approaching Lily and Erin, penning the customer in. "This isn't about *him*; it's about the thousands of jerk-offs like him. And this isn't about *you*; it's about all of us. About making sure we have somewhere to go. A job that never looks too closely, that lets you take three-hour lunches. Where you can get promoted despite literally never stepping into the store while sober."

"This mall?" Erin added. "This is the one place where *we* get to be in charge. The one place where hourly wage monkeys like us are *respected*, or fucking else. You've pretty obviously never worked before, so maybe you don't get it, but something like that, like real autonomy? That's absolutely worth killing for."

"So the Suncoast," Lily started, "and the Borders, and all the others, the stores that are supposed to be closed, they're still here because—"

"Because corporate oversight is the real evil," Bern said. "Because even an extradimensional hog-monster is powerless in the face of a billion-dollar international conglomerate." He smiled sideways. "There's a million ways to kill a person, Lily, and the Intercessor is far from the worst of them."

"And Leonard's? Is it really closing?"

"You do this, take care of him"—he tapped the customer with his sneaker—"and everything'll be fine. It always is."

"How many—"

"Don't worry about it," Erin said. She put her hands on the customer's shoulders. "Let's focus on this guy first. There's only so many hard truths a person can swallow at once."

"Swallow," the customer repeated, giggling in between snotty sobs.

"I'm not like you," Lily said, ignoring him.

"Aren't you, though?" Erin replied. "You don't have to hide anymore, Lily. I've seen the cracks, the hint of the real you underneath. The way you looked at me in school, here, in the food court. The awe—and the envy. I don't know if it's your church or your parents or being from South Carolina or all of the above, but you're free here. You can be your own person here. The real you."

"I can't—I can't *kill* a guy. Even if he is an a-faced clown-h-er."

"He's a *customer*," Erin said, "not a guy."

"And you're not killing him." Bern pointed a thumb over his shoulder. "She is."

"You're just . . . not stopping her."

Lily didn't reply then, didn't do much of anything at all. But nothing was enough. Erin and Bern looked at one another, exchanging some kind of secret glance, then grabbed the customer by each of his armpits, hefting the gibbering load to his feet. Dragging him, kicking and screaming, to the red stain on the roof.

Dragging him directly in front of Lily.

She didn't remember moving here, situating herself just so in front of the monster, in front of her bloodstained altar. She didn't even know if *she'd* done it, or if it was Erin and Bern, or maybe the Intercessor herself. But in that moment, she didn't care.

For once, Lily was going to stop thinking, stop dreaming, stop hiding. Stop forcing herself to be someone else, some stranger, the good girl everyone thought she should be. The girl she thought she *had* to be. Instead, she let herself feel—everything. Horror and fear and outrage—and anger.

Fury rose up within her, bubbling over like a pot forgotten. She was mad at everything, at the world. She was mad at having to leave home. She was mad about having to work. She was mad at the customer. She was mad at herself for trusting the customer. For looking for a bright side. For forcing herself to treat him like anyone else, even when she knew—she *knew*—he was a dickfaced chucklefuck. A festering abscess on the gaping asshole of the world. A rancid pile of meat and maggots and meanness in the vague shape of a man. Some sad and greasy Danny DeVito-looking motherfucker in a shitty suit, and with a shitty combover, too.

The rooftop rumbled. The Intercessor grumbled and grinned, twin tongues lolling from twin mouths. Bern and Erin stepped away, leaving the customer standing. He didn't run. There was no fight left in him anymore.

"Please," he mumbled, "please, please, please—"

Lily's hands were on his chest. She could feel his fear, the thunder of his heart.

She smiled, for the last time, for the first.

And then, eyes wide open, she pushed.

this place belongs to us

wendy dalrymple

Soft light spilled through the mold-speckled glass atrium ceiling on that humid Tuesday morning, illuminating the once grand food court of the Metro Mall. Stefani Myles ventured into the long-forgotten space and clutched her purse to her side, her pulse sloshing in her ears as a layer of grime and dry oak leaves crunched beneath her feet. The velociraptor scene from *Jurassic Park* came to mind as she eased around a table and overturned chairs in the cafeteria where she used to eat nachos with her friends. Stefani covered her nose and gagged as she passed the bathrooms and continued on down the dimly lit corridor. She could deal with debris and the dark, but the smell of mold and years of stagnant sewer water was almost unbearable.

Always and forever.

The words echoed in her memory, a long ago promise from someone she loved. A promise they couldn't keep, even if they wanted to. Those were the last words that he said to her, right in this very food court all those years ago. Back in a time when things were magic and when she still felt like herself. When there wasn't so much pain.

Stefani should not have been at the Metro Mall that morning—in fact, no one should have. The mall had been closed for over a decade since Hurricane Lorraine swept through town, ripping off half the roof and flooding the west wing. The owners took the insurance money and ran, of course, leaving the sprawling shopping center to be reclaimed by the swamplands that surrounded it. The building was a hazard and should have been razed long ago, yet it still stood in ruins, inhabited only by vermin and the occasional unhoused person.

After all this time and for reasons unknown to her, Stefani had returned to the place that still tugged at the softest, most nostalgic and secret parts of her heart. She wasn't sure how she even got there. Much of her everyday life had become a blur of caring for everyone else's needs but her own. She dropped off her youngest child at school that morning and found herself driving aimlessly toward the abandoned building as though on autopilot. Something called to her from deep within the dank guts of the decrepit mall, and it was a call she couldn't help but answer. Maybe she was running away from her life and responsibilities, or maybe the mask she always struggled to keep on straight was slowly slipping. She should have been happy with her nice house, her nice family, and her comfortable life. No one wanted to hear that none of it gave her pleasure or security in the way that it should have. No one would have cared. Stefani felt as though she was disappearing, and she only had herself and her memories to hold onto.

Breaking into the mall had been easy enough. Police had long ago stopped trying to keep people from living there, though now she suspected the rat population kept humans out more than anything. As she approached the entrance that day, Stefani carefully walked over broken boards and garbage to visit the mall for the first time in over a decade. The glass door leading to the food court was cracked, but with a little bit of work, opened easily enough to allow entry.

She didn't know what to expect upon seeing the place that used to give her so much comfort and joy now reduced to rubble and decay. The signage along the walls and various overturned kiosks featured outdated art, products that no longer existed, and ads for movies that were now free to watch on all the streaming platforms. Dirty toys, sneakers, and clothes streamed from every busted-out storefront, the remnants of looters from long ago. There was nothing much left of value at the mall these days, only danger in the form of tetanus, bacterial infections, or violence.

The further Stefani ventured into the mall, the more still and stale the air became. Even though it was October, the tropical climate caused the interior to steam like a sauna as moisture and heat pressed on her from all sides. She pulled out her phone and flipped on the flashlight, putting one foot in front of the other as long-forgotten memories bubbled to the surface. She recalled Christmastime and taking her eldest child to see Santa when he was a baby as she passed what used to be an open sitting area. To her left was the imitation jewelry store where she first got her ears pierced as a girl. To her right, the candle store where she saved her coupons to snag giant pumpkin- and cinnamon-scented candles for fifty percent off. The mall had been a haven for her during the hottest parts of the year when she was a new mother with an infant and had nowhere else to go. It was also a haven for her as a teen for the same reasons, and the place where she met Matt all those years ago.

Matt Lipnicki was all teeth and hair and big round eyes. He wasn't her first love, or her last, but he was the one who left the biggest hole in her heart all the same. Skinny as he was lanky, Matt caught her eye when she was fifteen and she still saw the world in high def. Everything was bright and new back then, a widescreen cinematic world in Dolby surround sound, and that summer, Matt Lipnicki was the star of it all. Their first kiss by the fountain tasted like salty pretzels and cherry soda. They held hands and threw pennies into that fountain and made wishes neither of them could make come true. Stefani met him at the mall almost every day that summer, taking the bus from her parents' house just to see him. They spent hours together flipping through CDs at the music store, trying on clothes, and running from the security guards. Her time with Matt at the mall had been fleeting, but had made her feel alive in a way that she hadn't been able to recapture since. As she ventured further and further into the abandoned mall, it became more and more clear to her why she was there in the first place.

Stef, watch this.

Stefani smiled and closed her eyes as Matt's voice echoed through her mind. He was there again with her dressed in an oversized black band shirt and equally baggy jeans that swallowed his slight frame. With a skateboard in one hand and a devilish grin set on his lips, he fell into a light jog toward the fountain and performed a perfect kick flip and grind against the ledge. They both ran from the security guard that day until they were out of breath, finally hiding in the cool, dark safety of the movie theater.

The earth seemed to shift under her feet as she opened her eyes. In a flash, the Metro Mall was alive again, restored to its previous glorious state. The grime-covered ceiling and walls were bright and clean just as they had always been before the storm damage. People milled about with their shopping bags and baby strollers, moving in and out of stores that were also once more filled with product and life. The still, stuffy silence was replaced by the air-conditioned hum of the crowd, footsteps on tile, and laughter between friends.

Stefani was transformed too. She glanced down at her hands, surprised to find her nails painted blue with silver rings adorning each finger. She was also dressed differently, her yoga pants and tee replaced by ripped jeans and a crop top. Even her hair had changed, cascading over her shoulder in the long, sun-bleached locks she had proudly brushed out every day in high school.

"Hey."

A gasp stuck in her throat as she glanced up at the familiar voice. Twenty-five years later and she would still know him anywhere. Matt Lipnicki stood before her with his sideways smile as though time had never passed.

"It's you," she said.

"Who else would it be?" He chuckled, holding out his hand. "Come on. There's something I want to show you."

Stefani took his hand in hers, the calluses on his palms rough and real as the last time they touched. He squeezed her hand, his skin warm and reassuring as he led her down the hall of the rejuvenated mall. They walked past all of their old haunts hand-in-hand, just like they did every day that summer, passing the novelty gift shop, the music store, the book store, the pretzel stand, and the movie theater. She continued to follow his lead as fewer people passed them, until finally it was just her and Matt once more.

"Hey, wait," she said, tugging at his hand. "What's going on?"

He turned to her, his forehead scrunched in confusion. "What do you mean?"

"Why are you here?" She asked. "This is . . . this is all wrong."

"You called me," he said, bringing a hand to her cheek. "I thought we were gonna hang out?"

Sparkles of adrenaline flooded her veins. He leaned in and planted a soft kiss on her lips and nostalgia drowned every last rational thought in her brain. Yes. Maybe she did call him. Maybe this was what she had really wanted all along. She leaned into his kiss, remembering the past, remembering the way that it used to feel to be with him. Then one day his skateboard shot out onto US-41 and a semi truck ended all of their Cherry Coke kisses and mall dates forever.

She pulled away from him, breathless and drunk on the moment.

"I'm . . . I'm old now," she said, pushing him away gently. "I shouldn't be here."

"Whaddaya mean?" He smiled. "You look the same to me."

"You're not real." Stefani frowned, the words breaking her heart. "I wish you were, but you aren't."

"I'm as real as you want me to be," he said, brushing a lock of hair behind her ear. "Don't worry so much. We're together now."

"I'm so unhappy," she said. "Sometimes when I'm having a bad day, I just close my eyes and come back here to be with you."

"I know. I like it when you do that," he said. "Hey, did you know they built an indoor pool here?"

"What?" She let out a laugh. A stray tear trickled down her cheek.

"Yeah, that's what I wanted to show you," he said. "It's right this way."

Stefani laughed again as he led her further and further down the empty, dark hall. She forgot all about her family and her responsibilities back home as her sneakers filled with water, the ground splashing beneath her feet.

"Wooo!" Matt whooped, his voice echoing through the dark. "Looks like we have the place all to ourselves!"

She laughed as he pulled her even further, the water pooling up around her knees now. A sulfurous smell filled her nose but she ignored it as he wound his hand around her waist and pulled her deeper into the water. His hazel eyes were dark and endless as he kissed her again, the water up to her ribcage now. She was dizzy and lightheaded as he pulled her further into his embrace.

"What would things have been like if you hadn't died?" she asked, holding him to her as the water hit her collarbone.

"Probably pretty rad," he said and placed a kiss on her forehead. "I know a way that we can find out."

"How?"

"Down there," he said, gazing into the black pool of water. "I want you to see."

"I'm scared."

"Trust me," he said. "Every day can be summer again. This place belongs to us."

Stefani bit her lip and nodded.

Matt smiled at her with long, sharp teeth.

He squeezed her hand tight and pulled her beneath the surface.

Her nose and mouth and lungs filled with stagnant swamp water as he pulled her down, down, down. Everything hurt and then nothing hurt.

And then, she opened her eyes.

And the mall was theirs again.

Always and forever.

how my self finds me

avra margariti

Later, when I would try to identify the exact moment of detachment, I'd always return to that day in the mall when my parents almost left me behind.

That was the moment I ceased to be me in my entirety. When I was split. One part of me returning to the home I'd known all my life. The other—the wild-kid part, the bad-kid part—staying forever abandoned.

I was six and holding my parents' hands—until I wasn't. Did they let go first, or did I? I remember whirling around, a lump in my throat, a chant of lostlostlost resounding in my ears. The lights were too bright, the people too boisterous. They towered over me, like fairytale ogres wanting to devour me.

I ran in dizzy circles until I spotted my parents. Then, I rushed toward them while they were about to pass through the automatic doors and disappear into the world outside. Panic made pulp out of my heart. Later, I would realize that my parents had only been pretending to leave. I had been throwing tantrum after tantrum during our start-of-elementary-school shopping spree. I wanted boy-clothes instead of the nice dresses my mother had picked out for me. This was my parents' way of scaring me into conformity: making me think I would be abandoned, swept away like trash, left with the lost and found if I didn't learn to behave like a good little girl.

When I reached my parents at the automatic doors, I hugged them rubber-band-tight around their torsos. I swallowed my tears and promised to be good, so good, even when I felt the lancing pain through my sternum. The split.

My parents hurried me along toward the parking lot. Yet, just as the mall doors slid shut, I turned back. I stared into the eyes of my child-self, abandoned by the out-of-order fountain. Burning incandescent with betrayal.

↑ ↓

I grow up, avoiding the mall for some time. I cannot explain this acrid anxiety thrumming through my system whenever my parents mention going to the stores, asking if I want to join them, if I need anything.

I say no. Obedient children need for nothing. I keep my head down, focus on my schoolwork and getting the best grades I can. It is how I acquire my new names: gifted child; precocious. I teach myself how to be good. No price is too high, including wearing the glittery pink dresses my mother brings back from her shopping trips. The dresses I once refused to wear, back when I was someone who was easily forgotten. Easily forsaken.

Eventually, I have no choice but to go back.

A preteen who avoids the mall is someone who cannot maintain any friendships. A friendless hermit is nobody's dream child. An unwanted child is, well—

My school friends, all girls, want to go shopping. We see the glossy magazine pages, the gigantic billboard ads. Opalescent nail polishes and frilly blouses. Colorful hair ties and pleated tennis skirts. Laughing girls, luminous girls, on every screen and poster.

When I am invited, I have no choice but to say yes. Girls who say no become outcasts. Outcasts become abandoned. And that will never be me again.

Yet, among the garish clothing racks, flocks of shoppers, and artificial grape air-freshener, I see myself. Not a reflection of my current image, so carefully poised and put together.

I see myself the way I once was. The old incarnation of me I left behind.

This child-self is dirty, bedraggled, androgynous. Not a she but an it—the vermin my parents wanted excised from the family photos. I am better now. I do things right. I am no longer unwanted.

But this child is.

And like all wild, forgotten things, the child goes unseen by the busy shoppers of the bustling department store. The shoppers evade the child's trajectory, maneuvering around it like a black hole they must instinctively avoid. Nobody asks the child if it's lost, if it needs help getting back to its people, its home.

I try to ignore the child, who squats in a pair of dirty overalls and a stained white tee, munching on fries picked up off the sticky floor. This child-self is like an animal. Like a thing I cannot bear to look at headlong.

So I follow my girlfriends deeper through the store, as they laugh and chat, popping pink bubblegum from pretty, lip-glossed mouths. I avoid looking at the clothes the disobedient part of me still craves: the loose cargo pants and baggy shirts from the men's section. I ignore the bra models and underwear mannequins too, worried that, if I'm caught staring, my friends will know about the magazines of half-naked women I hide in my room.

"Anna, are you coming?" my friend Katerina asks me, rifling through a basket of dangling phone accessories.

"Be right there," I reply, though the truth is, Katerina is another of those things I cannot look at head-on. Because, lately, my hand has been lingering in hers for too long. I have been sniffing her shampoo suffused through my pillowcase after she's spent hours sprawled out in my bed doing homework.

There are so many things to avoid in order to be good. But I've learned my lesson well. I will not be caught slipping.

At the sound of my name, the child tilts its head to the side like a filthy, curious owl. Not in acceptance of the name, but as though recognizing a word the child might have once heard in a dream. It follows me through the department store. The child carelessly bangs on sunglasses displays, while the employees rush to still the teetering piles of merchandise. Yet no one seems to spot the diminutive troublemaker weaving underfoot.

"What're you looking at?" Mikaela asks. She is the founder of our clique. The rich girl, the pretty girl. (The girl who once kissed me in the school bathroom, then said if I told anyone, she would make sure I would regret it.)

Before I can reply, Mikaela screams.

"What the hell?" She looks down at her leg, bare under her denim skirt, where my child-self has bitten her shin hard enough to draw blood. Its teeth take a chunk of meat from Mikaela when her kick shakes the child off. The child plays with the gobbet of flesh like a dog with a bone.

It's a real dog that gets blamed afterward. One of the little Pomeranians rich ladies bring to the mall. Mikaela's parents drive her to the hospital for antibiotics. Katerina clings onto me, her hand clammy with fear. And despite everything, I hug her back, savoring her touch. Forgetting, just for a second, my hidden shame.

I cannot forget it for long.

We keep coming back to the mall, only now without Mikaela, who declares the whole place haunted. There's nothing else to do in our suburb, no place the other girls' parents will let them visit unsupervised. My own parents have no opinions on the subject. A part of me wonders whether they'd be relieved if I never returned home after an outing. No matter how I've tried to mold and diminish myself, I am still not good enough.

Not the daughter anyone would ever want.

My child-self is there, every time I return. It takes to shadowing me throughout the mall. Laughing madly and shoving leftover food into its face whenever I discreetly try to calculate the calories of my skinny milkshake and plain burger. Sometimes it throws food at me. When I don't take the offerings, the child tangles itself between my legs in an attempt to trip me up. Making its displeasure known with a cascade of grunts and taunts.

The child splashes in the fountain when I pass by with my friends. We're in high school now, so boys have joined our all-girls group. Katerina's boyfriend is tan and honey blond. He holds her around the waist, slips his hand into the back pocket of her skinny jeans. I always feel like I'm third-wheeling when I'm with them, even with our other friends present. The child does not wash itself in the fountain to clean the accumulation of grime, oil, and dust. It just tosses water about like a sad pigeon bathing in a city square.

The child mocks me. "I thought she was your girlfriend," it says, stretching out the last syllable. "Why does your girlfriend have a boyfriend who isn't you?" The child has a lisp from a perpetually split lip. It likes to repeat things, like a chant or a compulsion.

Once, I saw it bang its head against the floor, yelling, "wrong, wrong, wrong," until I ran into the nearest music store to pull some display headphones over my ears and drown out the sound. My personal goblin making mischief, my squalid ghost following me wherever I go. It cries and spits like an arterial spray. Steals things from the pockets of passers-by. Rips things apart in destructive rage. Screams the way of feral things.

I cover my ears, hissing, "go away."

The insults vary each time. One afternoon after school, the child spots me sneaking alone through the mall. While Katerina is getting a new ear piercing at the jewelry kiosk, I edge toward a men's clothing store. Run my fingers down the simple cotton fabric of a men's button-up in blue and green check. The child jumps out from behind a shelf, screaming "boo!" through half-missing, half-rotten teeth. When I startle into a yelp, it cackles like a diminutive banshee.

"Boy clothes," it sing-songs. "You want boy clothes? Do you know what happens to little girls who want boy clothes?"

I look at the child, and I know. I know. Little girls who want boy clothes turn into my former self's fragment. They plummet from grace, slipping through the cracks of the world—no one there to break their freefall.

I let go of the shirt like it's singed my fingertips. Yet the child is still not satisfied. It tries to pull me back as I leave, screaming, "Where are you going?" Screaming: "You can't leave me!"

I find Katerina in the jewelry kiosk, picking adornments for her new piercing.

"Are you OK?" she asks me, while her boyfriend rolls his eyes. He held her hand while the needle pierced through her earlobe. He is cranky now, complaining about needing carbs and sugars after spending an hour doing "girl stuff."

"Girl stuff, girl stuff," the child repeats over my shoulder, having followed me again like my despicable shadow.

"I'm fine," I say, because when people ask, they only expect a certain kind of answer, even when it's the farthest thing from the truth.

I'm here with my school friends, but I'm also walking on eggshells. My parents made sure I knew from a young age just how conditional everyone's acceptance really is.

This time, when the child tries to follow me outside the jewelry kiosk, I spin a hoop earrings display, hitting my child-self in the face.

Howling in pain like a piglet being slaughtered, the child rubs its face in betrayal. Though it drops down on all fours and bares its teeth, it does not attack me. The child is angry, but more than that, it is hurt.

I walk away, and this time I do not look back.

I don't return to the shopping mall for a long time. I graduate from high school, then college, both with perfect grades. I go back to my suburb, marry a man my parents approve of, have a beautiful daughter. There is a moment of confusion in the delivery room, as if I was expecting a boy to come crying out of the blood of my belly, but that too is soon forgotten. I quit my office job, I enroll my daughter in preschool, I prepare to take care of my aging parents. By now I know how to perform everything that's expected of me. Yet I can't stop feeling like I'm walking through the world as a hollow husk. There is a part of me missing, and I know exactly where I left it.

I divorce, get a new job, I keep custody of my daughter. Tania is six and curious about the world and its wonders. Unlike me, she is still whole. We avoid the mall, but I take her to the farmer's market, where she wants to taste every fruit and flower. When I catch her being a nuisance to the market vendors, I remember my parents taking me to the mall, then pretending to leave me behind. All to teach me a lesson. For an eons-stretched second, I think about running away from my life, my daughter, her laughter turning to wails as she is left behind.

It's an intrusive thought that makes me want to scour my skin bloody in repentance.

While I grapple with memories and reveries, Tania has wandered to the florist stall. In her overalls and spiky short hair, she looks more boy than girl. She looks just like I did her age. It's why her father broke up with me. He said I turned our daughter strange, like I was. I shake my head to dislodge the last of my thorny thoughts, then follow Tania across the market, where the stall vendor has arranged a cornucopia of floral bouquets.

"Mom! They're so pretty," Tania says, pointing at the marigolds and pansies cradled in wax paper and twine.

I look up at the vendor, pierced and covered in variegated floral tattoos. "Yes," I agree. "They are."

↑ ↓

Milena sells flowers at the farmer's market and the mall kiosk during the day, then studies psychology by night.

"No one was made to be abandoned," they tell me between kisses, cuddled on my couch while Tania is asleep in her room. Milena's child psychology textbooks litter my coffee table.

I have had too much wine, spilled too much of my red-writhing guts. Yet I still can't bring myself to tell Milena about the feral child in the mall. Only about my last visit there as myself—my last memory before the split. "What about . . . Do you believe in the ghosts of our child selves haunting us into adulthood?"

Milena sighs, their fingers tapping over their tattoos in contemplation. Floriography. Ever since we started dating, I have learned the meaning behind every one of Milena's efflorescent tattoos. Regret. Anger. Self-forgiveness. They wear each flower—each word—with pride over the pale scars they once carved into their skin during their unquiet youth. "I believe that, to care for our current selves, we must heal our child-selves first."

But what if a child-self does not deserve any healing? I think about the feral child biting my old school friend Mikaela, wreaking havoc, screaming at the top of its tiny lungs in order to be noticed.

Milena kisses me again, but my mind is far in the distance, floating under too-bright fluorescent lights where the ghost of my flesh and my fear roams.

↑ ↓

"Tania?" I call out the car window, frantic, fevered with worry. "Tania, where are you?"

Our street is empty. The school called earlier to tell me my daughter is missing. She skipped class but didn't return home to me afterward. An older kid picked on her for her hair, her looks. The teacher on the phone didn't specify what the kid said, but I can imagine the razored words, the same ones that were thrown at me when I was her age. Words like broken glass wanting to cut and bleed. My parents no longer talk to me, so it's not her grandparents Tania might have visited. Her father, too, is out of town, always busy, only seeing her on holidays—and even then, barely looking at her head-on.

I drive around, my eyes scanning all the cafes and bookstores between home and school, but no sign of Tania. Then, I remember. It's Tuesday, which means Milena sells their pretty flower arrangements in the mall. If Tania didn't come home to me, she might have gone to the only other adult she trusts.

I drive to the mall for the first time in fifteen years. It looks smaller and shabbier than I remember, old stores closed, floors dulled with water stains, but still full of people and activity. I get the baffling urge to call my estranged parents, ask them: do you remember when you pretended to abandon me? Do you remember when you split me in two to teach me a lesson? But I doubt they would admit to it.

I dash through the mall and up the squeaky escalators, knowing Milena sets up her florist stall on the top floor, just past the food court.

How many times have I thought about coming here to visit my child-self, see if it's still around—still alive? Is it eating leftover fries and cold, stale pizza crusts? Is it sleeping by the floor's heat vents, or inside the expensive mattress shop, or curled up in the fake flower-beds like a flea-ridden kitten? What if I took hold of my self's hand and led me home? What if I chose me?

But no. I could not.

I am someone who gets abandoned. Someone who abandons myself.

I rush to the food court strewn with metal chairs and tables, following the fishhook pull behind my sternum. I need to find my daughter, save her from myself. I picture the feral child holding her down, bruising, choking, biting her body. My poor Tania acting as a surrogate for the child's rage harbored solely for me. Its long-overdue revenge. Yet when I reach the food court, the sight before me stops me dead in my tacks.

Tania and my child-self are together, sitting cross-legged on top of a table. The two of them share a height and build, with matching overalls hugging their skinny, scabby shins. My child-self presses a dirty-nailed finger into Tania's dimple. Giggling, Tania mirrors the motion. Then, she gently flicks the child's smudged nose.

All our years together, I have never caught it smiling. Caught them smiling, this genderless child-self of mine. Grimy, rash-afflicted, rat-nest-haired. Yet smiling as they share a secret joke with my—their—our offspring.

My birth-child and my child-self look perfectly alike under the stark fluorescent lights. When I squint, I cannot tell them apart.

I walk toward them, and with my eyes still squinted, I do not know who to hug.

So I hug them both.

Juice

ria hill

The man working the cell phone kiosk is watching me again.

I've been trying to ignore him since he got here, but I feel like every time I look up he's there, staring. I feel his gaze like a subtle crawling under my skin. I wish I could wash his glance off of my body as easily as I clean my hands of pulp and simple syrup after blending up a fresh drink.

I don't think I've ever seen him sell a phone. Not even a case. Our stand has been quiet, painfully so, for months now, but his kiosk may as well be closed. Only once have I seen him talking to someone else, but as soon as I peeked in his direction, his eyes were on me again.

He watched me over the customer's shoulder as she told him what she needed, smiling at me unsubtly until I made an excuse to step into the back.

↑ ↓

My manager has been pulling us aside nearly every day now to emphasize the importance of our commitment to the store. She squeezes my shoulder too tightly and tells me that we're a family here—and that when it comes to the success of our stand, the most important ingredient is our crew.

I just nod and smile as sweetly as I can and try not to feel the vibration on the back of my neck that means the cell phone man is watching me. Again. I know it must be lonely over there. At least here we have each other. Though my coworkers are dropping like flies, at least I have my manager. At least I have this countertop between me and the man at the cell phone kiosk.

I scrub the cutting surface again and don't meet his staring eyes.

Today, I see him up close for the first time.

My manager is on break when he walks up to the counter. He doesn't walk, he struts. His shoulders are too broad, his face the image of perfect symmetry. His grin feels like it has just been snipped free of its plastic casing and is feeling the stale food court air for the first time.

"Have you been working here long?" The nerve of the question takes my breath away, as if I didn't get here first, as if he hasn't been observing me every day since his arrival.

"A while," I say. "What can I get you?"

He doesn't look at the menu. "Classic."

I start to gather the ingredients. The classic blend consists of orange juice, ice, simple syrup, and a single scoop of that proprietary powder we stock in the back by the barrelful. Normally, I'd measure with my back to the customer, but the idea of turning my back on him even for a moment makes me feel queasy.

I assemble his drink as quickly as I can, pour the result into a cup, and set it on the counter near the register. He reaches into his pocket for a wallet.

"What do I owe you?"

I don't want to touch his money. I don't want to touch anything he's touched. He pulls out a twenty and holds his hand over the counter, but he's holding it folded in half and I don't think I can even take it without touching his skin.

"No charge."

His smile widens. It shouldn't be able to grow so wide.

"Thank you, beautiful." He winks and turns away. The slurping sound as he takes his first sip almost makes me hurl.

I know, I know, that I said the exact wrong thing.

Quince has been clutching her stomach all afternoon, and when six rolls around she's really starting to look green around the gills.

We close at seven, and I'm a soft touch. When she finally looks up at me, lip quivering and eyes wet, to say she doesn't think she can close tonight, I tell her I won't tell our manager. I tell her I can close myself.

"Clementine, I love you."

I can see the man standing at the cell phone kiosk, watching me in complete stillness, and I know I've made the wrong decision.

↑ ↓

When Quince is gone, the man arrives. I don't see his approach, he's just there.

"Clementine, huh?" he says. The question in his voice feels manufactured and I wonder how long he's been saving my name. "I knew you were sweet."

I don't dignify that. "What can I get you?"

The cluck of his tongue is sharp, more a snap than a click. I have never seen the food court so empty.

"Coy coy, juice girl." His head tilts by a few degrees, then a few more. "You know this place is dead, don't you?"

I decide right then that there are worse things than turning my back on this man. I can't talk to him. I can't look at him for one more second or my head will burst.

I face the back wall and scrub the counter. The sponge is rough and netted. We're supposed to throw them out at the end of the day, but I've been using this one for nearly two weeks. It's a colorful, sticky mess by now, but it hardly seems worth the waste with how few customers we have these days. The counter is spotless, but I scrub it anyway.

The cell phone man's voice rings out, echoing in the near silence of the food court. "Don't you want to get out of here?"

I lean closer to the surface, looking for spots I might have missed. Over the high-pitched scrape of my ragged sponge, I can almost hear the music. Or at least, I think there's music playing here. Hasn't there always been music on the speakers?

"Don't you want to see what it's like outside?" he says. "Feel the air on your skin?"

I can feel goosebumps rising on my arms. I don't even want his words to touch my flesh. I wonder if he's ever felt a chill. I wonder if he even knows what it's like to feel vulnerable. Every time I see him, his face is locked in that same rictus, that same brutally carved smile.

The next time I hear his voice, it's an inch from my ear.

"You'll rot if you stay here."

My body pivots, whirls a hundred and eighty degrees faster than the blades in the industrial blender on my right as I spin to face him.

His smile is wider, if that's even possible, than I have ever seen it before.

His arm bends, his movements stiff and his elbow locking in place like the hinge on a 2005 flip phone. His palm is hard and cold where it presses against my cheek.

"Don't," I say.

His laugh is a chime. "I'd love to squeeze you for everything you've got."

My leg folds. I'm not sure I even told it to, but before I can think I've brought my knee up and into the spot where his legs meet.

There's a snap, a pop, a hiss. He doesn't scream. It's not like the movies. But his body does pitch to the side, like I broke something inside him. I'm afraid he's not the only thing I broke. My knee is screaming with a searing, splitting agony.

I don't look.

"You little—"

I can't think. I shove the sponge in his face, in his mouth, down his throat.

His arm is still raised, an awkward wave to a friend he's not sure has spotted him. In my years in this food court, I've seen the gesture a million times. Soapy, beige water spills down his chin. With each gagging cough, blue sparks leap from his mouth.

"Stop!" This time, I do scream. My hand is slick where I held the sponge. The floor is slippery too. I strike the side of his face, knocking his neck at an uncanny angle.

He holds the pose like a doll might, head cocked farther than humanly possible. A fresh wave of sparking ignites a small fire just under his chin. Somehow, he's still reaching for me.

The knife on the counter is meant only for oranges, strawberries, and the odd pineapple. To break the thickest skins, it's kept as sharp as our limited means allow.

When I force it in under his ribcage, it's like sticking a fork in an electrical socket.

I must have picked it up with the blade inverted, because when the current tightens every muscle in my body, the upward motion splits his flesh and slams me back against the stainless steel counter.

His chest cracks wide open, a maw of blood and chunks of meat and wires and circuitry I don't even attempt to comprehend. Near where his heart should have been, a small, flat bar of white plastic sits. Slowly, as the runoff from the sponge leaks down his throat and over the plastic strip, the color shifts from white to red. His movements shudder to a halt as if the water has rendered him static.

Where a man might fall to his knees, whatever this is topples like a telephone pole.

I limp back, away from him, toward the cordless phone on the wall and the chair that stands next to it. I need to sit down. My knee is in agony and my heart is in my throat. I lift the phone from its cradle, then collapse into the plastic seat.

When I look down at my lap, my white jeans are torn and stained with bright orange. I think I must have spilled a drink and coated myself in juice. Until I touch the wound with my fingertips and feel the unmistakable squish of citrus pulp beneath my broken skin.

kim, ray, trey, and morgan

christi nogle

The game was a terrible idea. One of them would go into a store and lift something, pass it off to the next one. If anyone seemed to have looked, they would pass it once or twice more, surreptitiously. Often the prize ended up with Morgan, who looked about thirty years old with her oversized mom glasses, her heels and shoulder pads and full face of makeup. She was the kind of person you'd need to be really sure about before you questioned them.

I saw them get tapes in Sam Goody this way. I saw them repeat the trick at Victoria's Secret (a lavishly embroidered lace push-up for Morgan), at Maurice's (gold-plated cross earrings for Ray), and at Woolworth's (this time a really expensive video game cartridge that Trey and Kim ended up fighting over until they lifted a second one from Shopko).

I never participated, convinced that my parents would not only maim me but entirely disown me. They were really moral people, so much so that when I contemplated anything bad, I imagined them at some future event, maybe a potluck:

"Do you have any children?" the couple opposite them at the picnic table ask.

"No, no, we *lost* our daughter."

Dad squeezes her hand and looks devastated.

Or Mom making dinner. The phone rings, and she wipes her hands with a tea towel before answering. It's me, begging to be bailed out of jail or something equally terrible. Sometimes I'm in trouble with the mob instead of in jail, but it's the same idea. I've done wrong; I need help.

"Please," I whine. "Please, I'm your only daughter."

Dad has lowered his newspaper, mouths *What is it now?*

"We don't . . . *have* a daughter," cries Mom. She slams down the receiver just as the tears break free.

I've watched too much TV, sure, but yeah, I don't even think these are exaggerations, not in my heart of hearts. And so I never was involved. I never touched the stolen things—only watched from a distance, from a store opposite or from a bench in the hall outside.

I wanted to make sure my friends were all right, so I kept an eye out for the security guards. There were three, an older man and woman who seemed pretty oblivious, and a newer boy who looked barely out of high school. He was the one I worried about because he'd seemed to look our way a few times when we walked the center aisles.

I told myself I would jump in if anything went wrong and went through the scenarios, too: kicking out a leg to trip a security guard rushing toward them. Faking a heart attack—or no, a seizure—to create a distraction.

I loved my friends with my whole heart.

All of them were new to the school, all with the kind of allure that made them a little intimidating. We called our group the New Kids at the start, me included because though I'd always lived here, I'd become someone new when they found me. Sometimes you're lucky enough to get in with a friend group a little above you, a group of people more charming and well-adjusted than you could ever hope to be, but they tolerate you and even love you. It's because of some other factor that you're allowed into their orbit. In my case, it was art.

Before the New Kids, I was the resident art nerd. But Kim, Trey, and Morgan were dabbling in art just then, and Ray went along wherever they did, so the five of us were brought together in Mrs. England's fourth period drawing class. We were friendly there—unlike most new teachers, she kept whatever the opposite of a tight ship is—but people are often friendly in class and it doesn't go anywhere. It was different with them.

The mall was where we truly started to hang out. I ran into Kim in Waldenbooks, already gathering a stack of the same Stephen King and V.C. Andrews novels I'd been planning to look at. We gossiped about Mrs. England. Did she have a bottle of vodka stashed in her desk drawer? Did she even—as Kim had heard—take sips during class? We compared notes and could come to no conclusions, but it was fun. We laughed. I bought *Pet Sematary*, and she bought *My Sweet Audrina*, and we promised to trade books when we were done.

As I walked past the arcade another day, Ray and Trey called me over.

"We already wasted endless quarters on this thing," said Ray. The claw machine was filled with these awful plush bird toys called "Derds." Teal and orange and purple, with their names stitched across their chests, yellow plastic bills and dark horns on their heads. There was a Party Derd and a Sleepy Derd, a Hungry Derd and so on, but I knew they were trying for Horny Derd. That was the one everyone wanted.

"I bet she's good at this," said Trey, narrowing his eyes like he was thinking deeply. "Because of the art and all that, seeing accurate angles and whatever."

Mrs. England had more than once praised me before the class for accuracy, and people like Tony Marten would turn around in their seats and roll their eyes. I was ready to be mortified, but no, Trey was smiling warmly. He was flirting.

As was Ray, maybe. He begged, "Win it for me, win it for me," doing a dumb voice, and I did. On my second quarter, I won them the Derd, and we all jumped up and down with glee.

With Morgan, it was clothes. She'd approach me while I was looking at things I wasn't sure I could pull off, and she'd be like: direct eye contact, waves of sincerity coming off of her, "You'll look gorgeous in that. You *have* to try it on," just like you'd imagine a young, cool mom acting. My own mom was too old and too proper, and I'd never had a friend quite like Morgan.

Honestly, everything about being with them was like being on a TV show—and I think that, and then I correct it. There are struggles and interpersonal dramas on a TV show, even a very silly one. No, this was more like being in a commercial or a print ad, just smiles and laughs and back-slapping. Just pleasure. It felt entirely fantastical and yet entirely real, so that I did not simply love them; I was in love with each of them individually and in love with the group and my place in it, in love with myself, our squalid little city, and our big beautiful mall.

↑ ↓

My parents felt differently. It wasn't big things but small ones. They didn't like how Morgan dressed—or how any of them dressed, really. There were little digs about the boys' earrings, the girls' stiletto shoes. It's not like my parents saw a lot of them, so it felt like they would hold onto any little thing and keep returning to bother. Riding a dead horse, I always thought it was called until one time I said it out loud to Kim and she laughed. "*Beating* a dead horse."

Kim had gotten a Cabriolet convertible that just fit the five of us. We'd go to the mall but go further, too, into the desert or out into the suburbs to have a cheap sit-down dinner in one of the strip malls.

So I found myself arguing about curfews, too.

I remember one night Mom cooked and I sat on the stool at the breakfast bar. I mentioned our group project for Mrs. England and Mom said, "*Group* project? Ugh."

"It's about, like, identity? I think it will be fun."

"You'll be doing it all yourself. You know that, don't you?"

"I don't know why you'd say that. They all like art."

"They dabble."

"Quality people always do," I said. By quality, I meant class, I suppose. They certainly all came from more money than us. "They spread a mile wide instead of burrowing a mile deep into something, and that's better. Like, Renaissance men, you know?"

Mom scoffed. "I think that sounds like something a stoned teenager would say. A teenager who worries her friends are a little better than her—but she's wrong. She's the one who's better."

I wanted to barf. Sincerity like that humiliated me unless it came from Morgan, Trey, Ray, or Kim. I was only interested in what they thought.

↑ ↓

Or, maybe there was one little area of struggle, an interpersonal drama between us friends. It was subtle, but it centered on the one thing I wanted there to be no question about: my loyalty.

The fact that I drew a hard line on the shoplifting was something they had all questioned at one point or another. They would hear my reasoning, nod and smile, pretend to understand, but this remained the one thing that set me apart from them.

The question was greater than that, though. I had a few other friends from before the group started. It's not like anyone in the group liked them all that much, but any time I complained about something they'd done or said, the others would go quiet.

"Don't you like Misty?" Kim would ask, for example.

"Yes, of course." I wasn't sure that was true anymore.

"Then why tear her down?"

I'd be ashamed, and stop, and then I would forget. At some point, though, they'd cured me of it.

↑ ↓

And Mom wasn't wrong about the drugs. I'd resisted peer pressure when it came to stealing, but when Ray turned around from the shotgun seat one day in the mall parking lot, five tiny pills in the palm of his hand, I took my share.

I held the pill in my own palm.

"Nothing will happen. Your parents will never know," Morgan said, and that was good enough for me. I didn't see it as a moral issue, like stealing. I saw it as a safety issue, like swimming after a heavy meal, affecting no one else but me.

The first time, the trip lasted hours. We walked around the mall just . . . *looking* at things. Seeing everything for the first time. Clothes and shoes and knickknacks—the little velvet flocked teddy bear pins that were everywhere that year, the displays of pastel colored storage bins—glowed with a newness they'd never had before, as though they'd come from another planet. The effect was not only visual; there was an emotional quality to it. I was so young, I barely knew nostalgia, and yet the feeling was distinctly nostalgic, as though we had been separated from this world for a long time and had just come back.

The come-down found us entranced with the aisle of funny greeting cards in the mall Woolworth. Each card would have to be read and passed around, each had us cackling louder than the last, until an actual security guard came and asked us to go. It was the boy. Up close, his skin was so freckled, I found myself gazing, imagining constellations, until he said under his breath, "The fuck's wrong with you?"

As we went out the doors, we caught the fear in the checkout girl's face. "What's so scary about us?" said Morgan, and the girl turned away. She was only young, and working alone.

"You're sure you didn't see them take anything?" the guard asked, and she nodded without looking back toward us.

"I've seen that guard looking at us before," I said after we were in the car. "He's onto us."

Trey said, "That guy? He's been trying to bust us all year. Where were you?"

"He's searched my purse—this was before you started hanging out," said Kim. "He was *humiliated* not to find anything."

"You said *us* just now," said Morgan, brushing back my hair with her fingers. "That means you have to play next time."

I was chilled for a moment, but soon we all went back to laughing.

↑ ↓

The second time, the trip went faster. We were behind on our group project for art class, and Trey had asked us over to finish it in his parents' garage.

I had never been to one of their homes before. It was a large house in a much nicer neighborhood than mine, expensive-looking but entirely plain inside like the furniture store displays at The Bon Marché. His parents sat in a large living room off the entry, the dad with a newspaper, the mother with a magazine. "Hi kids," she called. "I'll bring cookies later, just say when you're ready."

In the garage, some wordless rhythmic music was playing. Trey held out a hand filled with five . . . not *pills* exactly, but irregularly shaped objects. When I picked mine up, I was surprised at the way it felt, like a piece of cartilage from a chicken carcass, but I popped it in my mouth and swallowed without a moment of hesitation.

"I like to see that," said Ray, ruffling my hair.

"You trust us now," said Morgan.

A gigantic "canvas" lay on the floor, cans of paint arrayed around it, a variety of weighty, long-handled brushes beside each can like they were place settings.

The canvas had been primed white with gesso, but the shape, and the grommets at one end, told me it had been a flag. Trey, or one of them, had stolen a gigantic flag from a car dealership or someplace like that, and we were going to desecrate it. I lifted the corner, but the other side had been primed as well. No way of knowing if this was the American flag or something else, but it didn't matter. It was wrong to steal; it was wrong to defile something that someone else held dear.

But I didn't weigh that above this: being with my people, showing my loyalty and identification with them.

I was ashamed to realize that, like Mom, I had expected to do this project myself and let them claim ownership. I had run through all sorts of ideas to meet Mrs. England's prompt "Who We Are," and now it would be something so much better, a true collaboration.

They were off at the other end, taking off their clothes and laying them on an empty workbench. I joined them. When we had all stripped to underwear, we began.

The music grew louder, the thing like a dance, throwing paint at first, laughing, splashing up on our bodies. The lights seemed to strobe. Splashing paint on the walls, the unmarred floor, tracking it through into the house when we breaked for cookies, and the mom only smiled. "Looks like y'all worked up an appetite!"

When we hosed off in the perfect backyard, the mom waited, holding towels. When we stripped off our ruined underwear and tossed them all in a pile on the grass—everyone apparently unself-conscious except for me: hesitant, covering myself as best I could and staring at the grass—the mom did not bat an eye.

Yeah, that was weird.

By the time we'd dried ourselves with the thickest, plushest towels I had ever touched, ruining them with the little vestiges of paint from forgotten nooks and crannies, and got into our clothes again, and got into Kim's car, it was still light out. I was trying to remember what all had happened, but it was a blur. My eyes had closed and I slumped against Morgan.

"Am I still high? I can't go home high."

"It's worn all the way off," said Trey. "But we'll drive around until you feel better, OK?"

"You're just exhausted," Morgan said, rubbing my shoulders.

Sometime later, I woke myself with a loud snore and said, "Sorry." It was dark, and the others tittered a little. The highway made white noise going by.

"Go back to sleep," said Morgan.

I did, but I woke again for a second to hear Kim whisper from the front. "We have to make her some glasses. Her eyes are still way too human."

↑ ↓

The mall's front entry walls had shadowboxes filled with outfits or other arrangements of goods to advertise their wares. The back entrance was for community stuff. I had seen grade schoolers' art displayed there so many times it felt a little insulting, but here we were. Our entire art class, many with girlfriends and boyfriends, parents, siblings. Most sat in folding chairs—my parents had come early and gotten a seat, I saw—but the stragglers like us leaned against the entry wall, with a view of the art as well as the audience.

I was enraptured with our painting, as Mrs. England had been. Such life and rhythm in its broad strokes, and in the details in-joke references. The orange and purple of a Horny Derd, abstractions to echo albums we'd loved and food we had eaten together, the lace of stolen lingerie, on and on like that. A map, a record, of our time together.

And more. Shapes and colors I could not pin down but that called to me. Stars, galaxies.

Mrs. England stood at a lectern now talking about the importance of the theme "Who We Are," self-awareness and being true to yourself, accepting your loved ones for who they are rather than trying to change them, and so on.

Kim leaned in, whispering, "I think she's drunk even now." She held on her palm a single object, something like an oversized gummy candy. My eyes darted back to my parents.

Morgan said, "Don't worry. This one goes really quick." She took my hand.

When I'd swallowed the thing, Kim took my other hand, the residue sticky between our palms.

In an instant, the painting transformed from references to our past into the past itself, like rooms I could step into, rooms where we laughed and danced, rooms where we met for the first time. I could not have looked away on my own, but Morgan let go of my hand, and gently grasping my temples from behind, she turned me, first to the audience. I saw inside them like an x-ray, almost all of them filled with the things we had learned about: the regular lungs and entrails and such, but some of them different.

Trey's parents, Kim's parents, they had no organs in them at all. They had gears and wires and pulleys. I began to panic, to shiver, and I would have cried out if Morgan had not been close to my ear, shushing me. "It'll be over in a minute. Just try to see as much as you can, while you can."

Mrs. England had entrails, organs, but they weren't quite what we'd learned about in Biology. She had two tight, small hearts and something very round inside her. As did Ray and Trey, when Morgan turned my head to them.

"It's just opening you up. It's just taking off some of the filters," she whispered. She directed my gaze down the mall corridor, where for a second I saw inside the stores, every item at once, and the cars in the parking lot beyond, and the building beyond that, but then it was over. The drug had worn off already.

The audience was applauding, Mrs. England thanking them, and they all looked normal again. They were rising, coming past us to look at the art. My parents were to either side of us. I felt Morgan and Kim holding me up, preventing me from collapsing on my jelly legs. The drug had worn off, but I was in profound shock.

"It came out . . . nice," said Dad with a pained expression, gesturing at our work.

"It's good, isn't it? Your teacher thought so." Mom looked at it for a long moment, with a puzzled expression, and said, "Group work is always such a challenge." My parents moved on to see the other work.

Mrs. England approached. She'd overheard my parents and shook her head. She stood for a moment, waves of pride coming off of her, and then she clapped Ray on the back. "See you all soon," she said, moving off.

She and Ray were the same inside—Trey too. What did that mean?

The boys had come close to me, too. We were all a tight huddle against the wall.

"Did she see?" said Ray, and Kim nodded.

It was Ray who held out his hand this time, offering a pair of large, thick glasses just like Morgan's.

"I'm a . . . changeling, like you," Morgan said. "We miss some developmental stages, but these make up the difference."

I nodded, though I was far from understanding. I took the glasses into my sweaty, trembling hand.

"Come to the bathroom with me?" said Kim, and the three of us went together.

I stayed in the stall a long time, breathing deeply, trying to slow my heart and dry my sweat. In one hand I held the glasses, and the other hand I held level in front of me to gauge how much it shook. They didn't try to coax me out, but when I emerged, they moved close, and Morgan gathered my hair into a ponytail, securing it with a sequined scrunchie from her purse.

"You want to think about putting your hair back when you wear glasses, or it can look a little messy."

"It hardly matters," said Kim.

"It matters to us. When you're raised here, you care about things like that, don't you?" She smiled. We were all looking at ourselves in the mirror. "We care how we look, and I don't think that's wrong. It's not wrong to do the things you're brought up to do. You just need to be open to new things, too."

The glasses were still grasped tight in my sweaty hand, and when

Kim wiggled them free, they were badly fingerprinted and fogged. She ran them under the tap and dried them on the hem of her shirt.

"Are you ready?" she said.

I let her place them on me. We all turned back to the mirror. Nothing had changed.

"It isn't as involuntary as with the drugs," said Morgan. "You have to learn to focus."

"Nothing," I said. I saw only the shiny mall bathroom tile and three tired-looking girls.

"Crossing your eyes might help?" said Kim.

"You can try that, or no—try this: pretend you're looking, say, a hundred feet in the distance," said Morgan.

I tried that.

I gasped and then nearly fell to the floor. What I'd seen inside Ray and Trey was inside all of us.

↑ ↓

The boys sat back against the wall across from our painting, but everyone else was gone from the back entry. They stood, and Ray and Kim hugged.

He asked, "Is she ready?"

Kim said, "Almost. Let her get a good night's sleep and she will be."

"Tomorrow, then," said Morgan. There were waves of expectation coming off of her, as though she were going to get something long desired.

"Tomorrow what?" I said, but no one seemed to hear.

"So should we call it a night?" said Ray.

"The mall's still open another two hours," said Trey, checking his watch.

I caught Morgan's eye and said as clearly as I could, "Tomorrow what?"

Vivid, beaming, she said, "Tomorrow, we go home."

And so we turned back into the labyrinth of the mall instead of out to Kim's little car. We started at the bookstore and moved through the clothes stores. There were pet stores in malls back then too, and we wandered through saying hello to the puppies and guinea pigs.

Saying goodbye.

I found myself shifting focus—and it must be like bifocals—seeing things as I had for seventeen years and then focusing past the mall, seeing the insides of people, seeing the insides of stores and beyond, and then I would restrain my focus and feel afraid. I thought a hundred times of letting them slide down my nose to the hard tile floor.

My friends were lifting things left and right. A pair of socks with toes, a whoopee cushion from Spencer's, a pair of dangling fish-scale earrings. The mall was dead, no security to be seen, and yet they passed the things back and forth like always. When I focused, I saw the trails in the air where the things had been and saw where they rested, in a pocket or under a sweater, waiting to be passed. It was more than a game. It was a way to stay sharp.

Finally I selected a purple lipstick, passed it to Kim, and watched it travel all the way to Morgan, settling in her large hobo bag.

When we came out into the central corridor again, the shops were starting to close.

Goodbye, mall.

But now they were all so giddy from my transgression, they wanted more.

We drove for a time, Morgan beside me saying, "We came here for you, just for you."

"Tonight's for taking whatever we still want to take," said Trey. "What do you want?"

"I don't know," I said. I already had everything I could ever want.

"A party?" said Morgan.

"I could send my dad out for booze," said Trey.

"Gah, your house is so far away," said Kim. "Let's just . . ."

"There, jackpot," said Morgan, pointing to a group of young men within reach of a streetlight at the edge of the park right across from the Circle K. One held a half rack of beer.

"I don't want that shitty beer," said Trey.

"So we send them in to get something."

We parked and moved in a group toward them, Morgan and Kim in front, approaching quickly and calling sweetly, "Hey, hi there."

The men were in a little huddle, the ones on our side of it turning, the freckle-faced boy in street clothes turning, leering, and without a pause, taking Morgan's wrist.

I was still in the shadows. I stopped.

Everyone else was in the light, and I hung back in darkness as the men asked, "What's up, Trevor?" and he said "This is them. These are the punk kids I was telling you about."

Kim, Trey, and Ray were each trying something different—trying to get him to let go of Morgan, telling him to calm down, showing their hands: no threat. The other young men were hanging back, too, looking to defuse things, and then the freckle-faced one, Trevor, he called for help, and they started moving in to restrain my boys. I stayed in the shadows.

I wanted not to be there. This was all my fault.

Trevor wrestled Morgan's bag out of her grip. Morgan screamed and then Trevor did. Someone called for me, but I still couldn't move.

I wondered, had my parents taught morality or only cowardice?

Through the glasses, I focused out a hundred feet beyond, a hundred miles, and when I looked back to my friends, the circular things within them were rising up. The one inside me was rising too. I felt it.

The men were screaming now because my friends' mouths were opening wider than they should and something tar-like was ballooning out of them. Morgan's first, and Kim's, and then the boys'. Trevor shrieked like an animal, blood splashing up in the air like thrown paint.

My mouth flooded with saliva, my own jaw ratcheting wide, and I could not let that happen. I turned. To the accompaniment of men screaming like dying animals, I ran.

As I ran, the heavy glasses moved down. I pushed them up. I cried and they came down further and further until finally, lubricated by tears, they slid off my nose to the hard pavement and shattered.

I went back, eventually. Anyone would have. I told myself it was only the lizard brain that had forced me to flee, but now I'd come back to do my part, defend my friends.

They were gone, all of them.

The car was gone; the half rack of beer, gone.

I was miles from home and ought to have gone into the Circle K to call my parents, but I could not manage to do even that. Instead, I walked, terrified of every sound and sight in the dark and unfamiliar streets.

Terrified, most of all, of myself.

None of them were at school. I had not expected them to be. At lunch, I called Morgan and Trey. Their phones rang and rang, and I did not bother trying the others.

When I got to fourth period late, a new teacher stood at the head of the class. I tapped Tony Martens's shoulder.

He cringed like a spider or a rat had touched him, turned and whispered, "What the *fuck*?"

"Did they say what happened to Mrs. England?"

"Who?"

"The old teacher, you know."

He only rolled his eyes and turned back to the board. This new one was giving a complicated lecture about linear perspective. I wandered out of the room before she saw me.

There was not much else to do but find roundabout ways of asking my parents if they remembered my friends, if they remembered where I might have come from. As far as I could ascertain, they knew nothing. I walked to Trey's and strolled through the open door to find his parents frozen in place on the sectional. I cut into his father's arm, pulled out the batting, the springs, then wandered to the mall. Our painting was still there. None of the rest were, but ours still hung, the mall shoppers giving it a wide berth, not looking even as I slumped against the wall opposite gazing at it, crossing and recrossing my eyes, trying to see where they'd gone.

the temple of all

cyrus amelia fisher

Makoma approached the Temple from the west, as generations of king-widows had done before her. Her canoe was one of the worst her outpost had to offer, hammered together from rusting salvage; she lost a quarter of the day stopping to bail out its foundering hull. In a sack woven from strips of old-world plastic gone as soft as skin with age, her husband's bones awaited her final act of devotion. Picked clean by ritual beetles and anointed with scented oils, they were the prettiest thing in her run-down craft: certainly the most valuable.

Oh, my lovely. His death-words still rasped in her ear, clear as when he'd spoken them. *You won't survive this world without me.*

In the end, he had made sure of that.

Brown-black floodwater lapped at the crumbling rooflines as she paddled toward her destination. The Temple itself slumped half-submerged in the center of a vast lake, its decaying façade fallen open into a gaping mouth. The expanse of flat water rippled with wind-currents like the flank of a terrified animal as Makoma paddled into the sacred building's shadow. Even in the marrow-red light of midday, Makoma could make out the grid of ancient sigils on the submerged black stone beneath her.

The words on the sign that stretched above that ragged opening had long since bleached beyond reading. What remained was three encompassing sigils, which the preacher had augured from the old tomes: A-L-L. A fitting moniker for a crypt. Death was everything in this world.

↑ ↓

Makoma guided her boat through the entrance to the ruin. The space stretched out above her in a vaulted ceiling, reddish light moving in ripples across the corroded walls. Nearby, running water sloshed and crackled, masking the sound of any predators who might have taken shelter in the old ruin. No helping that. It was not much farther now.

She took out her map, adjusting it for her different course of entry. She checked her provisions, what little she had brought: the bag of her husband's bones, the knife she had whittled herself from his snapped humerus, and the plastic bottle of ceremonial old-world wine saved in the preacher's cellars for occasions such as this. She had tasted only a drop of it before, on her marriage day: today, she would drink it dry. She'd even been permitted a rare chemical light from the preacher's storeroom to guide her journey into the dark.

Disposable luxuries. After all, she would not be coming back.

This was how it had always been done. Whenever a member of their clan finished that long process that began the moment they took their first breath of poisoned air, their bodies would be consigned to the ossuary. These old places of the world had power, or so the preacher said. It was only within them that the souls of the dead could enter the glorious kingdom whose ruins housed their bones.

It was Makoma's role to guide him, to carry his remains like a beacon through the sunken Temple of All, and usher him to the ossuary where their forefathers had rested for generations. And there, when she had arranged his bones in their proper place and laid herself down beside them, she would drink the dregs of the ceremonial mead and plunge the fragment of his humerus into her heart so she might accompany him the rest of the way on his journey.

She had known this would be her fate from the moment the outpost's sovereign chose her as his wife. Every queen must see her husband to his afterlife; it was what she had been trained to do. She did not fear the knife, nor the dark. He'd held her hand all through his long dying, coughing up words into her ear to remind her of her duty. As if she had any choice but to comply.

He had always been a creature of great wants, and he never settled for anything less than the full scope of his greed. Fitting, then, for him to be buried in this temple of old world riches, which hadn't saved them either.

This is your final duty, my love. This is what you were born for.

She had never been able to prove otherwise.

Past the Atrium, the water coursed down a long avenue with a decaying promenade overhanging each side. Scarcely any of the red-tinged sunlight filtered through the various gaps in the roof to the water below. Little use in postponing it; she cracked the chemical stick with a sound like her husband's arm bone had made when she shattered it in half with a hammer, and a sickly greenish light poured out to color the water's surface.

In that first flash of light, she could have sworn she glimpsed the flash of eyeshine in the darkness above, looking down at her from the walkways that lined the upper level. Her breath froze in her chest; the ossuary, after all, had its guardians. They would make little distinction between graverobbers and her.

And then, unbelievably, Makoma laughed. What did it matter? She had come here to die. As long as she reached the ossuary and laid out her husband's bones, her place in the next world would be secure.

Inside, the glyphs marking the inner caverns were better preserved, though no more meaningful than the ones outside. She pushed her canoe past row after row of alcoves, their epitaphs grim: Claire's, Francesa's, Spencer's. The names of old families who watched over them still. In some windows their treasures still gleamed in the light of her glow stick, following her like glinting eyes. A fitting burial for her husband. He'd always loved precious things and been loath to let them slip through his fingers.

You're nothing without me, my love. Never forget that truth.

Time meant nothing as she paddled through the tomb, consulting her map as needed. She navigated past the wide amphitheater of the food court, now festooned with fungal growths; she gave the tomb of JCPenney a wide berth, for it was rumored to be infested with flesh-eating rats. By the time she reached her destination, her arms were sore and her light had begun to wear down, its glow illuminating less and less of the red-tinged darkness around her. It didn't matter. The journey was over.

The strange, metal steps stretched up above her, leading to the crumbling upper level. The ossuary's sigils stood emblazoned at its height, their letters dark with mold yet clear even now: Regal Cinemas. Though the meaning of the second word had been lost to the ages, the first made it clear: this was the burial place of kings. For her sovereign husband, nothing else would do.

You belong with me.

She ascended into the ossuary.

Unlike the ancient graves in the rest of the tomb, the ossuaries were left unmarked. The ground here groaned beneath every step, and in certain places the floor had collapsed through to the level below as if exhausted of holding up its weight. The slosh of water was farther away now, sharpening her sense of hearing. She found herself listening for footsteps, remembering the glowing eyes. There was nothing; only the distant crack of a building sliding into its own decay, closing tighter around its dead riches like a greedy, rotting fist.

The preacher's instructions were clear. She moved down the dark and windowless hall, her light scarcely illuminating the ground three feet ahead of her. Sweat slicked her palm no matter how she wiped it on her trousers. Her fear was irrational. This was what she was meant to do. All her life, she'd known this was where it would end.

At last she found the door. It had been marked with the crest of her husband's family, the knife thrust up through a burning wheel. The hinges had long since rusted away; she had to lift the door out of its place so she could enter the darkness beyond, as rich and thick as loam.

She almost thought to leave the door propped ajar, so she would not have to move it again when she left. But of course, she would not be leaving. She maneuvered it back into place, ancient paint falling away on her callused palms.

Sealed inside, the smell rose to choke her: of dust and age and rot, thick as a wad of rancid cloth stuffed down her throat. For a while she stood still, forcing herself to breathe through it. In the narrow space, the floor sloped upward into an echoing void.

You must drink the wine at the threshold, child. Then you will be ready to face what lies ahead.

The bottle was warm in her hand, its smooth plastic surface still speckled with dust as fine as the velvet of a peach. She wiped it away from the reddish label with its bold white glyphs, the color still vibrant after its decades in the preacher's cellar. The cap twisted off far more easily than she had expected: before she could give herself a chance to smell what lay inside, she tilted it up and drank.

The taste burned down her tongue like an oil fire, coating her throat and burning through her nose. She coughed and retched, then drank some more, her husband's bones clicking against her back like an echo of his dry, humorless laugh. By the time she was done, her head was swimming; she was no longer afraid. There was nowhere else to go. She followed the path sloping upward, holding her light ahead of her.

Then she stepped forward and could feel how the air opened up around her; the open space moved across her skin like the ghost of words. The smell was far worse here, a flesh-stink mingled with mold in the damp, cool air. In a shaking hand, she raised her light. And she saw.

The space opened up into a vast chamber, the ceiling so high above that her dim light could not illuminate it. On a shallow stage, a tattered banner hung: her husband's clan sigil had been painted upon it, though age had worn away its edges. Across from it, seats rose like those in an amphitheater, neat as rows of teeth: all faced the same direction, toward the rotting cloth with its faded glyph.

Masses of mold and wild fungal growth sprawled before each pile of bones, perfuming the air with their living dust. Tendrils of mold dripped like the finest old-world lace from bodies bloated far past what the imagination could make of the human form. Some had bowed neatly before their husband's thrones; others had spilled out onto the floor as if trying to escape the death which found them as surely as the husbands whose bones they had carried here so diligently.

There had been no ritual beetles to strip their bones neat; no hand had laid them out in dignity and repose. This was their due. And there were so many more open seats, so many empty spaces on the floor for devotion to churn into rot. Makoma took a step backward, nausea rising in her throat.

Behind her, the door she'd left propped up fell to the ground with a crash.

Something burrowed out of her throat. She thought it was going to be a scream, until it moved past her teeth with the taste of acid and splattered on the rotting carpet. The vomit tasted like raw meat and left her shaking, hands gripping a dead man's throne just to stay standing.

She thought of the ceremonial wine, its acrid, awful taste. She thought of the preacher's instructions, and the way some women's bodies lay strewn so messily in comparison to their husbands. Of course, there could be no certainty that they would choose the knife in the end. Their husbands would need a greater assurance.

Even now something was shuffling up the narrow ramp, sniffing, intrigued by the noises of distress; but her head spun and the light had slipped from her fingers and rolled, and there was nowhere to go but deeper into that thicket of bone and mold, the rows and rows of grinning dead and their sprawling, luscious consorts.

A long, triangular head emerged into the dim light from the corridor. One of the guardians. It had followed her here, long-limbed and wraithlike, its skeletal limbs filthy as it loitered at the edge of her light, pointed ears raised, short fur mottled with bulging tumors. It lowered its long snout to the corpse of a sovereign's wife, sniffing gently at the rot that still bloomed there.

Then it moved forward with the leisurely steps of a predator that knows its prey is caught. She backed away as it came, father up into the amphitheater and away from her fallen light. It stopped to nose at the pool of her bloody vomit, and the fading light caught the tendril of drool that cascaded from its lips to the splattered contents of her stomach, as delicate as a spider's web.

It wanted her. Wanted to bear her to the stinking ground and devour her, bite by bite, under the banner of her husband's family. It would leave her moldering remains to spring up strange growths like the bodies around her, and all the widows who came to this place after her would see no difference between those who had died for their honor and one who had been slaughtered by a beast. And the cycle would continue.

The guardian prowled up the stairs, its skeletal limbs eclipsing the light. There was nowhere else for Makoma to go; she collapsed against the final row of seats, bent double over the agony in her stomach with a line of bloody saliva hanging from her panting lips. The light from her fallen torch was beginning to dim. The creature moved toward her without haste. It could see she was not a threat. Just another dying thing left to rot.

More vomit seared the back of Makoma's throat, but something inside of her had clenched to iron. She let the bones on her back clatter to the ground behind her; she would not die here, not for anyone's sake but her own.

You belong to me.

The guardian lunged. She raised the carved bone knife.

↑ ↓

It was two days before Makoma could gather the strength to make her way back to the light. She survived on cut strips of the guardian's flesh and the delicate growths from the wives' bodies, their earthy taste soothing the agonizing cramps in her stomach. She did not think they would mind; she could almost feel their approval at the blood that soaked the Regal carpet, a sacrifice for them alone. Every morsel of food roiled in her aching stomach, but in time, the fever went down; the poison left her dizzy, but she did not die.

When at last she limped out of the darkness of the ossuary, she carried her husband's bones with her. Though the crumbling balcony sagged toward the water below, she stepped onto it without fear. It held, even when she reached the railing. She stared across at the alcoves, the tombs of Victoria's and Kohl's and the modest monument to Auntie Anne's. And then she upturned the sack of her husband's bones and let them fall into a nameless grave in the water below.

It took many trips to bring the remainder of the bones to that spot, but the ossuary held no horrors for her now. The dead women there had helped her survive; she would repay the favor by setting them free. One by one, she dropped dead kings into the murk.

She kept her husband's humerus and a selection of his ribs. They would make good knives, when she found the time to whittle them. For there were more guardians in the ossuary, and she'd found their flesh was to her taste.

It was the first time since her marriage that she did not know how she would die: at the tooth of a guardian or some wasting sickness of their ruined world. But she intended to find out for herself. And if some other widow came calling here with a dead man's bones in her hand, Makoma would be there to meet her.

Connnor Boyle, "Hard to Be a Mall God"
  • graphic violence, harm to children, ableist attitudes

Coyote Victoria Dembicki, "The Basement of Crowley's Artefects and Interests of the Occult"
  • blood, violence, possession

J.R. Santos, "A Quick Trip to Ryan's"
  • addiction, bodily harm, sexually suggestive themes

Liam Burke, "Posers"
  • suicide

Pines Callahan, "The Silver Sneakers"
  • suicide, murder

Lor Gislason, "Closing Time"
  • transphobia, body horror

Rick Hollon, "Layaway"
  • death of children, homophobia, bullying, blood, drug and alcohol references, reference to masturbation

Wan Phing Lim, "Let's Go and Sit by the Pool"
  • references to self-harm, bullying, racial slurs, homophobic slurs, physical violence, sexual harassment, blood

Jude Deluca, "Generation Dead #37: Why I Won't Eat at the Food Court"
  • body horror, eye trauma, birth horror, extreme gore

J.A.W. McCarthy, "Cherry Cola Lips"
  • homophobia, blood, gore

Eirik Gumeny, "The Intercessor"
  • misogyny, murder, language

Wendy Dalrymple, "This Place Belongs to Us"
  • suicide

Avra Margariti, "How My Self Finds Me"
  • queer/transphobia, child abuse

Ria Hill, "Juice"
  • sexual harrassment, body horror

Christi Nogle, "Kim, Ray, Trey, and Morgan"
  • blood, violence, drugs/alcohol

contributors

Connor Boyle (he/him) lives in Santa Fe, New Mexico. His writing is influenced by Harlan Ellison, Julio Cortázar, and Mark Twain. He's a big fan of the *Trancers* movies and Ed McBain's 87th Precinct books. His work has appeared on the *Shotgun Honey* website and in the aquatic horror collection *Rampage on the Reef*. His favorite mall food is the Double Doozie from Great American Cookies. You can follow him on Instagram via @thylacinebooks.

Liam Burke (he/him) is an independent author with a passion for juxtaposing biting humor along with the sharp teeth of horror, razor code of cyberpunk, and back alley deals of urban fantasy. His most recent publications include "Augmented Orpheus" in *Orpheus + Euridice Unbound* (Air and Nothingness Press), "Death of a Tree" in *Loki's Torch Volume IV*, and "No Version Like Home" on the *Kaleidocast Podcast*. He is a member of the Brooklyn Speculative Fiction Writers group, the SFWA, and the HWA (NY Chapter). Find out more at ssjliam.square.site.

Pines Callahan (she/her adjacent) is a former geriatric psych nurse with a degree in history. She now works with native plants, a transition that has significantly lowered her blood pressure. Her writing is inspired by the vulnerable people and places in Florida, the experience of being queer and neurodivergent in a red state, and how we struggle against a cultural lack of empathy. She is a sucker for kids (especially her own), tells awful dad jokes, and says "no worries" way too much for someone with anxiety.

Anjum N. Choudhury (she/her) is a Climate Policy Researcher from Bangladesh, and the author of *The Divining Thread* (Harper-

Collins India, 2022). Her work has also appeared in *Selene Quarterly Magazine*. For more details, visit her website anjumchoudhury.com. You can also find her on Twitter @AnjumWrites and Instagram @anjumnchoudhury.

Wendy Dalrymple loves to explore the beauty in horrific things. She holds a BA in Journalism from the University of South Florida and is a member of the HWA. When she's not writing Florida Gothic horror, you can find her hiking with her family, painting (bad) wall art, and trying to grow as many pineapples as possible.

Inspired by H. P. Lovecraft, M. R. James, Shirley Jackson, Robert Aickman, and a ton of fan fiction, **Cassandra Daucus** (she/her) writes soft horror and dark romance. She is intrigued by how the human mind responds to the unknown, and also enjoys a good gross-out. She has stories in *Ooze: Little Bursts of Body Horror*, the *Dark Blooms* anthology, *Mouthfeel Fiction*, Kangas Kahn Publishing's *October Screams Halloween Anthology*, and *It Was All a Dream 2* from Hungry Shadow Press. Cassandra lives outside of Philadelphia with her family and three cats. Her social media and website can be found at linktr.ee/residualdreaming. To her shame, Cassandra has never had an Orange Julius.

Jude Deluca (he/him/they/them) loves the mall. They wish the mall could be their ringtone. A proud 90s mall trawler, they put all their knowhow of the mall and 90s comics into their story. A nonbinary aegosexual Capricorn, Jude's specialties are magical girls, slasher fiction, YA horror, superhero dads, and big beautiful men. As a professional horror detective, they've uncovered several lost stories from the 1990s, including *Goosebumps: Dead Dogs Still Fetch* by R.L. Stine and Braden Thomas Gardner. Their dream is to professionally write about Roy Harper, his adorable daughter Lian, and the Legion of Super-Heroes for DC Comics. They're THE #1 Lightning Lad fan of all time, and still have a bone to pick with whoever came up with *Justice League: Rise of Arsenal.*

Primarily an androgynous weirdo, **Coyote Victoria Dembicki** also works as a chef, driven by a love for both fire and knives. Born and raised in urban Alberta, they now live in rural British Columbia. They are very interested in exploring and playing with themes of identity, place, gender, alienation, and the supernatural. Msit no'kmaq.

Derek Des Anges (he/him) is a multi-genre trans author living in London and toiling in the night reading newspapers for PR companies, as well as growing mushrooms in a cupboard in his flat, sometimes even on purpose. His work can be found in anthologies from Parsec Ink and Other Worlds Ink, with a full list at derekdesanges. wordpress.com/books

Cyrus Amelia Fisher writes queer tales of shipwrecks, mycelium, and horrors of the flesh. After years of driving around the United States in a beat-up minivan, they finally returned to the mossy fens of their birth in the Pacific Northwest. Now they while away the hours communing with their fungal hivemind and writing about cannibalism. Naturally, they also love to cook. Find them on Twitter at @hubristicfool or at their website, cyrusameliafisher.com.

Lor Gislason (they/he) is a non-binary homebody from Vancouver Island, Canada, the author of *Inside Out* and the editor of *Bound in Flesh: An Anthology of Trans Body Horror*. Their nonfiction work has appeared on numerous websites discussing our relationship with horror from a neurodivergent perspective.

Eirik Gumeny (he/him) is the editor of Atomic Carnival Books and author of *Beggars Would Ride*, *The Greatest Gatsby: An American Werewolf in West Egg*, and the *Exponential Apocalypse* series. His short fiction has appeared in, among others, *Impossible Worlds*, *Kaleidotrope*, *Defenestration*, and *Soul Jar* (Forest Avenue Press). His nonfiction has been published by *Cracked*, *Wired*, and *The New York Times*. In 2014, he received a double lung transplant and technically died a little. He got better. Find him at EGumeny.com or on Bluesky.

Ria Hill is a writer, librarian, and nonbinary horror who lives in NYC. They are delighted to continue the family legacy that began when their mother worked at Orange Julius in the 1970s. Thanks, Momma! They spend the bulk of their non-work hours maintaining their recreational spreadsheet collection and interrupting their spouse's train of thought with deeply worrying story pitches. Their work has appeared in *The Book of Queer Saints Volume II* from Medusa Publishing Haus and is forthcoming *It Was All a Dream 2* from Hungry Shadow Press. If you see them in the wild, they are very unlikely to eat you. They promise. They can be found online at riahill.weebly.com and on various social media platforms @riawritten.

Rick Hollon (they/them or fey/fem) is a queer genderfluid author and parent from the American Midwest. Feir writing has appeared in *Fantasy & Science Fiction, Strange Horizons, Delicate Friend*, the *HELL IS REAL* anthology, and elsewhere. They collect old pulp magazines as well as much older rocks. Read more of their stories and poems from their website: mimulus.weebly.com.

Somto Ihezue is a Nigerian-Igbo editor, writer, and aspiring filmmaker. He was awarded the 2021 African Youth Network Movement Fiction Prize. A British Science Fiction Award, Nommo Award, and 2022 Afritondo Prize nominee, his works have appeared in *Tor: Africa Risen Anthology, Fireside Magazine, Podcastle, Escape Pod, Strange Horizons, Nightmare Magazine, POETRY Magazine, Cossmass Infinities, Flash Fiction Online, Flame Tree Press, OnSpec, Africa In Dialogue*, and others. Somto is Original Fiction Manager at Escape Artists. He is an acquiring editor with Android Press and an associate editor with *Apex Magazine* and *Cast of Wonders*. He is an alumnus of the Milford SF Writers '22, and Voodoonauts '22, and will be attending Clarion West '24. He is a member of SFWA, ASFS (African Science Fiction & Fantasy Society), BSFA (British Science Fiction Association), BFS (British Fantasy Society), and Codex. Follow him on Twitter @somto_Ihezue

Wan Phing Lim was born to Malaysian parents in 1986 in Butterworth, Penang. Her short stories have appeared in *Catapult, Ricepaper Magazine, Sine Theta Magazine, Portside Review, Kyoto Journal*, and more. *Two Figures in a Car* (Penguin Random House Southeast Asia, 2021) is her first short story collection. She lives in Penang.

Angela Liu is a Chinese-American writer from NYC. She researched mixed reality at Keio University's Graduate School of Media Design in Japan and now works in IT consulting and Japanese-to-English translation. Her stories and poetry are published/forthcoming in *Strange Horizons, Clarkesworld, The Dark, Cast of Wonders, Dark Matter Magazine, khōréō*, and *Uncanny Magazine*, among others. Her debut short story collection, *Beautiful Ways We Break Each Other Open*, will be released in September 2024 with Dark Matter INK. Check out more of her work at liu-angela.com or find her on Twitter/Instagram @liu_angela

Avra Margariti is a queer author and Pushcart-nominated poet with a fondness for the dark and the darling. Avra's work haunts publications such as *Vastarien, Asimov's, Strange Horizons, F&SF, The Deadlands, Lackington's*, and *Reckoning*. Avra lives and studies in Athens, Greece. You can find Avra on Twitter (@avramargariti).

J.A.W. McCarthy is the Bram Stoker Award and Shirley Jackson Award nominated author of *Sometimes We're Cruel and Other Stories* (Cemetery Gates Media, 2021) and *Sleep Alone* (Off Limits Press, 2023). Her short fiction has appeared in numerous publications, including *Vastarien, PseudoPod, LampLight, Apparition Lit, Tales to Terrify*, and *The Best Horror of the Year Vol. 13* (ed. Ellen Datlow). She is Thai American and lives with her husband and assistant cats in the Pacific Northwest. You can call her Jen on Twitter @JAWMcCarthy, and find out more at jawmccarthy.com.

Christi Nogle is the author of the Bram Stoker Award winning and Shirley Jackson Award nominated novel *Beulah* from Cemetery Gates Media and the short story collections *The Best of Our Past, the Worst of Our Future, Promise: A Collection of Weird Science Fiction Short Stories*, and the forthcoming *One Eye Opened in That Other Place* from Flame Tree Press. She is co-editor with Willow Dawn Becker of the Bram Stoker Award nominated *Mother: Tales of Love and Terror* and co-editor with Ai Jiang of *Wilted Pages: An Anthology of Dark Academia*. Follow her at christinogle.com and across social media at @christinogle

Jennifer Lee Rossman (they/them) is a queer, disabled, and autistic author and editor from the land of carousels and Rod Serling. Their work has been featured in dozens of anthologies, and they have been nominated for Pushcart and Utopia Awards. Find more of their work on their website jenniferleerossman.blogspot.com and follow them on Twitter @JenLRossman

J.R. Santos (he/him) is a Portuguese author of weird short stories. Previous contributions include *Archive of the Odd, Well, This Is Tense*, and others. His second self-published short story collection *We Living Failures* was released in September 2023. Find him @ccskeleton on Twitter.

editors

Jennifer Jeanne McArdle (she/her) lives in New York State and works in animal conservation. Her story, "The Mules," was a Brave New Weird 2022 award winner. This is her first time editing an anthology of short fiction. As a child, her favorite mall activities included reading in B. Dalton bookstore, getting thrown out of Spencer's Gifts, smelling things at Yankee Candle Factory, and convincing her mom to buy her one of those sprinkle covered sugar cookies at Great American Cookie. More info at jenniferjeannemcardle.blogspot.com

Michael W. Phillips Jr. (he/him) is a writer, editor, filmmaker, film curator, bookseller, and publisher based on the south side of Chicago. His work has appeared in *Grievous Angel* and *Disturbed Digest* and is forthcoming from the *Magazine of Fantasy and Science Fiction*. He's the editor of *This World Belongs to Us: An Anthology of Horror Stories about Bugs* and *Fettered and Other Tales of Terror by Greye La Spina* and the co-author of the nonfiction book *Gold: Nature and Culture* (with Rebecca Zorach, 2016). He is an active member of the Horror Writers Association. Mike's short documentaries about Chicago artists and musicians have screened around North America and Europe.

This World Belongs to Us:
An Anthology of Horror Stories about Bugs

"As engaging as it is varied, this collection will make your skin crawl in all the best ways." – Christopher Hawkins, author of *Suburban Monsters*

This World Belongs to Us is an anthology of horror stories about bugs, writ large—we're not scientists, so spiders and worms and leeches (oh my!) are in here too. This collection will terrify you with nineteen stories about the creepy-crawlies that were here before us and will be here long after we're gone. Featuring stories by Bram Stoker Award winners Kealan Patrick Burke and Cynthia Pelayo and Bram Stoker Award nominees Paula D. Ashe, Laurel Hightower.

ISBN: 979-8-9875743-0-0

$13.99 at frombeyondpress.com

Fettered and Other Tales of Terror
by Greye La Spina

"In this essential collection of lurid stories by the legendary *Weird Tales* author Greye La Spina, you will find mad scientists, ravenous vampiresses, werewolves, grave robbers, magi, elaborately coded messages—really, you'll find just about everything except a hint of restraint. They're marvelous."

– Molly Tanzer, author of *Vermilion* and *Creatures of Will and Temper*

Although she's mostly forgotten now, in the heyday of the pulps, Greye La Spina was more successful than H.P. Lovecraft, with more than one hundred stories and serial novels published in magazines such as *Weird Tales* and *The Thrill Book*. This volume is the single largest collection devoted to this unjustly neglected queen of pulp horror.

ISBN: 979-8-9875743-3-1

$10.99 at frombeyondpress.com

This Is Life: Rediscovered Short Fiction by Frank London Brown

"From existential soliloquys, to meditations on unfulfilled experience, to the healing balm of laughter, this collection is life writ large by a man who lived it fully, if not for very long. "

– Sandra Jackson-Opoku, author of *The River Where Blood Is Born*

Frank London Brown was one of the most important voices in Black Chicago literature, whose 1959 book Trumbull Park is a vital portrait of segregation in the North. He died of leukemia in 1962 at the age of 34. Between November 1959 and November 1960, he wrote "This Is Life," a series of very short stories (most of them around 200 words) for the Chicago Defender. These poignant, vibrant vignettes observed episodes of Black life in Chicago in Brown's trenchant style.

ISBN: 979-8-9875743-2-4

$10.99 at frombeyondpress.com

www.ingramcontent.com/pod-product-compliance
Lightning Source LLC
Chambersburg PA
CBHW021149310726
48971CB00002B/551